FRAGMENTED:
PHENEX

Jerrica K. Godwin

Copyright © 2025 by – Jerrica K. Godwin – All Rights Reserved.

Cover Illustrated Copyright © 2025 by – Jerrica K. Godwin

Cover designed and drawn by Jerrica K. Godwin

No part of this book may be reproduced or transmitted in any form by any means, whether graphic, electronic, or mechanical, including photography, recording, taping, or by any information storage or retrieval system without prior written permission from the author.

Any similarity to individuals, whether real or imagined, living or dead, is entirely coincidental. This includes places and events. If you find a character closely resembles you or someone you know (Yes, even that person), it could simply reflect your confidence though it might be worth a bit of self-examination. Keep in mind that this is purely fictional and absolutely intended for entertainment.

*The strongest women in my life nurtured my love for reading:
G-ma Marsh, Granma Shirley, Momma, and Aunt Helen.
You encouraged me to explore the worlds between the pages,
I fell in love with the delicate scent of paper & the touch of ink.
Your influence ignited a lifelong passion for the written word.*

This book contains depictions of child abuse (with physical abuse heavily implied and overtly described but not depicted on page, and emotional and mental abuse represented), physical assault of a child, and self-harm (cutting; heavily implied). It also addresses themes of loss, racism, and mental health throughout the narrative.

Although the disclaimer includes a humorous tone, the depictions of people and events are fictional. Some experiences are drawn from my own childhood, with certain events and moments exaggerated or minimized for the sake of the narrative within this fictional story.

Please ensure you are in a supportive headspace before reading and prioritize your well-being. While some may find this nuanced or "not heavy" I want to stress that though some including myself are able to handle these discussions with ease, your well-being is top priority in your life. I hope if you read this, you find a release and maybe some peace.

NAVIGATIONAL FRAGMENTS

CHRONICLES OF CHOICE	- 1 -
FRAGMENTED DREAM	- 15 -
FRAGMENTED CIPHERS	- 30 -
REPEATING TEEN TURBULENCE	- 46 -
FIFTEEN AGAIN	- 63 -
CHOICES DIVERGE	- 76 -
WAKING REALITY	- 92 -
DIVERGENT PATHS	- 107 -
SHIFTING FRAGMENTS	- 116 -
FATE'S DIVERGENCE	- 132 -
BUTTERFLY KISS; PARADOX	- 143 -
EBB OF TIME	- 152 -
FRACTURED DREAMS	- 159 -
FRACTURED BARRIERS; CONVERGING WORD	- 166 -
TIME'S RIPPLE, WATER'S DROP	- 180 -
THE PRICE OF FRAGMENTS	- 190 -
ORIGINS OF FRAGMENTS	- 201 -
TIME DIVERGING	- 211 -
A FRACTURE IN TIME	- 220 -
ALTERED FUTURE	- 228 -
CONVERGENCE	- 240 -

CHAPTER 1

CHRONICLES OF CHOICE

"Hands down, Echo and the Bunnymen over the Beatles any day. No comparison on the Liverpool hotties," Mikhail declared as "Stars Are Stars" began to play.

"Gag me with a spoon, Mish. Fleetwood Mac's *Rumors* that Stevie Nicks is absolutely fantabulous," Phenex said, lying upside down on a bean bag chair with her feet on the windowsill. "The Runaways, Sandy Pesavento, could drum circles around Pete de Freitas, Pete Best, and Ringo any day." She drummed on her stomach for emphasis, the bangles on her wrist adding a soft jingle like a tambourine to the hollowness of her stomach.

Their shared room was an amalgamation of their personalities: neon colors and band posters splattered the walls, with paint smeared in artistic chaos. A Tokio lamp's black light gave the room an eerie, mysterious vibe.

"Aren't drum circles about love and peace?" Mikhail laughed. "I guess you could make a point with that, but I am talking about attractiveness." Even in the purple-illuminated room, Phenex could see her sister's dark hazel eyes flash with excitement.

Phenex blushed, a warm rush creeping up her cheeks. "Heh, right-right. My bad." She paused, the playful atmosphere around them shifting as she suddenly heard heavy footsteps echoing down the hallway. Her heart sank, the sound triggering her anxiety like a sudden summer storm gathering on the horizon.

Seconds felt stretched; her breath caught in her throat as she turned toward the doorway. With a loud creak, their bedroom door flew open, flooding the room with harsh light from the hallway. The brightness was blinding, illuminating every corner and casting long shadows across the floor. In the doorway stood a familiar silhouette that sent a chill racing down her spine.

"What are you two doing in here?" The voice was gruff, tinged with impatience and laden with authority. Rhett Nemain, their stepfather was a short man with sandy brown hair styled in a crew cut, a habit from his military days, though Mikhail wasn't sure how it was a habit since he had only served the mandatory two years from being drafted—stood in the doorway. "I've told you it's time for bed," he said sternly. "That means shut up, lights out, and asleep."

"Mami allows us to stay up 'til ten," Phenex said quickly, spinning into a crisscross sitting position. Her voice was quieter, almost a whisper, a sharp contrast to just a few moments ago.

"Your mother is working, meaning I am in charge. Thana and Enoch should have been ready for bed over an hour ago." He stood with his arms behind his back in the at-ease position, his voice demanding a palpable tinge of annoyance.

Phenex scrambled to her feet and grabbed her pajamas from the top bunk before disappearing into the bathroom across the hall.

Mikhail stood, a shadow cast over her face as her expression darkened, her eyes seeming to glow an amber hue, "You're the parent."

"I beg your pardon?"

"I said, you're the parent. It isn't my job to care for the kids. As you said, Rhett, you're home. You," she pointed at him to punctuate her words, "you, take care of your children. I'll take care of Nixx and myself." Mikhail's voice was a little stronger this time. She remembered all too well the times Rhett had shirked his responsibilities, leaving her to care for Thana and Enoch. "If you want us in bed at eight, well, isn't getting the little ones ready for bed is too much responsibility, wouldn't it, sir." She spat out the word "sir" as if it were poison.

As she reached for an oversized T-shirt and started to walk past Rhett, he caught her by the arm, his grip like a vice. "¡Ey! ¡Suéltame!" She yanked her arm back, but his grip tightened, like a constrictor wrapping around its prey. Her heart pounded in her chest as she fought to mask her fear. Memories surged—she was four again, feeling the sting of his belt on her thighs for having an accident after near begging to go to the bathroom. "Just a minute," he had said, his eyes glued to baseball cards, leaving her to wait and wait.

Rhett brought his face close to Mikhail's, a shadow cast on his face because she was slightly taller than her stepfather. "You listen up and listen close," his jaw twitched in anger as his face reddened, "you ungrateful brat. I have been in your life since you were three. I am the only father you have known, and you will respect me as such. I have told you this is America; we speak English."

"Because *my dad* died, you piece of…" She was careful not to raise her voice too much as her anger began to bubble deep within her; she had her opposite fist clenched, fighting the urge to swing at him, "You're only a stepfather to me, emphasis on step so back off.

If you were a real man, you would show Mother how you treat us." She continued to hiss, "Vete a la mierda." She pulled away as his grip loosened slightly.

Following Phenex into the bathroom, she quickly closed the door and locked it, leaning against it as her heart raced. The thumping was so hard and loud that it seemed to reverberate through the door, echoing in her skull. She let out a slow breath and closed her eyes, memories flooding back. Rhett's voice echoed from when she was seven, shoving her from his and her mother's room after a nightmare. "Grow up, get a spine, and go back to bed," he had barked, harsh and unforgiving. In contrast her youngest sister and baby brother would still climb into their parent's bed despite being ten and nine and Rhett welcomed them with open arms even occasionally encouraging them.

Mikhail sighed in relief as she heard Rhett muttering, his footsteps fading toward the living room. Her breath steadied as she changed into pajamas—shorts and an oversized T-shirt that fell to her knees. For a moment her mind wandered back three years ago, she'd tried talking to her mother after a long day, but Rhett had blocked her, ordering her back inside. His interference had crushed her hopes of connecting with Colette for good.

As she exited the bathroom, her eyes meeting Phenex's dull topaz briefly. Though they were not twins, like all siblings, they had a specific and special bond, like a psychic link they could always feel. This quick look they shared was Mikhail telling Phenex she was fine, and they were okay. Phenex, though she had faith in her sister, was worried for her as she glanced at the obvious outline of a handprint on her arm.

Phenex finished brushing her teeth, the minty taste lingering on her tongue as she glanced at her reflection in the mirror. After rinsing, she sat on the edge of the tub for a few moments, her heart pounding in her chest. Pressing the heels of her hands hard against her knees, she tried to still the tremors that threatened to shake her apart. A shiver coursed through her, unsettling and persistent, making it hard to inhale deeply.

Why is he like this? The thought echoed in her mind, sharp and unnerving. She inhaled slowly, held her breath for a brief moment, and then exhaled, releasing the tension that had coiled tightly within her. As the air slipped out, she allowed herself to scream internally, a silent cry that reverberated through her thoughts, hoping it might somehow alleviate the weight of dread settling in her stomach.

The vivid memories of tense encounters flashed through her mind like snapshots—his anger, his unpredictable mood swings, the way his shadow loomed larger than life. Each thought felt like a slap, each scenario drilled into her with an unsettling certainty that left her feeling small and trapped. She squeezed her eyes shut, grounding herself in the present, trying to summon the courage not to let fear dictate her actions.

Taking one last deep breath, Phenex opened her eyes and focused on the tile beneath her feet, the coolness a stark contrast to the warmth of her anxiety-riddled skin. It was just a moment of weakness, she assured herself. Her fingers brushed against the smooth side of the tub, and she felt the sharpness of an unseen reminder of the emotions she kept hidden, the faint sting was a solace that she craved and loathed. The paradox clouded her mind, a fantastic painful release that clawed at her with guilt. The contrast of pain brought clarity as her breath steadied, comforting stillness in the throes of her chaotic thoughts.

Rhett had never struck her or Mikhail, but his yelling and the way he spoke to and about them were like razor blades across the skin. She didn't always claim or show that she understood the tension between them. Rhett was capable of being kind and caring as he had been with Mikhail and her when they were younger, and he showed his love to Thana and Enoch. That's when the attitude shifted, the stepchildren, like her and Mikhail were just baggage Colette brought along with her.

When Phenex walked back into the bedroom, the overhead light was on, and Mikhail was sitting on the lower bunk, back against the wall and knees close to her chest. She was clenching and unclenching her fists while doing a few deep breathing exercises. "Hola."

"¿Estás bien?"

Mikhail responded with a soft smile, "Of course, Phe-Phe. Are *you* okay? I know you hate when I push back like that, turning it into a screaming match." Phenex nodded without saying anything. "I try not to engage," Mikhail continued, "but he's like scabies, gets under my skin." Mikhail absentmindedly traced a figure eight on her thighs with her index finger, preparing to say more, but Phenex crawled onto the bed and pushed Mikhail's legs down to lay her head in her lap.

"Forgiven?" Mikhail asked quietly, running her fingers through Phenex's chestnut hair. She smiled, "Te quiero, manita."

"Te quiero, carnala." She responded quietly as she quickly drifted off to sleep.

Mikhail threw a stuffy at the light switch on the opposite wall; it hit perfectly, and the light went out. It would have been more impressive had this been her first attempt, but there were four other objects she had thrown at the switch piled on the floor. She stared at the door in the darkness, the light from the hallway glowing around the frame.

Mikhail traced the thin scar on Phenex's cheek, a faint line that ran along the right cheekbone, starting from her temple and ending near her upper lip. A wave of guilt and shame washed over her as memories flooded back—Beau swinging his fist, the rock clenched tightly within it. Mikhail had stood by, frozen in horror. "Lo siento, manita. Yo siempre te protegeré."

The scent of the griddle and sweet bread wafted through the air, warm and inviting like a cozy embrace. It carried hints of buttery sweetness, a subtle aroma that mingled with the faint undertone of vanilla and blueberries. "Morning, Mijas. How did you sleep?" Colette asked as her elder children entered the kitchen. Enoch and Thana were already at the table eating breakfast. "I made pancakes."

"Thanks, but no thank you, Mother." Mikhail said, reaching for the cabinet above the refrigerator. "I'll just have a strudel." She pulled out a box of apple-currant Pop-Tarts.

"I'll have some!" Phenex exclaimed, quickly taking a seat at the table just as Rhett entered the kitchen. Leaning closer to Thana, she whispered, "Pass the eggs," trying to keep her voice down amid Thana's excited squeals about her sisters joining them.

"Hey, hey, Thana-banana," Rhett said sweetly amongst the morning chaos. "No need to scream, indoor voice please." He kissed Colette on the cheek, giving her a playful squeeze on her hips. "Enoch, going for a record of five pancakes, I see! My growing big boy." His tone quickly changed to a flat affect, "Phenex, be sure to save some for everyone."

Mikhail glanced at Phenex's plate, which held one and a half pancakes—slathered in peanut butter by Thana before she decided to share—and a single egg. In the center of the table, a towering stack of at least ten pancakes loomed, alongside five sizzling fried eggs in the pan. Mikhail couldn't help but growl softly, "Yeah, Nixx, save some for the starving army of ants… or maybe that oversized scabies *mite*," she said, playfully directing her gaze at Rhett with a smile, then winking at Phenex

"Your mom made breakfast. Why are you grabbing a Pop Tart?" Rhett asked, directing his attention to Mikhail. A harsh tone in his words.

A car's horn cut through the air outside, followed by quick rapping on the door. "Mikey, we're going to be late!" a voice carried through the door.

She rolled her eyes, loathing the nickname of *Mikey*, "I have a thing and my ride is here." She smirked, a sideways grin that lit her eyes up with a mischievous glint as she ran out the door, extending her middle finger towards Rhett before shifting it into a peace sign so she didn't flip him off, but the sentiment was obvious, "Gotta bounce. Te quiero, manitas y manito."

"We love you," Colette called after her eldest daughter as she ran out the door. She turned her attention to Phenex. Her voice soft and airy as she spoke, "Do you have plans today, Phe, honey? I need to stop by the office and grab a few files, but we could spend the day together.

Rhett interjected before she could answer, "She's a teenager, babe. It's our day off together. We can take the kids to Nana Daisy's and spend the day together." He kissed her on the cheek, wrapping his arms around her waist from behind. "Isn't that right, Phenex? You don't want to hang out with your mom all day, do you?" He glared at Phenex over Colette's shoulder, giving her a look that said, "Don't you dare contradict me."

Phenex's shoulders slumped as she hesitated, her voice barely above a whisper, "Yeah... I do, sorry, Mami. Maybe next time?" Her eyes darted away, and she avoided eye contact. "I should get going," she said, hastily tossing the remainder of her uneaten food into the trash. With a quiet excuse, she slipped away to her room and retrieved the duffle bag she and Mikhail kept hidden, a stash of cash, books, and non-perishable supplies that had become a trusted companion on their weekend retreats to the treehouse they'd built seven years ago. Though they'd once fantasized about running away, their plan had never been more than a fantasy – a way to spend their summers and most weekends hidden away in their secret sanctuary.

As she turned to leave, Phenex found Rhett standing in the doorway. His presence was both commanding and intimidating, a mix of authority and horror that made her heart stop. She stared at the floor, dread pooling in her stomach. "When we get back, I don't want to see you in my house," he said, his voice low and cold. "You're out all day, and you better tell that ungrateful brat of a sister the same." He stepped closer, looming over her with an oppressive intensity. "Is that understood?"

"Y-yes, s-s-sir," she muttered, forcing herself to meet his gaze after realizing she had been staring at his feet. Anxiety washed over her as she remembered how frequently he had berated her for avoiding eye contact, insisting that it showed a lack of respect. Her heart raced painfully in her chest as she fought to take a shaky breath. "May I—may I go now?" Her voice trembled as she continued to exhale slowly, afraid to draw attention to herself by breathing too quickly or loudly.

Colette stepped into the room. "Here, some money for pizza for you and the Morell twins." She smiled, handing Phenex a twenty.

"Sorry you're busy, but I agree, next time. You, Misha, and me, okay?"

Phenex smiled politely while pocketing the cash, "Gracias, Mami." She forced herself to sound excited but knew the chances of having alone time with her mom were absolute zero. Rhett couldn't handle the younger ones by himself, always calling her over to help him and keeping her within earshot when they were out. When he was off work and Colette had to work, they would go to her office every other hour so he could talk to her, and when they got home from visiting her at the office, he was on the phone with her. Mikhail had once voiced that she was amazed that their mother still had a job with Rhett constantly hanging off her.

As Mikhail returned home around two-thirty, she noticed two subtle changes that caught her eye. The lawn gnome, previously facing north, now pointed west, and the pink garden rock that had once sat underneath it now stood sentinel in front. These rearrangements were just one part of the secret code she and her sister had shared over the years. A glance down the driveway confirmed that the family car was missing.

She knew that meant Rhett was out, and she had a key to the front door, but Rhett had found a way to keep tabs on them while he was away. He often wedged a match in the door frame, which would fall out when they opened the door, alerting him to their presence. The match was a signal, a warning that their rules were being disobeyed. The consequences typically included extra chores or menial tasks, punishments that seemed innocuous to outsiders, but were a constant reminder of Rhett's watchful presence.

Mikhail felt the anger of the previous night still simmering inside her, as well as the unease from the morning's events. Instead of following Phenex, she headed to the side of the house toward their bedroom window. They'd removed its screen ages ago, so all she had to do was push against the glass and climb inside.

She checked for the duffel bag, but it was missing. *Awesome, Phe. Camp tonight, blow off steam.* She thought while cautiously and quickly tip-toeing through the rest of the house. She opened the fridge and poured about eight ounces of milk into a bottle of Rhett's shampoo she had found in the trash a few weeks ago. She then added the exact amount of water to the milk jug, giving it a good shake. She added an egg to the shampoo bottle, ensuring it came from inside the carton since the ones in the door were counted, even unintentionally.

Silently and quickly, she moved like a shadow through the house. Armed with a bobby pin and makeshift tension wrench, she expertly picked the lock to her parents' bedroom—a skill she had perfected over time. Bottle of milk and egg mixture in hand, she rummaged under the sink and discovered vinegar alongside baking soda—Collete's makeshift substitute for toothpaste. A sly smile spread across her face as she imagined the eruption that would occur when Rhett used the concoction. But then, the thought of the smell—a rancid blend of curdled milk and sulfur—made her gag as she envisioned the putrid pungent explosion.

She added vinegar almost to the top and shook the mixture, then took a single sheet of toilet paper and peeled away a layer. Carefully, she wrapped a pinch of baking soda in the single-ply, setting the makeshift packet atop the other half around the screw cap. This was the tricky part: she pushed the rest of the baking soda in just enough to delay the reaction.

As she checked the bottle in the shower, she estimated it would be at least a week before anyone discovered the tampering, giving her plausible deniability. Carefully, she placed the altered bottle at the front of the cabinet. Then, as quietly as she had entered the house, she slipped away.

On her way to Triplet Creek and their hidden camping spot to catch up with her sister, she stopped at the pay phone outside Ray's Good Day, a small gas station near the hiking trails. There, she left a message on the machine for her parents, saying she and Phenex were camping with friends and would return by dinner on Sunday.

Mikhail entered the convenience store to use the restroom and pick up a few essentials, grabbing a couple of colas and a candy bar as she went. She then set off along the V. Richard trail, jogging at a steady pace as she made her way to their secret sanctuary. After about a mile, she veered off onto a hidden path that wound its way through the trees, leading her to a secluded clearing by a stream.

Their hidden retreat, which they called the "treehouse," looked more like an earth house, with a sturdy tree-like exoskeleton that had grown around it. The tree itself had been blown down but still lived, its roots taking hold in the ground. Over time, erosion had created a small hollow, which the girls had carefully excavated further by hand, careful not to damage any living part of the tree. They wrapped some branches around the roots to create a hut-like shape and added a wooden framework from the scrap yard. They smoothed out the mud walls, carefully heating them to form a structure more akin to mud bricks or mud cement, transforming the space into a cozy little hideaway. Despite its impressive design, the treehouse remained surprisingly undiscovered, well-hidden by the surrounding landscape. After seven years of construction and gradual adjustments, the treehouse had become a cozy refuge, a tiny home away from the world, specifically, a retreat from their parents, school, and the residents of Wakford.

Inside the treehouse, Phenex lay on her bed, a makeshift arrangement of pallets topped with a thick, homemade straw mattress. Despite its potential itchiness, the mattress was surprisingly comfortable. Light streamed through the trapdoor window, inspired by the clever designs of trapdoor spiders. With her headphones on and the volume cranked up to maximum on her Walkman, she listened to "Silence is Out of Fashion" by Mama's Boys, passionately lip-syncing with her eyes closed. As she playfully drummed the air, her head sank deeper into the duffle bag that served as a temporary pillow, enveloped by the familiar comforts of her sanctuary.

At home Phenex or Mikhail would flash the lights to get the attention of one another, a trick their friend Saria taught them. In the tree house because the lighting was less traditional, they had to be more creative, opening and closing the trap door instead.

Mikhail opened the trap doors wider to let in more light, grateful for the coolness that being partially underground provided—a welcome relief from the unexpectedly humid September.

As Phenex lip-synced to "Nyx" by Muttering Gibberish, the bass reverberated so loudly that she felt her eyes rattle. Just as she was about to hit the fourth verse— "I scream and shout, but I have no voice. It feels as if I am choking and dazed"—she sensed the sunlight flickered away, prompting her to open her eyes and turn down the music.

Peering down at her was Mikhail concern evident in her gaze. "Hey, Phe," she said softly, her voice cutting through the fading echoes of the song.

Tears brimmed in Phenex's eyes. "I hate him, Misha," she said, her voice trembling as she pulled her sister close, seeking the comforting embrace of her sister's warmth. She buried her face in the crook of Mikhail's neck, searching for solace amid her anger and pain.

Chapter 2
Fragmented Dream

The tea kettle's high-pitched whistle tore through the air of the treehouse. Mikhail (Misha) swiftly lifted it from the alcohol burner, pouring hot water over a mixture of crushed mint leaves, lemon peels, and whole cloves. She handed the concoction to her sister, Phenex (Nixx), who reclined on the beaten-up futon in the living area of their treehouse. "Here, drink this," Misha urged, the spicy aroma filling the small space. "It's an immune booster, far more palatable than pine needle and bark tea."

Nixx looked at the concoction with curiosity. Her sister had been studying survival tips for nearly two years, using Phenex as her test subject. The memory of the pine needle and bark tea made her shudder, recalling the bitter, sour tang of turpentine. She hesitated before taking a sip, sputtering as the liquid went down the wrong way, prompting a roaring laugh from Mikhail. "Easy there, Phe-Phe. No dying on me!" she teased, settling on the opposite side of the futon to face her sister. Leaning forward with her elbows on her knees, she asked, "So, when do you plan to come home?"

"How about never?" Nixx retorted, rolling her eyes as she took another sip of the tea. "At least this is better than the poison you gave me last time." Her tone was sharp, but the edge of her voice wasn't aimed at her sister. Mikhail smiled solemnly, "Of the places to runaway to, the tree house isn't exactly the best. A few days, couple weeks maybe, but here people would find you." She reached out placing a hand on Phenex's knee, "That opossum might come back."

"Since you've been gone, all the responsibilities have fallen on me. I'm expected to be an adult, managing Enoch and Thana!" Phenex shouted, her frustration boiling over. "I have to keep the house in order, tend to the massive yard and garden. If the little ones misbehave, I'm the one who gets punished! If my grades slip, if Enoch gets into a fight, or Thana talks back, it's all on me!" Her heart raced as anger bubbled within her. "And don't even get me started on the twins! After you disappeared, Mami and Rhett decided to replace you and had another! Surprise! Hunter and Ryder were born!" She shoved Misha's hand away, punctuating her words by punching her thigh.

Misha nodded, listening intently as Nixx continued. "You know the worst part of it, Mish? It's not the feeling of helplessness or hopelessness." She stared at her leg, where the impression of her fist was still visible on her jeans. Swallowing hard, she fought back tears that felt dry and suffocating in her throat. "It's feeling worthless and knowing that our younger siblings can sense it."

Listening empathetically, Mikhail reached out placing a hand on Phenex's cheek using her thumb to wipe away a tear, "I'm sorry Phe-Phe. You know college it was expected that I would lea—"

"It wasn't college!" Nixx's voice trembled as she began to shout again, "You disappeared, Claudia! No body, no note, nothing! No closure!"

Misha's expression darkened, her eyes flashing in the pale moonlight that filtered through the makeshift trapdoor window "I would never," her expression changed for a moment as if realizing something; she shook her head before grabbing Nixx by her shoulders and locking eyes, "¡Podemos cambiarlo. Puedes tener--!"

"Where are you, Misha? Can't I join you? Couldn't you have taken me with you?" Nixx pleaded, seeming to ignore Mikhail's urgent and anxious tone.

Misha pulled back. "Phenex, please listen. I don't think I have the time. It's possible."

"No!" Nixx protested as the world began to dissolve around them. Furniture flickered and faded, followed by the room itself, swallowed by an encroaching blankness. A high-pitched, shrill beep echoed around them, growing louder and faster with each repetition: BEEP, BEEP, BEEP! "No... it's too early," Nixx pleaded, her voice laced with desperation. "Please, just a little longer! ¡Lo siento!"

"Por favor, manita, the journals." Mikhail cried out as she was ripped away as though being erased or shredded apart vanishing in a flicker of pieces like a pixelated puzzle.

⌛ ⌛ ⌛

Phenex sat up, jolted awake by the insistent alarm. "Stupid dream again," she muttered, frustration and sorrow warring within her as she slammed her hand on the snooze button.

The familiar setting of their childhood treehouse unfolded, but this time, it felt strange, as though Mikhail had been there in realtime. It was a dream she had had before and until this time, had always been the same. Mikhail responding with what felt to be preloaded responses, just another character in her dream, but this time dream Mikhail went off script.

Time was cruel, just over a decade had slipped away since Mikhail's disappearance. A decade without answers. A decade without her sister. A decade without closure. As she stood, the weight of responsibility settled heavily on her shoulders. At twenty-six, she had become the anchor for her family. Clasping her necklace, adorned with three class rings, provided a small comfort, grounding her in the present moment. Yet, her thoughts relentlessly drifted back to Mikhail. *Where had she gone? Why had she left? And why did those haunting dreams refuse to fade away?* They had plagued her over the years, but since January, their frequency had intensified, pulling her deeper into an unsettling past.

The unanswered questions had haunted her for years, a constant ache in her heart. Six years later, in '93, tragedy struck, leaving her to raise her four younger siblings. Now, with Thana and Enoch out of the house, she found solace—and occasional frustration—in the love of Hunter and Ryder, her youngest treasures. She pushed the thoughts aside as she adjusted her glasses on the bridge of her nose before making her way down the hall.

As she stood at the kitchen counter, adding the final touches to breakfast, a spark ignited within her, fueled by the recent dream. Mikhail's last words before she faded out like the end of a Twilight Zone special, *'the journals.'* She needed closure. She needed to uncover the truth about what happened to her sister. If the dream was somehow a key, then she was going to use it. Her heart began to beat faster, she could hear the palpitations in her skull, her hands began to sweat. "No…" she muttered, "This is nuts." she muttered to herself, exhaling slowly in an attempt to calm her growing nervousness. Her eyes drifted to a small box on the desk in the corner of the office, filled with Mikhail's belongings, a poignant reminder of a past she and her mother seemed reluctant to let go of.

She made her way to the small desk nestled in the corner of the room and placed a shaky hand on the cardboard box. *This is ridiculous.* Her mind reeled as she opened the box, to discover several worn notebooks, a few stuffed animals, and an old jacket. She pulled out the hoodie and stared at it for a moment. It was from a band that she and her friends had enjoyed as teenagers, "Muttering Gibberish" was slapped across the front in bold letters, a faded image of Medusa in the background. The sleeves had thick red thread stitched into them in the shape of an X. The jacket had once belonged to Phenex's best friend in high school; Bryce Ripley. She pulled the hoodie over her head, it still fit, though a little tighter than it had been back then. She smiled remembering how comfortable it was back then, the faint scent of sandalwood still clung to the fabric.

A gentle smile teased at the corner of her lips as she took a moment to remember Bryce's strong arms, that had embraced her when Mikhail vanished, a moment of light in that dark time. She placed her hands in the kangaroo pouch of the jacket to immediately retreat her hand feeling a sharp pain on her finger. She reached again this time pulling out a pen with a broken cap, its sharp edge had stabbed the tip of her finger. Twisting the pen's tip slowly revealed a yellow sticky note, seemingly untouched by time. A single word was scrawled across it as though it had been freshly written, bearing the simple yet urgent yet cryptic message: *"Encuéntrame! 98: 2-28"*

"¡Oye! Niñito, ¿Dónde está tu bolso?" Nixx inquired as her ten-year-old brother, Ryder, hurried past her, snatching an apple from the counter. "Preparé el desayuno." She motioned towards the table, where eggs, sausage, toast, and oatmeal were laid out. Admittedly, as she glanced at it, she realized that adding fruit would have been a good idea.

"Lo siento, Mana," he exclaimed, skipping over to the table and sitting down. "Gracias. My bag is in the car; I didn't have homework, so I left it there last night.

Man, I wish I had that energy first thing in the morning, she thought as she took a drink from her second cup of coffee. "¡Hunter! ¡Desayuno! Hurry up, o te dejo con un cereal bar!" A girl with wild curls and bright amber eyes appeared in the kitchen almost as though she manifested out of the shadows, "Crap, where did you come from? Sit. Eat."

"Genetically? Mom." Her tone was as flat as the humor in a poorly written sitcom, devoid of emotion but oddly amusing. "I'm just grabbing una naranja."

Nixx nearly choked on her coffee; Hunter's unexpected sarcasm cut through the air, reminiscent of her eldest sister, Mikhail. The similarities were striking; even her eyes flashed with excitement in the same way. Seeing the orange in her baby sister's hand, she said, "Alright, alright, I hear you. I should have included some fruit," Nixx chuckled as she settled beside her youngest siblings to share breakfast, "Obviously, you kids are being raised secretly by someone other than me." She grabbed an orange from the basket, "Need to follow your examples."

As she dropped the kids off at school, she waved goodbye as they ran up the sidewalk to join their friends in the courtyard before the bell rang for class. Phenex drove away, her mind lingering on the dream and the note, the single phrase "Find me" scrawled across the paper in Mikhail's rough handwriting.

Though she often thought of her sister and sometimes dreamed of her, this dream had felt different, it was different, the note she had found was proof of that. A dark thought flashed in her mind; *History had a way of repeating itself, was this a premonition?* Ryder and Hunter were not yet born when their eldest sister went missing, but they had heard the stories. Enoch and Thana, only ten and eleven when Mikhail disappeared at seventeen, had fewer memories, yet they spoke of her often.

As Phenex drove, her thoughts swirled until she reached the edge of the woods where their old treehouse lay hidden. "If you're trying to tell me something, Misha, I could use a sign now," she said aloud, cracking the window slightly and turning off the engine. With a heavy sigh, she tried to steel herself. *Let's do this*, she thought as she stepped out of the car and onto the familiar hiking trail. The carpet of fallen leaves muffled her footsteps as she ventured deeper into the woods, the towering trees standing like sentries, casting long shadows on the forest floor.

As she walked, breaking away from the semi-worn trail to a path hidden by years of growth, she couldn't shake the feeling that she was being guided, as if Mikhail was leading her deeper into the woods. She reached a clearing where sunlight filtered through the canopy above, casting beams of light on the weathered remnants of the structure they had built together. The wooden planks were warped with age, the ropes frayed and hanging limp. It was a stark reminder of the passage of time, of all that had been lost.

She traced her fingers over the rough wood. "Misha," she whispered, her voice shaking, "¿Dónde estás? Where are you?" In the stillness of the clearing, she paused, hoping for a sign. A whisper. Anything that would give her solace. The only sound was the gentle rustle of leaves in the breeze.

As she sat there, lost in her thoughts, a sudden gust of wind swept through the clearing, blowing dust and knocking over one of the planks that seemed to be holding on just for that moment. It fell, revealing a small box that appeared untouched by time. The silver of the lockbox shone brightly, a stark contrast to the weathered and rotting wood of the dead tree they had once called their Earth-treehouse.

Just then, a painfully familiar voice drifted from behind her. "Ya era hora, you finally show up." Nixx spun around in disbelief, her breath catching in her throat as she dropped to her knees. There, illuminated by shifting ribbons of sunlight through the overgrown tree's canopy, stood Misha, her smile radiant. Relief, joy, confusion and anger washed over her as Mikhail reached down, her crooked smile growing brighter, "Hey, Nixx."

Phenex felt a wave of dizziness wash over her as her mind struggled to grasp the reality of the situation. Misha stood before her, unchanged and familiar, as if no time had passed at all. The sharpie that painted her nails still looked fresh, a stark reminder of the last moments they shared. As Phenex tried to focus on Misha's eyes, tears flooded her vision, making it feel like she was peering through a shimmering pool of water. "How is this possible?" she whispered, disbelief lacing her words.

A maelstrom of emotions and questions swirled within her, threatening to consume her. How could Misha be here after all these years? How had she not aged a single day? Yet, amidst the turmoil of her thoughts, one truth stood out like a beacon, shining brightly in the darkness: her sister was here, real and tangible, a presence that filled her with a mix of excitement, wonder, and trepidation. Her heart pounded in her chest, as though trying to break free from its confines, while her throat constricted, making it hard to breathe. It was as if she were struggling to inhale through a narrow straw or gasping into a soft pillow that offered little resistance. The sensation was suffocating yet exhilarating.

""Mish... how...?" Nixx began, struggling to find the words between her surprise and her tears. Her voice cracked as she tried to speak, as if the words were stuck in her throat, waiting to be freed. She wrapped her arms tightly around her sister, holding her close as if she feared that if she let go, Misha would vanish once more, leaving her with nothing but memories and longing. "Mikhail, I... I don't have words," she stammered, her voice trembling with emotion. Tears streamed down her face, mixing with the rain that had started to fall around them, creating a blur of water and color. Anger, joy, sadness, and fear swirled inside her, a vortex of emotions that threatened to consume her. It was the five stages of grief, but faster, and more unstable, like a rollercoaster that couldn't be stopped. "I've missed you so much, mi carina," she whispered, the words tumbling out in a mix of languages, a Spanglish that was imperfect and raw. As she spoke, Nixx was struck by the awkwardness of her own words, the way her mind was combining

Spanish and English in a way that felt unnatural. But in that moment, it didn't matter. All that mattered was the truth of her words: she had missed Misha with every fiber of her being

Mikhail returned the embrace, holding her sister close. "I'm here now, Phe-Phe," her voice soft but filled with a sense of determination. "I don't know how much time I have, but can we go home?" She placed a hand under Nixx's chin and lifted her face to make eye contact. "I know Nixx," she said as though understanding Phenex's hesitation in letting go, "but we have got to get out of here. I promise we will talk all about everything at home." She helped her sister to her feet and grabbed the silver box. Nixx took Mikhail's hand as they quickly made their way back to the trail. Phenex held her sister's hand tight, afraid she would disappear if they were not in contact with one another.

As they pulled up to Nixx's childhood home – *their* home, the one she'd shared with Mikhail before everything fell apart – a barrage of questions clawed its way to Nixx's throat. Eleven years... nearly eleven years had bled by, and yet Mikhail hadn't aged a single day. She looked *exactly* the same as the day she vanished: still seventeen, with that familiar mischievous glint in her eyes.

And then there was the jacket. The "Muttering Gibberish" jacket. It was practically a uniform from their rebellious youth, a style borrowed from their friend Bryce before college scattered them to the winds. But the two jackets... they told starkly contrasting stories. Phenex's was a road map of their lives: faded, softened with countless washes, patched haphazardly with scraps of fabric and defiant hope. Mikhail's... Mikhail's looked almost new, pristine, untouched by the passage of time. *How?* The question echoed in Nixx's mind, a growing unease battling with the overwhelming joy of her sister's return. This was *wrong*. This was impossible. And Nixx was desperate to understand why.

Misha paused in the foyer, studying the family photos that lined the walls. Most captured a blissful family with four children and their parents, but as Mikhail aged in the images, the smiles seemed to wane. Her fingers brushed against one photo of Phenex, proudly wearing her cap and gown at her high school graduation, a college acceptance letter clutched in her hand. In later pictures, two unfamiliar children appeared alongside Phenex. The most recent images featured only her and the two children, with occasional glimpses of Enoch and Thana, now depicted as young adults.

Mikhail's eyes widened. "Phenex Alejandra, *do you have kids?*" She seemed genuinely astonished, but there was an underlying caution in her tone, as if she was treading on delicate ground.

"Oh yeah," Phenex said, a grin flashing across her face, "The miracle surprise twins, Hunter and Ryder." A mischievous glint mixing with a shadow that momentarily flickered across her features, a spark in her bright earthy eyes. "But *technically* they're our siblings. Mami and Rhett thought I needed more responsibility... in eighty-nine." She paused, the smile fading slightly. "It was a whole thing," she added with deliberate vagueness, hinting that the story was more complicated and potentially darker than she was letting on.

Misha flinched, a barely perceptible movement, at the mention of Rhett's name. A wave of cold dread washed over her, dragging up a riptide of suppressed memories. It seemed the moment Thana was born, Rhett's disdain for the elder children, especially Mikhail, had become fervidly evident. He'd been a simmering pot of anger ready to boil over at the slightest irritation, and Mikhail had been his constant target.

She remembered the impossible demands, the way he'd set her up to fail. *Dishes!* he'd bark, and before she could even finish rinsing the last plate, his voice would boom again, contorted with rage, *"Laundry!"* The air always smelled faintly of his aftershave. She'd learned quickly. Explanation was useless, defense perilous. The **crack** of the belt, sharp and sudden, still echoed in her ears. The first searing encounter – the leather a brutal brand on her skin – had taught her that lesson. She remembered the way her breath hitched with each strike, the way her thighs burned. Later, she'd tried to reason with him – *"I was almost done with the dishes, Rhett"* – but his face had darkened, and the belt had come down again. The unspoken threat hung heavy in the air: *"Do not talk back to me."* Each strike reinforced the lesson until her defiance faded into quiet, terrified obedience.

A particularly sharp memory pierced through the fog of years: being forbidden from the kitchen at six years old. She'd sneaked in, just to grab a quick drink, but Rhett had been waiting, his eyes blazing with righteous fury. Twenty strikes to the back of her hand with a switch. Each crack was a brutal echo in the silent house, each blow sending jolts of pain up her arm. "Disobedience equals discipline." The memory lingered like phantom pain. She couldn't shake the bitter conviction that Rhett treated her and Nixx differently, with a cruelty reserved only for them, perhaps fueled by the fact that they weren't biologically his. This theory had been solidified in her mind when Thana had done exactly the same thing when she was six, to be met with Rhett explaining kindly that she just needed to ask before yelling at Mikhail to keep better watch on her youngest siblings.

"Hey," Phenex put a hand on Mikhail's shoulder, "you, okay? You went all Sprocket for a moment." Her brows knit close together with concern.

"I am... No, I'm not. Sorry. I think reality is hitting me a bit hard." Mikhail looked at her sister, her eyes sparkling with wonder, "You're an adult now. We have siblings I've never met..." She sat—or rather, dropped—onto the couch. "How are Enoch and Thana?"

"Enoch has really channeled all that pent-up anger and energy into something positive," Nixx said, a smile creeping onto her face as she sat beside Mikhail. "He's taken up martial arts, inspired by Bruce Lee and Jackie Chan. Can you believe he's fifteen and one in competitions now? The kid's been tearing it up down in Kentucky! I don't really understand the details but he's been so excited about it, I can barely keep up."

Nixx chuckled, remembering the way Enoch would light up while talking about his latest victories and training sessions. "And then there's Thana. She's buried in books, contemplating her future. One day she talks about becoming a doctor: the next, it's law school. I swear, she's got a running joke about becoming Doctor López, Esquire. Ambition is definitely not something she's short on."

Staring at Mikhail, Phenex's eyes lit up with genuine affection. "She stays with Saria and Sprocket in Boston during the school year. Saria keeps her grounded, focused. It's clear that the two of them push each other to aim higher, and I'm so proud of that drive."

"López? But that's our last name... she's Rhett's."

"Yeah, she and Enoch both changed their last names when..." Nixx paused, a realization washing over her. Her sister had been missing since 1987, and their parents died in '93. "Oh," she whispered, her voice barely audible.

Her face softened, eyes widened as she realized the heavy truth of Phenex unspoken words, "How did it happen?" Mikhail asked, feeling a pang of disappointment and heartache.

She gazed down at the floor, her voice laced with sadness and pain as she recounted the events of that night, "Car crash. An unfamiliar road, just like any other day an argument between them caused a distraction, I suppose... The car rolled over into a ravine, trapping them upside down. Rhett... didn't survive the impact. Mami, she was upside down in a ravine." A faint tremble crept into her voice as she locked eyes with Mikhail's, a somber gaze mirroring the sadness in her own.

"Hours later the car and their bodies were discovered. I was twenty-one. As their family member, I was granted custody. Daisy tried to gain custody even threatened court. Luckily, her past-history made that possible." There was a pause, and then she corrected herself, her voice barely above a whisper, "I meant impossible." A hint of resignation crept into her expression as she spoke. "Abuelos were too old to care for young children full time, I couldn't in good conscience do that to them. So I came back." The distance in her eyes seemed to deepen, as if she was lost in memories.

Mikhail sat quietly for a few moments, absorbing the information. "Wow... I am so sorry, Phenex. I can't imagine... You're incredibly strong, Phe-Phe." She reached out and touched Phenex's cheek softly, her thumb brushing against the warmth of her skin. "Good to know you still mix your words," she teased lightly, a small smile breaking through her concern.

"Way to ruin a moment, Misha." A small huff laugh escaped through her nose. Phenex smiled solemnly, "Thank you." nuzzling her cheek against Mikhail's hand like a cat seeking affection. "I appreciate those words coming from you." She glanced at the silver box still tucked under her arm, her brow furrowing. "Mish, my mind is swimming. How are you here? What happened?"

Mikhail sighed, "You'll need to remember some painful memories, Nixx. The red journals will help. But the main one is the leather one that Bryce gave you. If you can decipher the information, if you can remember, we might be able to change things, change them so there is no, are not any disappearances." Her tone was somber, each word weighted with unspoken fear and desperation.

"Nixx!" Hunter's voice cut through the house from the foyer; both Misha and Nixx looked in that direction, "You're not going to believe what happened at school today, Mr. Dickerson," her voice grew louder and softer as she approached the living room, "-- Who were you talking to?"

Chapter 3
Fragmented Ciphers

"Oh, this..." she turned half her body to gesture where Mikhail had been sitting but she was gone, and the silver box she had been protecting left in her place.

It took some convincing for Hunter to believe Nixx when she dismissed her question, claiming she was talking to herself about the latest tech trends. She explained that she was currently working on a portable computer, a device small enough to carry anywhere—from home to coffee shop, hotel, or beach. Laptops existed, but she wanted to make something smaller and more affordable.

Her room was a wreck of a dismantled Talking Battleship game, a few screens, and a motherboard spread across every surface. "I was just working through some ideas out loud," she said. "Packing half a desk into something only an inch thick is proving to be quite a challenge." She hated the act of lying itself, a bitter taste on her tongue. It was a betrayal, a twisting of the truth that ran counter to everything she strived for in her relationship with her siblings. The promise she'd made to them when their parents died, a sacred vow to always meet them on their level, to be honest and open, echoed in her mind, amplifying the guilt. Even the subtle art of omission felt like a lie, a deliberate withholding of information could chip away at the foundation of their trust. Justification for the exception laid in the evidence, the silver box, devoid of any proof connecting it to Mikhail. It was this lack of evidence that allowed her to justify her actions, to tell herself that this deception was different, a necessary evil in a complex and dangerous situation.

Phenex's usual day job was computer programming and building custom computers and hosting LAN parties in her shop downtown. It all started as a hobby, a way for her to escape the stresses of daily life and indulge her passion for technology. After her parents died, leaving her to care for her younger siblings, she knew she needed a stable income. With determination and self-discipline, she dove deeper into self-study, absorbing everything she could about computer repair, software development, and electronics. Her dedication paid off when she managed to open her own small computer repair shop in their hometown.

In the beginning, it was solely Phenex and an almost endless stream of coffee, toiling away for long hours to repair neighbors' computers and construct custom ones from spare parts. She also sold electronics and home appliances, building a small but varied inventory that drew a consistent customer base.

Her business took off when the owners of Foxburns hardware store and the Shelley cousins who owned the bookstore recognized her dedication and drive. They started recommending her to their customers for technological needs and even assisted her in getting better prices on parts and materials. To further support Phenex, Foxburns stopped selling small appliances, allowing her business to thrive, in exchange for a small discount on her services and products.

With their support and her growing reputation for reliable, high-quality service, Phenex's shop began to thrive. Word of mouth spread, and soon, it wasn't just locals coming in but people from neighboring towns as well. She earned enough to hire a small yet reliable staff, each member carefully chosen for their expertise and customer service skills. This allowed Phenex to focus more on the programming side of her business, taking on larger projects and even some custom software development.

By the time Ryder had returned home from school, Hunter was convinced that Phenex had in fact been talking to herself about complex math, logistics and blueprints. While the younger children worked on their schoolwork, Phenex made a light dinner. As they sat at the table, Hunter started excitedly recounting the day's events, including Mr. Dickerson's unfortunate wardrobe malfunction.

Somehow, the teacher had managed to rip his pants, from the zipper to the waistband, in front of nearly the entire school during an assembly. "It was seniors and juniors versus the teachers in this ultimate relay race. Mr. Dickerson was at the table crawl, where you're supposed to crawl under the tables. But since they were in the gym for the pep rally, he was in socks and tried to slide under them."

Phenex laughed, "Dickerson is in his late fifties! He shouldn't be doing that."

"That's what Dillon and I said!" Hunter continued, "When he jumped up, he just looked scared." Hunter and Ryder chuckled, but their laughter was tinged with sympathy for Mr. Dickerson.

Nixx had genuinely liked him as a teacher during her school years, and she couldn't help but feel sorry for him now. He had been the history teacher when she was a student, he still taught history, he was now also the principal, overseeing the elementary school students.

"I don't think I've ever seen Mrs. Schon move so quickly. She covered him with one of the burlaps from the sack race," Ryder continued where Hunter left off. "James McKnight, who was racing against him, didn't even realize what had happened and was already doing the Roger Rabbit."

Nixx shook her head bringing herself back to reality from staring at the silver box, "Sounds like an interesting day. So, you two not going to the game tonight?" she stole another glance as the kids started speaking again.

"I wanted to go to the movies with Dillon and their parents if that's okay. Mr. Foxburn said it was okay but told me I had to ask you, too. They're going to watch Ernest in the Army." Hunter looked at Nixx with pleading eyes.

"Homework?"

"It's Friday, Phe-Phe, please? I'll do dishes all weekend!"

"Stop with the puppy eyes, that's manipulation!" Nixx laughed as she feigned defeat. "Call Dillon, tell 'em it's fine, but I want to speak to David or Monika before you hang up." She smiled. "If you promise to clean the downstairs bathroom, I'll throw in a fiver, but if you forget, you owe me ten."

"Deal!" Hunter shouted, running to the phone in the living room.

"What about you, papito?" she asked, pulling a five-dollar bill from her wallet on the table. "Movies with friends, game, or is it you and I tonight?"

Ryder looked up at the ceiling for a moment, as he usually did when weighing his options. His dark eyes darted from one corner to the other. "How did you know I was invited to the movies?"

"David... Mr. Foxburn called earlier in the week," Nixx allowed herself to laugh after checking to see if Hunter was still in the other room. "Don't tell your sister," She winked.

"Mana malvada, muy evil" he laughed, enjoying their shared secret. "What can I do for five?"

"Uh... upstairs bathroom, and trash." Phenex narrowed her eyes realizing that Ryder would spot the loophole, "All trash, including the garage."

"Extra three, and I'll vacuum the car."

Nixx laughed. "Oh, good negotiation, you have a deal. But done by seven on Sunday night, okay? Or you owe me fifteen." She gave a ten-dollar bill to Ryder, "Give the change to Hunter, I owe her two dollars anyway."

"Hey, Nixx, Mrs. Foxburn is on the phone for you," Hunter said as she walked back into the dining room, extending her hand with the cordless phone.

⧗ ⧗ ⧗

The house settled into a silent stillness, a welcome relief after the twins' energetic farewell as they left with the Foxburns. Phenex savored the silence, a brief respite from the whirlwind of life with two nine-year-olds. Her gaze, however, was drawn to the silver box, a tangible echo of Mikhail's departure. Her hand, usually steady with a pen or soldering iron, trembled as she reached for it. The metal surface caught the dim light, reflecting her own hesitation. *It's just a box,* she chided herself, but the knot in her stomach remained. She studied it, a simple silver rectangle, unremarkable save for its unusual presence. Smooth, cool steel, a single handle centered on the lid, designed for easy carrying. A small, four-digit combination lock, an integral part of the box's structure, dominated the front, each dial displaying the numerals zero through nine.

Turning away from the silver box, Phenex forced herself to focus on routine; bills, monotonous cleaning, anything to distract her from its magnetic pull of the mystery inside the lock box. The steady, rhythmic ticking of the clock seemed to amplify the tension in her chest.

Her thoughts drifted back to the day's bewildering events, including the dream, and how it felt impossible that, in just over twelve hours, so much had occurred, and yet she felt more lost than ever. *The box is here, isn't it? It has got to be real.*

As she organized the order forms from work, her gaze drifted to the box of old notebooks from high school that she had rediscovered earlier in the day. Her brow knit together with cautious curiosity as an urge to revisit the contents of the cardboard box tugged at her. She carefully pulled the flaps open once more. Inside, various black cardboard-bound composition notebooks filled the box, each labeled with the year, grade, and the names of their previous owners. Some had her name scrawled in blocky letters across the standard white label that read "Belongs to," while others bore the names of her friends.

One notebook, labeled "*Keep out! MIKHAIL'S EYES ONLY!! AGE 13*", particularly piqued her interest, but she decided to set it aside for now. Instead, her eyes landed on a cluster of notebooks tied together with an oversized rubber band. A yellowing sheet of paper tucked beneath them had caught her attention; it was marked "1987-1988 Bryce, Saria, Casey, Nixx; Quantum Annoyance and Misha's Missing," written in her own handwriting, albeit a little less refined as her handwriting changed with age.

As she combed through the notebooks, one in particular held her gaze. Bryce's name was written in blue marker across the front, drawing her full attention. She set her glass down, her hand hovering for a moment as her eyes remained fixed on the calendar inside the notebook. The amber liquid swirled lazily inside the glass, a warm glow spreading through the dimly lit room. She ran her finger across the hand-drawn grid, the worn paper creaking softly beneath her touch. Bryce's neat, slanting script and her own messy handwriting were etched into the calendar, a chaotic blend of notes and reminders that seemed to mock her now.

She scanned the grid, dates and appointments blurred together, but one entry made her pause. The paper seemed to shimmer before her eyes as her finger lingered on the year of Mikhail's disappearance. She traced her fingers along the date, *Nineteen ninety-eight that's this year. Fifty-three. Seventy. What the...* The memory was elusive, slipping through her grasp like sand between fingers. She looked at the calendar on her wall, dates and times carefully mark with events throughout the week and month. Dates that bills were due, and silly messages in the margins. She focused on each day. The calendar in the notebook only depicted February until May of '87, cutting off on May 10th. She looked again; *no way is it this easy.*

She spun the dial of the lock box, a rhythmic *click-click-click* echoing in the hush. "Okay... Not that. Not my birthday. Not when she vanished. ¡Pensad, Alejandra, think!" The Spanish, a reflexive outburst in moments of intense pressure, hung in the air. Frustration, a hot, stinging wave, washed over her, and she collapsed onto the couch in a messy heap, a blend of tantrum and utter exasperation. In these moments of heightened stress, she would often slip into using her middle name, "Alejandra," a habit she associated with Bryce, who had used it affectionately, or sometimes with playful exasperation, during their shared, often-turbulent, teenage years. The stubborn lockbox was relentlessly pushing her towards that raw, unguarded edge.

She flipped through a composition notebook, a drawing of a dragon or some other less identifiable creature had been carved into the cardboard cover. There were the same calendars on one page, some random notes to one another on another. Memories that had been pushed aside or hidden away started to surface like bubbles in water. Camping trips in the woods. Lunches at Sova's Diner. Prom. Moments suspended in time, documented by the only witnesses.

She grabbed another notebook, this one appearing to be a journal kept by Mikhail—a collection of moments Phenex couldn't recall, stories filled with unshared memories and events that she had deliberately kept from her. With a sense of trepidation, she slowly turned the pages, her fingers tracing the details of the words within. Each page unveiled mundane exchanges: musings about the future, gripes about their parents' quirks, and the usual sibling achievements and aspirations. One page, however, caught her attention; it was scattered with their familiar code, hastily written in a style that broke from Mikhail's typically meticulous penmanship.

As she examined the puzzling combination of letters and numbers, curiosity ignited within her. "What are you trying to say,

Misha?" she murmured, her mind racing to connect the dots. She pulled out her multi-colored pen and began to scrawl the cryptic symbols next to her sister's writing.

She muttered to herself, staring intently at the notebook page as her eyes danced over the ambiguous notation: "*71/GN14, (nBN_BM23)*" The scribbles seemed to leap off the page, taunting her in a cryptic code she didn't understand. A spark of insight flickered to life within her mind as she pondered the possibility, *a code*.

As her eyes roved over the symbols, the thrill of a connection began to build within her, a spark growing as she realized the code was a simple number and letter switch, a double cipher using their favorite band and the alphabet. Her gaze snapped to the scribbles as she hastily sketched a new interpretation on her hand running out of room on the page: "53/36N (-97W)." The format now unmistakable, a set of geographical coordinates, pointing to a precise location on the map. Her heart quickened, her mind racing with the potential implications of this discovery.

With a sense of purpose, she seized her atlas and began to flip through its pages with growing urgency. Each map spread whispered possibilities, and as she finally landed on the section for Wakford, Oklahoma, her breath caught in her throat. This wasn't just any ordinary town; it was her hometown, a place where nearly all her memories were woven into its landscape. Summers spent chasing her friends through sun-kissed streets, swimming in the Buresh's cattle pond on sweltering afternoons, and catching fireflies on warm summer nights all came flooding back, mingling with the memories of more recent times.

The pain of those days still lingered, an open wound. She remembered the blue truck racing down the main street, Mikhail's blood-curdling scream echoing through her mind, and the stark contrast of a teacher's brutal slap across Bryce's back for falling asleep in class, met with utter apathy. The incident was dismissed, attributed to Mrs. Schon's medication allegedly causing lapses in judgment.

"What are you trying to tell me, Claudia?" Her thoughts were laced with bitterness. Calling her by her first name – Claudia – was Phenex's way of needling Mikhail when she was irritated, a name Mikhail absolutely detested. In the decade since Claudia's disappearance, using the name, even internally, felt like a strange connection to her sister, albeit one without the usual satisfaction of getting under Mikhail's skin. Now, after ten years, she was chasing some dream, a manifestation of the guilt and shame she felt for daring to be happy when her elder sister's disappearance remained a mystery. She circled the spot on the map where the coordinates pointed. "Boomer Cave?" she muttered. An echo from the past cried out in her mind, correcting her: "Sooner Cave."

Phenex felt a mix of hope and fear swelling within her. She traced the coordinates in the atlas with her finger, confirming just a few miles outside of Wakford off the hiking trails around Triplet Lake and the falls. "I have to go there," she decided, resolve igniting within her.

She leaned back in her chair, closing her eyes as she pinched the bridge of her nose, as she sighed as she glanced at the clock. The second hand seemed to slow to nearly a stop as she realized it was just after one in the morning. *I need the code. Four digits. Something even Misha would know.* She let out a light groan of frustration, nearly six hours of combing through journals, notes, decoding and chasing a literal ghost for her to have only come back to her original suspicions from when Mikhail first disappeared.

With sleep clinging to the edges of Phenex's mind, a single thought broke through the fog—the combination. It surfaced around two in the morning, a long-buried memory finally rising to the surface. With a sigh of relief, she sank onto the couch, the lockbox now resting on the coffee table, its secrets within her grasp. She attempted spinning the dial again, feeling the click of the dial as it rotated, each number a heavy thump as she stopped on each number. Click-click-CLUNK. The sound of the latch sliding to the open position caused her heart to leap excitedly, the coordinates had been the key. Slowly she lifted the lid of the box terrified yet excited for what contents may be inside.

The steel lockbox contained a small stack of journal pages, ripped from the binding. Flipping through twenty or so entries, she saw the dates ranging from March 3rd to May 8th. *March third... wasn't that?* Her hand instinctively went to the back of her head, fingers tracing a subtle indentation. The hair there, once dark mahogany, now grew back a pale, ashen shade, concealing a scar at the base of her skull. As she read the March 3rd entry, vivid images flooded back – cold water washing over her, the sensation of being pulled under, the taste of water in her nose.

A few words seemed to jump out at her, "Different. Changed. Older," etched on a page, but their impact was lost on her tired eyes. After hours of pouring over the journals, her hands shook as she flipped through the pages, seeking a brief respite from the endless flow of words. She pulled out a stack of polaroid pictures, their faded colors a welcome change from the strain of reading. As she gazed through the photographs, more memories surged back, memories long forgotten.

A particular picture caught her eye - Enoch, tiny and wrapped in stuffed animals, a testament to Thana's desire to introduce her newborn brother to the world of play. Another snapshot showed Bryce and Phenex, laughing and covered in mud, their joy infectious. A third image revealed Casey and Saria, their middle fingers raised in a playful gesture, their lips locked in a kiss under the mistletoe at a Christmas party. A tinge of confusion sank her heart as she stared at the image a moment longer, *I don't remember this*. Casey's hair was buzzed short, a hair cut he had adopted after high school. The faint stubble of a beard graced his jawline.

Hesitation and anxiety started to envelop her as she continued to browse through the photos, one image brought the group together - all five of them, smiling and carefree. A memory that she held fondly. Mikhail sat cross-legged on the floor, engrossed in a vinyl record, while Saria lounged on the beanbag next to the bedroom window, the warm glow of sunlight streaming in. Casey, Bryce, and Phenex herself hung upside down from the top bunk, their laughter and joy palpable. The scene was a celebration of Bryce's emancipation, a milestone marked by their group's unwavering support. Each of them, aged between thirteen and sixteen, had come together to toast Bryce's newfound freedom.

Between the photo of the five of them celebrating Bryce's emancipation and the next one was a news clipping, she unfolded the paper.

The headline read in massive bold letters: "Missing Teen; PHENEX ALEJANDRA LÓPEZ."

Phenex felt a cold dread grip her. The world seemed to tilt, the edges blurring. Her breath hitched, a strangled sound in the sudden silence of the room. *Me?* The thought echoed in her mind, a painful throb against her skull. Eleven years. Eleven years of imagining, hoping, grieving and this was wrong. The date of the paper read; Thursday, May 14, 1987.

A wave of nausea hit her, and she stumbled backward, bumping into the wall. Her vision tunneled, the sounds of the room fading into a dull roar. *Missing...Mikhail...* But it was her photo that stared back at her. Her name in the article.

Phenex Alejandra López, 15-year-old resident of Wakford, Grant County, Oklahoma, last seen 12:30 P.M. Sunday. She is 5 feet 3 inches tall and weighs approximately 146 pounds. López was wearing a black jacket, denim jeans, and no shoes.

If any information, contact the county sheriff's office or Colette and/or Rhett Nemain at 594-2584.

She flung the papers back into the lockbox, slamming the lid shut with a frustrated thud that nearly caught her fingers. "No, no, no, this isn't right!" The words escaped her in a rush, each syllable tinged with rising panic. She needed clarity. Diving into her pocket, she retrieved a tin of mints, twisting it open like a lifeline. With urgency, she popped one into her mouth, biting down hard. A vivid explosion of eucalyptus and mint surged through her senses, sharp and invigorating, offering a brief respite from the chaos swirling in her mind.

Her pacing came to an abrupt halt. Gripping her necklace tightly, she focused on the cool metal rings, each one a silent promise to herself. She pressed her fingers into the smooth stones embedded within, hoping they would anchor her in this moment of turmoil. Sitting down, she forced herself to inhale deeply, letting the air fill her lungs, a slow, deliberate act that, while not a cure, helped temper the panic lurking just beneath the surface.

With each exhale, she willed her racing heart to slow. She leaned back, her eyes locked onto the ceiling, and began to tap her fingers against her thumb, three beats for each finger. The rhythmic repetition soothed her, guiding her racing thoughts as she synchronized the movements with the stroking of her left index finger over the rings on her necklace. Round after round, the familiarity wrapped around her like a comforting blanket.

But suddenly, she felt the weight of realization settle over her— this wasn't just a passing moment; she had slipped back into an old anxious habit. The very act of counting had become a frantic ritual, a reminder of the anxiety she thought she had left behind.

In the back of her mind, Rhett's voice echoed, "Why are you looking stupid like that?" She halted, forced her fingers into a fist, and set her hand beside her before jumping to her feet once more, pacing back and forth.

Why am I listed as the missing person? That's me... I was staring at myself. She felt her knees shaking as her mind rushed to process what she had read and what she knew. *This is not happening.* She quickly gathered a small backpack, her GPS, a refurbished Garmin 75 model GPS unit, the lockbox, and a small first-aid kit. She glanced at the analog clock on the wall: 6:17. *Have I really been up all night?* The kids likely would not be back until early in the afternoon; she had time, and she would be back before the twins returned home.

Her heart raced as she drove to the Creek Trails. She made a quick stop at Ray's Good Day for a cup of coffee before continuing. Once she arrived, she parked and locked her car, double-checking her backpack to ensure she had everything she needed, including water. She made her way back to the tree house, occasionally clasping at her necklace as if it were assuring her she was doing the right thing. This time, things seemed different as she veered from the path heading to the clearing where she and Mikhail had spent so many weekends, shared memories, and conversations—before it became the place of painful memories where her sister had disappeared, where she had found her sister's strange appearance and the lockbox.

She paused at the clearing, her eyes scanning the remnants of the treehouse before following the path guided by the geographical coordinates she had programmed into her GPS. For a moment, she stopped to remember the large creek that had once flowed behind the treehouse. Over the years, drought, town expansion, and shifting land had reduced the once nearly five-meter-wide creek to less than two meters. The rocks that had once been nearly invisible due to the creek's depth were now exposed, serving as easy steppingstones to hop across.

She was nearly halfway across the almost dry creek bed, staring intently at the flickering screen of the GPS as she tried to decipher its blinking icons and squiggly lines. The world around her began to dissolve into a hazy blur. Colors swirled, and shadows danced at the edges of her vision as if reality were slipping away, leaving her adrift in a dream. A wave of nausea rolled through her, settling in her stomach like a heavy stone, while dizziness unfurled in her mind, warping her sense of balance. She fought to focus, but the sensation of vertigo threatened to pull her under.

CHAPTER 4

REPEATING TEEN TURBULENCE

"PHEEEEEEENEEEEEX!!!!" The sudden, piercing screech of her name sliced through the fog, reverberating off the trees like a frantic siren. The familiar voice jolted her back to reality, and she spun around, her heart pounding wildly in her chest, to see her sister Mikhail hurtling toward her, panic etched across her features.

Phenex felt her feet slip out from beneath her. "What the—CRAP!!" Before she could fully process the loss of her balance or make a desperate attempt to catch herself, she was hurtling into the rushing water. The frigid water slammed into her, stealing her breath and shocking her muscles into an unbearable, painful clench.

The icy water engulfed her, a suffocating embrace that threatened to drag her into the depths. Her backpack, a heavy anchor, pulled her further down, each movement a desperate struggle against the relentless current. As she fought to break free, at first, it was darkness, then a kaleidoscope of colors swirled around her, a surreal dance of reds, oranges, blues and greens that seemed to mock her plight.

Panic ensnared her, a stealthy predator creeping closer to its prey. Her lungs burned, a desperate plea for air, and her limbs grew heavy with the weight of the water. She thrashed, struggling erratically, trying to free herself from the backpack, but the river's grip tightened, pulling her deeper into its frigid embrace.

She desperately attempted to regain control and swim, freeing herself from the weight of her backpack. But the current was unforgiving, hurling her hard against the embankment, slamming her with brutal force. Her head snapped back, striking the base of her skull with a sharp thud on what she thought was a rock. An excruciating pain reverberated in her mind, causing her to cry out in agony just as she managed to snatch a faint breath. The shock of the impact left her lungs empty, and she plummeted downwards into the icy creek, the water's edge a distant memory. Her thoughts screamed in panic, *how is the water this deep?* as she stretched out her arms, straining desperately to reach the surface and the sliver of light beckoning her upwards.

Her body was feeling weaker as it began to sink as though filling with concrete, her limbs heavy. *This is it...* The edges of her vision dissolved fading into blurred shades of grey, leaving only the darkness directly ahead, closing in around her. Just as the blackness was about to engulf her, a strong yank pulled her upward by the hood of her jacket. A garbled voice, barely recognizable, cut through the water as her head broke through the surface.

Her lungs protesting as she gasped for air as she was pulled to the bank. The cold water seeped into her bones, numbing her senses. She clung to her savior, her body trembling uncontrollably. A wave of relief washed over her as she realized she was safe, at least for now.

Phenex coughed violently, expelling a mouthful of water as her body began to convulse with uncontrollable shivers. A sharp, numbing sensation, like a thousand tiny needles, coursed through her limbs. Scrabbling on her hands and knees, she collapsed and rolled onto her back, staring at the sky and gasping for air. Mikhail loomed over her, her voice muffled and distant as Phenex struggled to process the near-drowning experience.

"Nixx, Nixx, dios mío, ¿estas bien?" she said, panic and fear etched into every syllable as she hovered over her sister.

After a few agonizing moments, gasping for air, Phenex could feel her heart hammering against the ground with frightening intensity. She pushed herself to her feet, a storm of confusion, anger, and fear contorting her features. Stepping forward, she gripped her sister's shoulders tightly and began to speak rapidly and erratically in Spanish, the urgency of her emotions overwhelming her ability to be coherent. Realizing she was rambling too quickly for Mikhail to understand the full weight of her distress, she switched to English, slowing her pace to punctuate each word clearly, "How are you here?" she finally exclaimed. "You disappeared again, Mikhail!" Her anger flared, and she began to flap her hands, trying to cool them down, focusing on her breathing.

"Whoa, Phenex, slow down," Mikhail said calmly, taking a slow step forward as she placed a gentle hand on her younger sister's shoulder. She was afraid of escalating Phenex's panic and spoke in a soothing tone. Her hands were open, hoping to project a non-threatening posture. She slowly reached out, gently taking Phenex's hands and holding them between her own. Glancing down as she stepped closer, she noticed an worrying shade of red staining the ground where Phenex had been lying. "Oh, miércoles," she muttered under her breath. Without hesitation, she carefully but quickly spun Phenex around to examine the back of her head. A small, no longer than her first knuckle but deep cut was revealed. "Jesus Cristo, Phenex, sangre." She pulled the bandana she carried in her back pocket and placed it against the wound.

Phenex instinctively brought her hand to the back of her head and took over pressing on where Mikhail was holding the cloth. She turned slowly and stared at her sister in disbelief. Mikhail seemed to ignore her words as she spoke. Though replaying her own words in her mind, she could understand that her sister would be confused and looking for a head injury had their roles been reversed. "Why… No…" the throbbing pain at the back of her head distracted her. She closed her eyes tight trying to bring everything into focus again.

"Oh here, I found these where you fell in." Mikhail said holding out a pair of rectangular black framed glasses.

As she reached out to take her eyewear she froze. It wasn't anything major, but her nails were painted, the tips of her fingers had smears of black ink from the running sharpie. *¿Qué demonios?* Her eyes quickly scanned the area, looking past her sister she saw the waterfalls again, still pristine. She realized the area was different, cleaner, almost untouched. She placed her glasses on her face, and looked at her free hand, her arms bare, the bright tattoos that adorned her left arm were gone, leaving behind a fresh tapestry of cuts, as if the artist had painted them anew. She quickly pulled her arm back into the sleeve of her jacket. *What's going on?*

⧗ ⧗ ⧗

Mikhail guided Phenex back to the treehouse, the silence between them thick with silent questions and unresolved tensions. As they sat on the worn futon, the familiar creak of the wooden slats beneath them seemed to echo the uncertainty that hung in the air. Phenex's eyes darted around the space, her brow furrowed in confusion. "Mikhail?" she whispered, her voice trembling like a leaf. The memories she had been trying to grasp slipped through her fingers like grains of sand, leaving her with more questions than answers.

As she struggled to piece together the fragmented recollections, the events of the morning came flooding back - the frantic search for clues about her sister, the desperation that had driven her to search again, despite the decade that had passed since Mikhail's disappearance in nineteen eighty-seven. The weight of her emotions threatened to overwhelm her, each twist and turn leaving her breathless and disoriented. Yet, here she was, sitting in the treehouse, surrounded by the musty scent of moss and earth. The space was alive again, untouched by time.

Phenex's gaze fell upon her hands, and a jolt of realization ran through her. They were familiar, yet foreign, like a distant memory that refused to be grasped. She turned them over, studying the lines and creases, the shape of her fingers. The truth hit her like a ton of bricks: she was no longer twenty-six. The realization sent a shiver down her spine, leaving her wondering what had happened, and how she had gotten here.

Mikhail reached out her hand, placing it against Phenex's cheek. "Phe-Phe, ¿qué te pasó?"

Phenex's face sank into Mikhail's hand, and she closed her eyes, her breath slowing. For a moment, the world around her stilled. Then she opened her eyes, a frown etching across her face. The tree house looked... different. Not like it had in her memories, with its weathered wooden planks and overgrown vines. This one was sturdy, with fresh wood grain shining in the sunlight.

She touched the back of her head, wincing as her fingers brushed against a tender cut and the image of a large festering purple bruise flashed in her mind. "I..."

Mikhail's hand cradled her face, a gentle smile on her lips. Phenex felt a sense of calm seep back in, but it was fragile.

"I remember I was looking for you," she said, her voice barely above a whisper. "Climbing the ridge near the waterfalls. Is it a dream? I've had it before, this exact one."

She trailed her fingers down her wrist, her eyes following as she gazed at the three deep gashes across her skin. Her tattoos, once a protective barrier over her scars, were gone. Every single one.

Mikhail's hand moved, guiding Phenex's face away from her palm. "You're okay, Phenex," she said softly. "Let me take a look."

Phenex's eyes flicked up to her sister's face, then quickly darted back to their feet as Mikhail examined the bruise on the back of her head. Mikhail's eyebrows drew together, her lips pressed into a worried line. "Es no malo," she murmured, the Spanish words laced with concern. "What day is it?"

"I don't know, Saturday?" Phenex replied, her voice hesitant. The day was a guess, pulled from a foggy memory triggered by the journal's pages. In '98, for her, it was Saturday, March 7th. She clung to that certainty, hoping her assumptions about the dates were true.

"Full name?"

"Yours or mine?"

"Either."

"Claudia Mikhail y Phenex Alejandra López."

"You're only getting by with calling me Claudia because of the bump on your head Nixx." Mikhail teased. "What year is it?"

"Ninety... Nineteen eighty-seven?"

"The good news is I don't think you have a concussion. Your eyes are dilating properly, and you answered the questions correctly." she said, "You'll be okay. We should head home; how does it feel when you stand?"

Phenex grabbed her jacket from the back of the futon. A slight dampness clung to the thick fabric, a lingering reminder of the unexpected swim, despite the fireplace's warmth that had already dried the rest of her clothes. With a flicker of disappointment, she tied it around her waist. Rising to her full height, she stared at the floor, as if searching for a forgotten thought. "Misha," she said slowly, "Do we need to go home? Can we not stay here another night?" The cut on her head throbbed with each pulsation of her heart. She reached for the bandana that had been used to clean the blood from her head, stiff with dried blood. With a sigh, she tied the dark bandana around her wrist to hide the tapestry of thin red lines that marked her arm.

"I don't think so," Mikhail reminded her, her voice even. "The... *mouth breather* has been on us about curfew and chores lately." She paused, her brow furrowing with concern. "Are you sure you're okay?"

"Yeah, just a bit confused, head pain," Phenex said, nodding slowly. She paused, carefully choosing her words to conceal her true feelings. "I don't know, it's like déjà vu, but backwards—jamais vu. I know I've done this before, but it's like I'm disassociating, watching what I'm doing and being part of it at the same time."

With a slight shiver, she forged ahead through the woods. The early spring air was crisp, tinged with the first whispers of warmth as snowmelt trickled into the nearby creek. Sunlight poured through the bare branches, now beginning to bud, casting intricate patterns on the ground where last autumn's leaves lay in quiet decay beneath their shoes.

As they navigated through the overgrown dead grass, which still bore the last remnants of winter, patches of green began to peek through. Delicate wildflowers, bold in hues of violet and yellow, poked through the undergrowth, signaling spring's arrival in this quiet corner of Oklahoma.

They climbed over a massive fallen tree, its wood damp from recent rains and cool against their skin as they maneuvered across it. A few insects scurried away in protest, disturbed by their presence. Each step was practiced, and deliberate as they dropped from the tree onto the trail that led back to Ray's Good Day, back to town, and back to their house, where chaos would surely greet them.

Mikhail raised an eyebrow as they continued to walk toward their home, "I guess that makes sense with the emu egg on the back of your head. We will need to tell Mother about it so she can keep an eye on you. We can tell her–"

"That I- you- hit it while taking the two-hundred trail. You were on the rocks, and because–" They were speaking in unison, Mikhail's voice faded off, "I slipped." Phenex finished.

Mikhail stopped walking, captivated by the sight of Phenex receding. She carried herself with a newfound confidence, a subtle power in her stride. The hesitation in her speech remained, but it was tempered by an unexpected depth of understanding that surprised Mikhail.

"Coming, Mish?" Phenex called, walking backward, her tone edged with playful impatience. "Rhett will be on our case if we're late for chores. We might need to jog the last half, you slowpoke." She spun around with a laugh and took off at a sprint. "Race you, Mikhail!" Her voice trailed behind her as she ran.

The girls were laughing by the time they made it to the front porch, Phenex shouted, "I win!" as she leaped over the three steps and touched the door. "When did you get so slow, Misha?" she teased, pulling her key from her kangaroo shoes.

The laughter vanished as they entered the house. Rhett sat in his chair, the lamplight painting a dark shadow across his face. Phenex stopped short in the doorway, her breath catching in her throat. Mikhail, following close behind, bumped into her, a small "oof" escaping her. The cold fury in Rhett's eyes seemed to freeze the air itself, silencing the girls instantly. "You're late," Rhett said, his voice dangerously calm.

Mikhail checked her wristwatch, then muttered, "It's not even six." She gave a gentle nudge, urging Phenex forward before Rhett could erupt in anger about the door being left open.

"Excuse me?" his voice rising as he stood, his dark blue eyes seemed to flash for a moment, his brows knit together.

Phenex stepped closer, narrowing the distance between her face and his to just a few inches. "What are we exactly late for, Rhett?" she asked, her tone a mix of exasperation and irritation. "Curfew? Saturday's curfew is nine." An almost smug smile played at the corner of her lips, "When the big hand is on the twelve, and the little hand is on the nine." She paused, her eyes flitting to the clock before looking back at him again, "Right now, the *big* hand is just after the twelve and the *wittle* hand is on the six. I don't think I can simplify it more than that." She leaned in a bit, directing his gaze with an exaggerated gesture toward the clock on the wall. Each time she mentioned a part of the clock, she punctuated her words by pointing dramatically, ensuring he grasped every detail.

"Phenex…" Mikhail quickly pulled her back, stepping protectively in front of her. She locked her arm around Phenex's waist, securing her behind her. "¿Qué demonios!?" she exclaimed.

"You don't speak to me like that, ungrateful little girl," Rhett snapped, taken aback by Phenex's defiant tone. He was accustomed to Mikhail addressing him with such boldness, but Phenex was typically compliant, quiet, and calm; he had instilled a sense of dread in her, making her feel as though she had faced the wrath of God and would again if she ever went against him. So why was she suddenly confronting him with such reckless insolence?

"She hit her head, Rhett. We were hiking the two hundred trails, and she fell. Probably just dazed, a head injury aggravated, like when Enoch hit his head at the park last year. I don't know, maybe the wind knocked her off balance." Mikhail spoke quickly, almost inconsistent, her eyes darting between Rhett and Phenex as she wrapped a protective arm around the other girl's waist. She steered Phenex away, guiding her toward their room, half-leading, halfshoving her along as if trying to contain a wild animal. Mikhail's voice dropped to a hushed, harsh whisper. "What the hell was that Nixx? Why were you like that? You scared me."

Phenex's brow furrowed in confusion, echoing Mikhail's own anxiety. "I... I don't know where that came from," she said, her voice remarkably steady, betraying none of the inner turmoil that churned within her. She reached a hand to the familiar weight at her throat, the corded necklace she always wore. But as her fingers brushed against the pendant, a jolt of disorientation ran through her. The familiar three rings weren't there. Instead, her fingers traced the outline of twisted wire wrapped around four separate, rough-hewn rocks and stones.

How did I not notice that earlier? The thought screamed in her mind, amplified by the growing panic that threatened to consume her. Her mind began to race, a dizzying carousel of conflicting information and sudden revelations. The realization hit her like a physical blow: *Her* adult consciousness, the accumulated experiences of her adult life, was trapped within the body of her teenage self.

Mikhail had noticed earlier that Phenex seemed to speak louder, almost more confidently. It was subtle. Most wouldn't notice except for the complete personality shift when she sarcastically explained a clock to Rhett. Mikhail was uncertain if she needed to praise her younger sister or if they needed to go on the run. Rhett seemed so taken aback by Phenex's sudden hostility that he was thankfully at a loss for words and stayed back in the living room. She took a step forward, a mixture of concern and confusion etched on her face as she reached out a hand to Phenex, hesitantly touching her arm as if offering a lifeline. "Phe, what's going on?" she asked, her voice barely above a whisper. "What's happening?" She searched her sister's face, her eyes scanning her features as if hoping to find an answer etched somewhere on her expression.

Phenex sat on the lower bunk bed, her back rigid as though under inspection. Her features were a battleground of conflicting emotions: shock and bewilderment warring with a flicker of something else, a defiance she hadn't dared to acknowledge in years. *Holy hell… I said that.* The words echoed in her mind, a jarring replay of her own unexpected outburst. *What is happening to me?* The sensation of being adrift, of observing her own life through a distorted lens, was overwhelming. She needed to be alone, to process the chaos, to understand the words, the tone, the raw emotions that weren't her own. "I have to pee," she mumbled abruptly, almost bolting across the room and into the bathroom across the hall. The need for physical separation, for a moment of unobserved clarity, consumed her. She locked the door, then placed the small toilet paper stand in front of it, a symbolic, albeit ineffective, barrier. The stand wouldn't stop anyone, but its displacement would serve as a primitive warning, a subtle indicator of intrusion. *Just… breathe.*

Alone in front of the mirror after taking a shower, she stared at her reflection, a ghost of her younger self peering back at her. The steam clung to the glass, softening the harsh lines of adulthood and reminding her of a time when innocence still lingered. As she dried her thick hair with a towel, it tumbled over her face in dark waves, a curtain that momentarily shielded her from the world. She was cautious, mindful of the raw, tender cut on the back of her head, a faint reminder of a recent struggle.

With each careful swipe of the towel, she felt the coolness of the fabric against her skin, grounding her in the present. Confusion had clouded her mind earlier, but now, dressed only in shorts and an undershirt, she examined herself critically. The soft glow of the bathroom light exposed every imperfection and scar, reflections of battles fought and endured. She took a deep breath, steadying her racing thoughts as she scrutinized the woman in the mirror, searching for the strength she knew she possessed but felt she was losing.

She ran her fingers lightly over her face, her arms, and down to her thighs. Occasionally, her touch lingered over faint scars and a few fresh cuts, reminders of moments of pain she had experienced days and at the same time years ago. She paused on her right wrist the longest; her first tattoo, and only tattoo on that arm were her sister's handwritten words, *Te amo, -Mikhail* "was gone. She had it since she was seventeen, she and Bryce had gone to Mexico while she was visiting Bryce at Baylor University in the summer. *My best friends.* She removed the cord from her neck and examined the stones, each a representation of one of her closest friends. The stones would be replaced in a few months with the class rings of her friends as they left for college that she would continue to wear into her adulthood.

Her hands trembled as she realized that this was the year Mikhail disappeared. The year everything changed. She was left behind, and though she didn't blame her friends, she was alone. *I can see Casey and Saria… I can tell…* "Bryce" she whispered remembering the scent of sandalwood from the hoodie she found earlier.

She splashed cool water on her face, trying to ground her mind, spiraling as she forced herself not to focus on Bryce, or Casey, or any of her high school friends and hoping to pull herself from the surreal situation. She retraced her skin; a mix of disbelief and a lingering sense of numbness washed over her. *I was drinking alone; could this be an insane intoxication-induced dream? No… I would have woken up at this point. Unless I'm dead?* "Wait… reading." she reached for a shampoo bottle, remembering something she had read in a magazine that people cannot read in their dreams. She stared at the shampoo bottle for a moment. The words were clear as she read the ingredients. Admittedly, half the ingredients were chemical compounds she could not pronounce, but she was able to read, so it did not count. "Okay, that was a bust." she tossed the bottle into the tub, not caring to place it back where it had been.

Okay. You're fifteen, it's nineteen eighty-seven. And it is– She stopped, "The journal." Suddenly, she realized what some of the entries meant. The lines she had glanced at in Mikhail's distinct handwriting. *Phenex hit her head. Acting differently. Beyond years.* She touched the back of her head and winced; the injury was still fresh, she could feel the cut about three centimeters long, and the bruise was extremely tender. She thought for a moment, she did remember this, but it was fuzzy like she was looking at it through frosted glass. *No way.* She thought, looking for the small magnetic bank calendar they kept in the bathroom.

There was a nearly silent click, Mikhail slipped inside after picking the lock. The metal toilet paper stand clattered on the floor, shattering the uneasy silence of the small bathroom. A cascade of toiletries followed, adding to the sudden disruption. Phenex, her face obscured beneath the sink in a frantic search for the tiny calendar, didn't react. Mikhail, perched against the tub's porcelain side, finally broke the quiet. "Hey," she said softly, her voice carrying the weight of unspoken questions. "What was that?" she asked, her eyes locked on her sister, still half-hidden within the cabinet.

Phenex backed out of the cabinet but remained staring into it, a glazed look in her eyes as she continued searching, "I just was tired of him treating you… treating us–"

"Nixx, look at me." Mikhail's voice was firm, almost commanding.

Phenex shook her head pulling herself out of whatever trance she caught herself in and stood. She closed her eyes and sighed before making eye contact with Mikhail, "I'm sorry, Mish, I am just so exhausted. I never stood up to him when… I mean, I didn't…" She swallowed the lump that formed in her throat, hoping the right words would come to her.

"You're her, aren't you?" Mikhail asked quietly before Phenex could say anything more.

"Yeah, of course, I'm your sister. I thought I was the one who hit her head." Her tone was playful but dismissive.

Mikhail raised an eyebrow as she stood, stepping closer to Phenex as they locked eyes.

"You know that's not what I meant, Phe-Phe." She placed her hands on either side of Phenex's head and touched her forehead to her younger sister's. "Please, Nixx, we don't lie to one another."

Phenex had forgotten how much taller her sister was, about ten centimeters, but she realized that if they were both adults, they would have been nearly the same height. She tried not to give any indication that something was wrong as she stared into Mikhail's almost red eyes. She had forgotten how fascinating they were, changing colors with her emotions, flashes as they lovingly called them. Her irises flared crimson and amber, the color of a warning flare, when she was angry or worried. When she was happy, they seemed to shimmer a vibrant and bright dark seafoam green, like the ocean after a heavy storm. She exhaled slowly, relaxing in the safety of the forehead touch.

Misha stared into Phenex's dull topaz eyes as though searching for a clue. She took a slight step back and sank onto the side of the tub. "You're not just my sister, are you? You're the one from my dreams."

Phenex's face fell at her sister's words. She tried not to show a reaction. There was the pang of guilt, the lie by omission to Hunter earlier. Being dishonest about who she had been talking to. *I will never lie to you.* The words of her promise echoed in the recesses of her mind, a promise, a bond she had with each of her siblings. The origin of the promise was Mikhail, a promise she carried to each sibling especially after Mikhail's disappearance.

"You know about my dreams, Nixx," Mikhail continued, never breaking eye contact. "Vivid, remarkable conversations with you, only older, different... You're more confident in- in the way you speak, how you were sitting in our room, and the way you walk. It was how you confronted Rhett... You're Phenex from the future, aren't you?"

A chill ran down Phenex's spine as her face flushed with warmth. Mikhail knew. She always knew when Phenex was hiding something and even displaced in time, her mind was older than she physically was, Mikhail could tell. Phenex's nostrils flared as she inhaled deeply before answering. *Don't tell her, protect her! Save her!* "Yeah, no se como pero I am..." She felt a wave of relief as tears formed in her eyes. Wrapping her arms around Mikhail, she said, "I wanted to tell you the moment you pulled me out of the water. I'm so confused." She folded into her sister, nearly knocking her backward into the tub. "I'm terrified but so happy to see you again, I have missed you so much."

Mikhail caught her balance, preventing them from falling into the tub. "I don't know either, Phe-Phe, but we'll figure it out together. Te prometo que, Manita."

Chapter 5
Fifteen Again

Blistering unearthly white walls, the familiar irritating buzz of fluorescent lighting paired with the annoying droning tick-tock of the analog clock on the wall. The nearly tangible stench of overused body spray and perfume filled the halls. Quick socializing, bullying, and laughter, as well-trained as Pavlov's dogs, were abruptly halted by the piercing screech of the school bell. The resulting silence was short lived, quickly overwhelmed by the shuffling of feet and squeaking of tennis shoes as students scrambled to class.

Phenex shifted uncomfortably in the hard wooden chair. Memories of her first school experience flooding back. Back then the constant suspicion from teachers and mockery from classmates was overwhelmingly taxing and a major source of her anxiety. Now, with the benefit of hindsight, she recognized their narrow views for what they truly were—an unwillingness to accept that she and others like her could genuinely excel. Later in life she would use this realization as a springboard, allowing herself to embrace her potential and run her successful business. Looking back from her adult perspective, she couldn't help but feel a mix of empathy and begrudging disdain for her teachers' and towns people narrow views and unchanging attitudes toward the ever-evolving world.

Wakford, Oklahoma, was a town shrouded in shadows and steeped in secrets. Here, echoes of the past drowned out the whispers of the future. Most residents dreamed of greener pastures, following the adage, but few ever made it beyond their familiar surroundings, and even fewer found the prosperity they sought.

Many lived in fear of anything or anyone outside the invisible lines that defined their borders. Clinging to their prejudices, they filled their hearts with anxiety and clouded their minds with superstition.

That wasn't to say that everyone shared the same sentiments. In fact, it seemed that the intolerance that plagued the town gradually diminished with each passing generation. Younger residents began to question the entrenched beliefs of their elders, fostering a sense of curiosity that contrasted sharply with the prevailing attitudes of the town. Unfortunately—or perhaps fortunately—this shift in perspective often created tension among the populace. Those who embraced forward-thinking ideas found themselves facing pressure to conform, forcing them to either remain silent about their beliefs or, in some cases, seek a fresh start elsewhere. As a result, the community risked losing its more progressive voices, leaving behind a landscape that was increasingly stuck in its ways.

The sensation was strange; her teenage mind, body, and experiences were melding with her adult perspective. She could now see and understand moments and viewpoints that her teenage self, caught in the immediacy of experience, had been unable to grasp. Trying to articulate this feeling, the conversation with Mikhail the previous night came to mind. It was as if she possessed The Contra Code but still had difficulty navigating the controls.

She glanced down at her completed assignment, wishing only for the bell to ring. Her thoughts drifted back to the conversation she and Mikhail had shared the previous night. They had agreed to keep their plans secret, and the weight of their unspoken resolve pressed heavily on her.

Absently, she clasped her necklace, momentarily confused by the stones that dangled from the cord instead of the class rings. She traced the edges of the tourmaline, its smooth, flat surface contrasting with the rough, unpolished ridges where her fingers caught. The stone felt cool against her skin, a solid and grounding presence. Its uneven texture reminded her of something raw and unrefined—much like the thoughts tumbling through her mind.

In contrast, the copper wire wrapped in delicate, twisting patterns felt warmer, its surface smooth yet firm. She knew the stone intimately; it was a gift from Saria after a summer trip to her grandparents in Nigeria. Years of familiarity allowed her to identify it by touch alone, its unique texture providing a small comfort amidst the chaos.

"Miss López," Mr. Rilbecti's booming voice cut through the mostly silent class, "since you seem to have nothing better to do than annoy us with the tappity-tap-tapping, please come up here and answer this equation for the class." Chip Charles "Chuck" Rilbecti was a large skyscraper of a man whose two balding spots didn't quite meet in the middle. He had a long ponytail that he usually wore braided that went to the middle of his back. He had black pinprick eyes. In Phenex's opinion, they were too close together, and his nose was too small for his face.

Phenex sighed, muttering, "I'm sure this will be a delightful way to spend the last few minutes of class." As she began making her way up to the board.

"When I say go, you will have until the bell to answer correctly. If you do not, you will be the reason for the entire class having additional homework." There was a chorus of groans from the class and a few utterances of violence, but the class knew not to protest too loudly, or it would be their heads on the chopping block next; he may have been the mathematician of misery, but he was fair in his torment of students, and with less than a minute till the bell, it was a risk no one was willing to take. "This is an SAT-level question. Good luck and go."

Phenex took the chalk in her hand without hesitation. She jotted down the answer, "1044.579," before working on the how-to part of the answer. She knew she was slow when it came to writing; trying to keep her writing legible was always difficult, and even when she was twenty-six, she preferred to use a computer or typewriter than write anything down if anyone else had to read it. Before she could finish showing her work, Mr. Rilbecti stopped her. "You cheated; you had to have seen the answer."

"I wear glasses, Ch-uheer, Mr. Rilbecti." She said flatly with an eye roll, "Even with twenty-twenty, the font in that book is microscopic from my desk halfway across the room, so tell me, how did I cheat?" She tried to stop herself, but her annoyance had already boiled over as the bell releasing students for lunch cut through the stiff air. "Can I go now?" Phenex moved to her desk to gather her items, quickly throwing her bag over her shoulder before dashing out of the room. She glanced back at Mr. Rilbecti, whose face was turning a deep shade of red.

⧖ ⧖ ⧖

"Dios mío, Phenex, it's only halfway through the day, and I have heard about you making teachers hella mad already," Mikhail said, joining her sister at the lunch table.

"I'm bored, Mikhail. We hardly had a chance to talk last night, and I'm in my mid-twenties, trapped in my fifteen-year-old body. School is tedious. Puberty sucked the first time, second time is awful," Phenex responded quickly in a rushed and quiet whisper, "I forgot how cu—"

"What about hormones?" Casey Cabrera asked, sliding into the seat next to Mikhail. "Going to hit that growth spurt, kiddo?"

"I am three years younger than you, Sprocket. Please stop with the kiddo," Phenex said in a mock exasperated tone. She smiled as she took a bite of the ham and cheese sandwich she had brought from home. "At least my next class is with you. Maybe I'll hold my tongue better if you're around, Misha."

She looked at Casey, "You might make it worse, Space boy." She smiled at how naturally she felt teasing him, having always had a soft spot for him. When he was younger, he said he wanted to be an astronaut. 'Diplomat to all the 'verse!' His favorite show was *The Jetsons* in childhood, which inspired Phenex to called him "Space Case." As they grew older, she called him "Spacely" before it devolved or rather evolved into "Sprocket." He loved the nickname; it was even on his varsity jacket.

"After what I heard you said to your stepdad," Casey started laughing, "I doubt it. Please, in excruciating detail, what did his face look like when you explained how the clock hands work," his laugh infectious "I would have loved to have been a fly on the wall for that moment". Casey was the running back for the Wakford Red Warriors. An attractive young man, having just barely turned eighteen. His dark brown jheri curls styled in a fade. He was one of the few in school who was friendly to Mikhail and Phenex and maintained a semblance of popularity, though that had to do with his football skills and that he was the star pitcher during baseball season.

Girls seemed to fall for him, but he never dated—partly because his mother insisted, he wasn't allowed to until college. The other reason he believed that most girls were too easy, constantly flirting with him by batting their eyelashes, giggling at everything he said, and finding excuses to touch his arm or shoulder. To him, they never seemed authentic. He often expressed his appreciation for Mikhail and Phenex, who never cared about his abilities or social status; he could truly be himself around them. They also had a way of lovingly bringing him back to reality whenever his popularity threatened to inflate his ego.

Casey was wolfing down his lunch when he paused, "Rhett is going to kill you, isn't he?"

"Think my head injury is a valid excuse for the next three years?" Phenex asked almost sarcastically. "I'll try to behave the rest of the day. Hopefully, Mami is the one the teachers talk to, and I can show her the goose-egg. She will be more understandable." Her eyes widened confusion spreading across her face, "She will be more understanding."

Mikhail reached out and placed her hand over her sister's, "Hey, it's okay. We will be fine. Estamos bien prometido."

"English, Miss López." Sheryl-Louis Schon said. She was the high-school English teacher, AP teacher and this week's lunch monitor. Her ears would home in like bat sonar on them. Of all the bullies in the school, Mrs. Schon was the best of the worst; as a teacher, she had authority, and with her tenure, she could deny it and get away with it and she did.

As many did in Wakford, Mrs. Schon donned a mask of acceptance and tolerance, but upon returning to the safety of their picturesque vision of the world, their disdain and biases resurfaced. This facade maintained the illusion of a perfect utopia, a cherished oasis in Middle America—so long as everyone remained compliant, silent, and unquestioning. However when it came to the girls and her friends, that mask was transparent in her abhorrent disdain.

"Cuidado, la bruja está escuchando," Casey whispered before all three of them started laughing. Witch may have been the kindest word Mrs. Schon's was called.

"Phenex! Michael! I will see you in my classroom in fifteen minutes," she snapped.

"Oye, they said nothing. Estoy hablando español, señora boba. It was me." Casey said in their defense. "I should be in trouble."

She snorted before speaking in her gruff, troll-like voice that resonated with surprising depth for being so high pitched. "I don't care that you also speak it. They were the ones laughing, Casey. If you know what is good for you, you will not interrupt me again."

Mrs. Schon resembled a Trolls doll with her wild, spiky red hair and a square face that sagged with droopy cheeks, not unlike the villainous Heat Miser from those old Christmas specials. Despite her small stature, Mrs. Schon possessed a voice that could command the attention of the entire room. Her voice, like the screech of chalk on a blackboard, could silence the entire class with a single, discordant note. The nuances in her tone were subtle yet revealing.

With most students, her gruffness would soften, offering fleeting glimpses of hidden kindness. However, for a select few—like Phenex, Mikhail, and their friend Bryce—her tone turned razor-sharp, tinged with impatience. This harsher edge often left certain students feeling unwelcome and dismissed, as their heartfelt questions were met with curt, clipped responses that reverberated in the silence like an ominous warning.

Casey opened his mouth to say something and instead made an odd high-pitched squeak as Phenex kicked his shin under the table. "Ouch, Nixx." He glared at her, to be met with her innocent eyes as Bryce Ripley and Saria Pascel joined them.

"The lunch line was ridiculous today. Can you believe it? We get thirty minutes to eat, but if the line takes forever, we have five minutes to stuff our faces and make it to class," Bryce said, starting to eat the applesauce from the small bowl provided with the tray. "It's a wonder we have awful eating habits." Bryce drawled, sarcasm dripping from their words with a venomous honey-thick bite.

"Taking that candy-striping extra seriously, I see," Mikhail said, reaching to grab a crouton from Bryce's salad. "How's that class going, by the way?"

"Not candy striping—I don't even think that exists anymore, Mikey. I am taking med aide night classes." Mikhail cringed at the nickname "Mikey," which most of the school used because they either assumed her name was Michael or couldn't be bothered to pronounce Mikhail correctly. "But having the certification will look great. The further I can get from here, the better." Bryce flashed a grin and winked at Phenex. "You'll come after me, right, Nixx?"

"Totally, Ripley, totally." Phenex felt her cheeks flush slightly; she tucked the chain back into her shirt, noticing she was tracing the familiar curves of the small selenite heart. The crystal was smooth but delicate, its surface almost silky beneath her fingertips. She knew if she pressed too hard, the soft mineral could scratch or flake, but she never did—it was too precious. The center of the heart was dark, like a storm frozen in glass, while the edges faded into a soft, milky glow.

The green copper wire, once bright, had deepened over the years, darkening into an earthy patina. She could still remember the day Bryce had given it to her in third grade, their small hands clutching the crystal with an awkward sort of pride. Phenex had missed the Salt Plains trip, stuck at home with chicken pox, but somehow, this little heart made her feel like she had been there too. "You'll have to wait for me; I'm two grades behind, after all."

"Are you two flirting again?" Mikhail asked, staring at Saria, who was signing. Mikhail signed back an affirming 'yes' before Bryce could answer with an eye roll.

Bryce casually draped an arm around Saria, their laugh a low rumble as they quipped, "Oh, I can flirt with you too, baby," nudging her playfully and winking. They were housemates and, of course, best friends. Bryce turned towards Casey, a playful glint in their eyes "Is it really flirting if I do it with all of you?"

Saria had become Bryce's roommate when her parents moved across the country for a considerable job offer with Boeing; they allowed Saria to stay in Wakford to complete her final year, providing her with money for rent and frequent visits. As the co-salutatorian, Saria aspired to become a pioneering deaf doctor, inspired by Dr. Judith Ann Pachciarz. Though she lost her hearing at ten, her hearing aids enabled her to fully engage with her environment. When she joined Wakford Public at twelve, the entire sixth-grade class learned sign language to communicate with her better.

Their laughter echoed throughout the cafeteria, a bright symphony that swallowed the hum of the fluorescent lights. *I sure miss this.* Phenex had forgotten the thrill of their games, the shared secrets whispered between bites of pizza, the effortless joy of her friend's group. Most of them left town when they reached adulthood; she, too, had left, but returned when Rhett and Collete died. Her past had become intertwined with her present, a new reality. Phenex shook her head, grounding herself in the now. She absently reached for the smooth, cool stones on the cord around her neck—gifts, each from a cherished friend, holding special meaning. Clutching all four tenderly, a content smile touched the corners of her lips, reaching her eyes.

When the bell rang, Mikhail and her sister went to Mrs. Schon's classroom. When they arrived, Casey was already speaking to her, "So why am I not being punished? ¿Yo también hablaba español oor is that rule only for those you-?"

Interrupted by a slight, high-pitched noise that pierced the air like a tired whistle, Mrs. Schon's lips curled into a saccharine smile that would terrify the Cheshire Cat. Her voice dripped with a honeyed sweetness that, to the untrained ear, might seem genuine. "Do you really want those types bringing you down?" she asked, her eyes glinting with a calculated sharpness that belied her almost syrupy tone. The warmth in her words was laced with an unsettling undercurrent, as if she were delicately steering the conversation toward a darker agenda. But those who knew her well could detect the undercurrent of mockery in her words.

"You're keeping us from our class," Phenex started to say but was elbowed in the ribs by Mikhail before she could finish the sentence. "Lo siento. My bad," she rolled her eyes, "What is it, lines?"

Casey sat on top of a desk near the door. "Still not leaving."

"If you do not get out of here, I will double their punishment, Mr. Cabrera."

"That's male bovine—"

"¡Cállate!" Phenex whispered harshly. "Appreciated, but, dude, hush."

In defeat, Casey put his hands up. "Claro, you win, Mrs. Schon, sorry. Hasta luego hermanas. Ten cuidado."

Mikhail locked eyes with Phenex. *Don't, it'll just be worse*, she thought, hoping that her sister would understand the words she could not speak.

Mrs. Schon was behind her desk, searching through a stack of papers. "What can you tell me about these papers?" Her voice was condescending. "I would think carefully about how you answer." She set down two papers with identical marks, each noun underlined, verbs circled, and corrected sentences written at the bottom of the paper in the essay section.

"Two passing papers that wrongly received a zero." Phenex's response was reactive, immediate, seeing the bold red "F" in Sharpie at the top of the page.

"You're both pathetic if you think I wouldn't notice how obviously you copied off each other," Mrs. Schon nearly shrieked.

Mikhail grabbed her sister's hand, sending a silent message to keep calm. Phenex exhaled, her jaw unclenching slightly as she spoke. "We had our mother double-check our work. She's the editor of the Wakford Herald."

A shrill, unnerving laugh escaped Mrs. Schon's throat, sending a chill through the room. Her eyes narrowed with cruel satisfaction as she spoke with condescending clarity, "Maybe she needs to reconsider her career. Read the instructions. Double underline the nouns.' Her words dripped with mockery, underscoring her disdain for the students and their supposed incompetence.

Phenex tightened her grip on Mikhail's hand, her knuckles whitening. She forced her voice to remain steady. "So? We misread, it happens. Have you checked Bolt Jacobson's, JJ Baker's, or Tyler Butler's papers? They copied off us and likely made the same mistakes."

"This is not about them," Mrs. Schon snapped, her voice rising with frustration. "This is about you two and your flagrant disregard for following simple instructions."

The tension in the room was unmistakable. Mikhail felt her sister's anger radiating, knowing it wouldn't take much to push Phenex over the edge. She stepped in, her voice calm but firm. "We respect the rules, Mrs. Schon, but we deserve fair treatment. If this is about discipline, then all students should be held to the same standard."

Mrs. Schon's eyes narrowed, her face reddening with anger as a terrifying grin twisted her lips, reminiscent of the Grinch and the Joker. "You think you're clever, don't you? This defiance will not be tolerated. You'll both serve detention for the rest of the week, and I'll be speaking to your parents about your attitudes.' Her voice dripped with venom, emphasizing her vindictive intent.

Chapter 6
Choices Diverge

"She's a total cara de perra, and her breath is just as bad," Phenex remarked as she caught up to Mikhail after detention. "I'm glad that she... Would telling you the future mess up some sort of continuity? Though I guess preventing your disappearance isn't exactly keeping continuity either. H.G. Wells didn't answer this."

"Well, that would involve a time machine, wouldn't it?" Casey appeared seemingly out of nowhere. "Why are we talking about time machines?" He fell into step with the sisters.

Mikhail glanced at Phenex, searching for a quick answer. "Required reading," they both replied in unison. "Jinx! Dang it, jinx!" They laughed, saying 'jinx' one more time before giving up, "Why are you here so late Sprocket?"

"I was hiding chicken eggs in la cara de perras' room, mostly in the ceiling tiles." He shrugged, "No one messes with my girls."

"Your girls?" Phenex raised an eyebrow. "I'll accepting only because I think it's hilarious." She imagined the eggs eventually filling the classroom with their pungent, distinct scent—an unbearable, nose hair-curling stench of rancid sulfur.

"Mrs. Schon might be right, English only." Mikhail teased, "Run that sentence in your head again."

Phenex paused for a moment, contemplating her response before breaking into a laugh. "Shut up," she said playfully, running to catch up with the others.

Casey chuckled, keeping pace with her. "It's okay, Nixx. I knew what you meant." He followed Mikhail as she turned onto Oak Street. "So, where are we goin'?"

Wakford was a quaint little town, with a population just over 1,500 residents. Despite its size, it stretched out over a mile and a half, boasting a charming mix of homes, local shops, and family-owned eateries that gave it a distinctive character. The warm, welcoming atmosphere was complemented by the rolling plains and open fields surrounding the town, creating a picturesque setting for a community deeply rooted in tradition.

Most residents of Wakford under fifty embraced a simpler life, strolling through the quiet streets while exchanging friendly waves and casual greetings with neighbors on their way to the local coffee shop or the park. Vibrant community events, like seasonal festivals and summer fairs, fostered a strong sense of camaraderie among the townsfolk, uniting everyone to celebrate the small joys of life.

For the newly minted sixteen-year-olds, getting a driver's license represented a thrilling milestone. They looked forward to driving to the local high school at the far end of town, their parents' old cars parked haphazardly in the lot. While Wakford lacked the bustling infrastructure of larger cities—no sprawling malls or fast-food chains—it thrived on accessibility and the strength of its friendships. Each day there was woven with the threads of shared traditions and simple pleasures, where every moment contributed to a cherished tapestry of memories.

"The littles usually have bowling on Mondays, but it was canceled," Mikhail said during their walk. "I talked to Saria during the last period. She said she and Bryce could pick them up, so we have a pit stop to make."

Phenex raised an eyebrow. "Ripley's place?" there was a slight hitch in her voice.

Bryce Ripley was an absolute force of nature. Having lived independently since twelve and officially emancipated at fourteen, they now juggled an impressive array of responsibilities at sixteen. On track to graduating two years early as valedictorian, Bryce also maintained a part-time job while attending night classes three nights a week. Despite these commitments, there was still time for sports, especially track and field—excelling in shot-put and proudly holding the school record.

With her fingers Phenex traced over where ink once decorated her arm, laughter exchanged, and the friendship that had once pulsed with vibrant energy. She could still picture them as carefree teenagers, hanging out at Sova's Diner, or at Bryce's house, where every secret was whispered like a solemn promise and every glance lingered longer than necessary.

As the years passed, life pulled them in different directions—a familiar path fading into the background. In 1998, Phenex occasionally caught snippets of Bryce's life through mutual friends; they still shared threads of connection, stretched thin by time and circumstance. She knew Bryce had been dating a college friend for five years now, and the chatter of wedding plans floated into her ears, a bittersweet excitement.

A twinge of longing tugged at her heart. She tried to push it away, reminding herself of the happiness she felt for Bryce. Yet, that flicker of what could have been—what might have bloomed if they'd dared to step beyond the bounds of friendship—lingered in the shadows of her mind.

"Yeah, Bryce's. You want to come with us, or are you heading home?"

"Um, yeah. I'll go with that, sure," Phenex found herself stumbling over her words for a moment, recalling a memory from the first time she went through this. *How is this the same?* There was a vague throbbing in the back of her mind; she couldn't quite recall what had happened, but she remembered going with her sister, and Sprocket was the unexplored option.

Bryce, with boundless energy and infectious laughter, chased the younger children around the living room, athleticism evident in every move. The door, thankfully left unlocked, was the only way they could have entered amidst the cacophony of playful shrieks and screams. Meanwhile, Saria sat at the roll top in the corner writing, her quiet strength contrasting Bryce's exuberance, observed the chaos with a serene smile, her hearing aids set aside as they immersed themselves in the vibrant, albeit noisy, scene.

"Hey, Sprocket! Misha!" Bryce shouted as they came to an abrupt stop, their momentum sending them sliding across the carpet and nearly toppling over. Phenex caught them, wrapping her arms firmly around Bryce's waist with one hand pressed against the middle of their back to steady them. "Oh, and my hero," Bryce teased playfully, their smirk growing as they looked up at her.

Phenex could feel the muscles in Bryce's arm that tightly wrapped around the back of her neck, flexing as Bryce's back tensed in response. "Oh boy, we're going down," Phenex tried to say, but what came out instead was more of a squeaking cry that sounded like a small rabbit, "Sorry, you're—I'm slipping."

Before the words had fully registered, Phenex felt her legs buckle as Bryce's feet slipped further on the carpet. In a split second, she instinctively lunged forward to cushion Bryce's fall, landing half on top of them in a tangle of limbs. "Ay, caramba! Sorry, Ripley, are you okay?"

She winced slightly at the awkward twist in her leg but forced herself to stay focused. With one hand pressed gently against the back of Bryce's head, she waited anxiously for a response, her heart racing as she assessed the situation. The room felt momentarily suspended, the air thick with concern, as she hoped fervently that her quick reflexes had been enough to soften the fall.

Bryce groaned as they hit the ground, trying to catch their balance but failing, which brought Phenex down with her. "I'm okay," placing a hand on Phenex's cheek and looking into her eyes with a caring smile. "What about you?"

Phenex felt a blush creep up her cheeks as Bryce's touch lingered, and for a brief moment, an intense connection suspended time. She admired the sunlight dancing on Bryce's freckles, a constellation of beauty that drew her gaze. But Thana's squeal jolted her back to reality. "I'm okay," she said, her voice a bit breathless. "Just shaken up, but fine!" Startled, she quickly pulled away, trying to regain her composure. "I'm good—great, actually! Knees aren't meant to bend that way, but it's fine!" Her words tumbled out as quickly as her racing heartbeat, while Casey and Mikhail helped lift them both back to their feet.

"Phenex, estás bien?" Mikhail said as she placed her hand just above the base of Phenex's skull and touched foreheads, "I know it's loud; this cannot be easy for you", she whispered. She spun around, and in an instant, a commanding authority radiated from her, "Thana, Enoch, you two get your packs and shoes." her voice firm, strong. It was how Phenex remembered Mikhail, a true leader, caring, loving.

Actually, it's just a momentary rush, nothing to worry about, she reassured herself, forcing a casual nod in response to Mikhail. The warmth in her cheeks and the flutter in her stomach hinted at something deeper, but she'd keep that to herself.

"Bwyce said we can keep the hawmony-cacas!" Enoch exclaimed, his lisp and small stature making him seem younger than his nine years. He hurriedly shoved his feet into his shoes. "And we ate helado; I had chocolate! Can we do this tomowwow?"

His adorable mispronunciation of "harmonica" sent a wave of laughter rippling through the group. Meanwhile, Bryce swiftly signed to Saria while she inserted her hearing aids, eager to fully engage in the conversation.

"No, Noch, Daddy is picking us up tomorrow," Thana said as she grabbed his school bag. "Bryce, how do you say thank you in sign again?" she asked.

"Ey, I know!" Enoch excitedly signed thank you and ice cream to Saria. Thana repeated the same movements.

Saria smiled. "You're welcome, little pikins," she said, signing slowly so the children could copy her. "I had fun, even if it was a bit loud." She laughed lightly.

"But unlike us, you can turn off your ears," Casey teased, covering his ears with his hands. "Wish I could do that during pelafustán cara de perra class today."

"I think I've mentioned it at least once a month since we were kids, but I'll say it again: it's not fair that you speak three languages," Bryce said, kneeling to help Thana untangle her shoelaces. "By the way, ¿qué es pelafustán?" She pulled at the knot with her teeth letting out a quiet victory yelp as it came loose. "How did you manage to get these so knotted, Banana Butt?"

Casey, Mikhail, and Phenex exchanged puzzled glances, their brows furrowed in concentration. "Uh... Pelafustán doesn't translate well," Casey began, scratching his head as he searched for the right words. His eyes darted between his friends, a hint of frustration visible on his face. "It means lazy, but…" He paused, biting his lip, trying to piece together the nuances. "There's more to it than that, you know?"

"Not good? Horrid?" Mikhail added, "Though it averages out, Casey speaks four languages, Nixx and I speak three, and the kids only speak one and two halves- since they aren't fluent in ASL or Spanish. No telling how many languages Saria speaks."

"And I'll never tell," Saria smiled before saying something in Yoruba that the others didn't understand but guessed it was either how many languages she spoke, or more playful banter.

They spoke a few minutes longer before leaving; Casey followed the girls home to hang out. Rhett was already there. Casey immediately started chatting with him as though they were best friends. "Hey, Mr. Nemain! Catch the game last week? Lakers and the Mavericks. What a nail-biter!" He drew out his words as he came in for an overly enthusiastic handshake. "Magic was unbelievable!"

"Hey, Casey, how's your dad—" Rhett's voice trailed off as the girls headed to their room. The younger two had been dropped off in the backyard to burn off their energy.

Phenex sat on the floor and leaned back against the beanbag chair, only to send a stream of polystyrene beads shooting into the air like a geyser. She shook her head, realizing she had forgotten about the hole—it had torn open last month. The memory felt oddly fresh yet distant, much like the rest of her life. Being in her twenties while trapped in her teenage body was disorienting, a constant loop of déjà vu and jamais vu, a sadistic strange salsa of yin and yang.

She sighed, "Not that I forgot why I hated high school, but I forgot how mentally taxing it was—the constant beratement and belittlement from teachers and students. College was better."

In the living room, she could hear Rhett's laughter, mixed with Casey's more tentative voice. She hoped Casey could hold his own against Rhett's sharper tones. Friends were supposed to uplift, but there was an undercurrent of tension she couldn't quite shake. She refocused her thoughts, reminding herself that she had created a space where they could feel safe, even amidst the chaos of old memories and new interactions.

Mikhail smiled. She had always been proud of her younger sister, but hearing she went to college, her heart leaped a little. "What did you study?" she asked hopeful that Phenex may share some of her stories from her older self.

"Aviation. Embry-Riddle in Florida," she replied, her fingers instinctively reaching for the small stones around her neck. She was momentarily surprised to remember they weren't the cherished class rings she had once dreamed of. "But after… I had to leave in my final year; something came up, and I couldn't complete my education. Still, I run a successful business—computers—thanks to the Foxburns and the Shelley… cousins." She paused for a moment before adding the last word reminding herself she was in the past. A dreamy smile crept across her face. "I'm very lucky; some things have improved in this town. I'm only here—" She trailed off, suddenly wary that she might be sharing too much.

Mikhail stared at her sister for a moment; in their conversations in her dreams, she never mentioned college. Though she did recall a few moments of vague mentioning, "Hunter and Riker?"

"Ryder. How do you know those names?" she raised an eyebrow.

"You told them to me in a dream." Mikhail's voice was somber, a distant echo of thoughts trying to resurface from the depths of her mind. "I've been having more dreams lately, but ever since your older consciousness arrived… nothing. It's like the connection has frayed." She hesitated for a moment, her gaze unfocused. "I even saw you older just a few days ago. There was a glimpse—brief and blurry—but I could feel your presence."

Her breath quivered slightly as she recalled the image. "I think I saw a picture, too. Hunter looks just like Thana, but her eyes—they're yours. I mean, the older you, the more confident version. And Ryder, he has the same look you do in pictures where you're concentrating."

Mikhail's voice faltered, and she raised a hand to her mouth, as if to catch the words. A heavy silence settled around them, thick with unacknowledged feelings. "How are—" she hesitated again, the question teetering on the brink of something precarious. "They're gone, aren't they?" The realization sank like a stone, and her eyes shimmered with unvoiced sorrow, as if the very thought had pierced through the fragile veneer of hope she had been clinging to.

"I thought her eyes looked more like yours." Mikhail's words stuck in the air, and Phenex shifted her gaze, unable to meet her sister's searching look. The bond they shared was profound; lying felt impossible. Deep down, she felt it, the certainty that Mikhail hadn't truly run away. Mikhail would never abandon her. The anger that had once bubbled within her faded into something bittersweet.

"Yeah..." Phenex nodded, tapping her fingers to her thumb for a moment before stopping herself, "That's why I dropped out. Thana and Enoch were nearing college; they didn't need me as much. But Hunter and Ryder... I couldn't let Daisy raise them. She couldn't even handle Rhett." The words tumbled out, tinged with frustration.

She shrugged; a gesture infused with resignation. "And los abuelos son demasiado viejos." A small laugh bubbled up, but it didn't mask the shaking sadness in her voice as it broke, "It's like they're talking with one foot in the grave and the other on a banana peel." The humor felt fragile, a thin thread holding back her emotions.

"I was twenty-one; I was old enough. I don't regret it, but…" Her voice faltered heavy in the silence. "I wish… I wish, I hadn't missed out on a few things."

"Like dating? Partying?"

Phenex laughed, "Yes, I was so focused on Embry that I didn't really try to have fun. Plus, it's hard to date when it's hard to tell who is attracted to you. At parties, I was usually the one talking to the dog or cat. I met a ferret once; his name was Wheeze-ell."

"That name just sound cruel." Mikhail laughed, "Well, I think"

They heard footsteps outside their room, and both turned toward the door, holding their breath. Casey flung the door open, half-closed it, then flung himself onto the floor as though he had no bones. "Mama Cole invited me to dinner since my folks are out of town. Rhett is making grilled chicken."

"Collette home?" Mikhail inquired; her tone more confirming than questioning.

"Yeah, she was pulling in when I was walking onto the porch." He laid his head on the beanbag next to Phenex. "I told her I wanted to hang out since it had been a while."

Mikhail laughed. "Dude, you ate dinner with us like three days ago."

"I didn't say it had been a *long* while."

Mikhail stood up. "I'll go speak to her. You two just hang out here."

"Gracias por el permission, Misha," Phenex said, rolling her eyes.

"I'll testify if I need to!" Casey called out as Mikhail left the room. "So, Nixx, have I mentioned you seem different today? I can't place my finger on it." He turned to rest on his elbow, facing her. "Everything okay?"

Phenex turned to face him, looking up slightly. "Sí, Sprocket." She covered her mouth as she yawned. "I just hit my head a few days ago, and with Rhett being Rhett... It's good I didn't have a concussion."

"Look on the bright side—Misha always has your back," he smiled. "You two have such an amazing bond. My brothers and I just punch each other, and my sisters slap me upside the head."

Casey was the youngest of seven in a blended family. He barely remembered his birth mother, who had passed away when he was two. His dad, Carlos, was left with Casey and his two older brothers and sister, doing his best to keep things together. When Rei-Lee became his stepmother just before Casey turned nine, it didn't feel like a big shift—she simply slid into their lives. With her came two additional sisters and a brother, expanding the mix.

Life was hectic. The siblings often wrestled and teased each other, teasing that came with being close. At every home game, the bleachers filled with familiar faces, all there to cheer him on. "That's my brother!" they'd shout, drowning out the noise of the crowd, their support a constant buzz in the background.

"Mikhail and I are all the other has. I mean, yeah, we have our younger siblings, but Mother and Rhett... she tries, and Rhett doesn't give a flying rat's—"

"I'm sorry." He sat up a little more, staring at her with his large brown eyes. They conveyed sympathy with bursts of gold and amber-like exploding clouds when he was excited, complementing his golden honey complexion. "Mikhail will be eighteen in a few months. You can move in with her, then get out of dodge like the rest of us, unafraid of chasing the stars."

Phenex scoffed. "Sometimes I wonder if it's worth trying to catch them. Some will forever be out of reach." *That was rather morbid... and out loud.*

"Rather morbid thinking, don't you think, Phe?" he smiled slightly as though reading her mind. *Did I say that last time we had a similar conversation, too?* "Well, you seem to be reaching for something; you never would have spoken to a teacher the way you did today. Well, from what I heard, anyway, I wish I could have witnessed it."

"Is that a compliment, Sprocket?" she asked, her voice laced with amusement and a hint of mockery. Her smile was sly, and her eyes sparkled with mischief. "Dios Mio," she muttered to herself, shaking her head. "Not that word. Bryce is the flirt, not you."

Casey shifted his weight, leaning in a little closer. "I thought that was just white girls in general," he laughed. "Always overly affectionate with each other."

"I mean, that's a theory, but of our constant friend group, Bryce is the only white girl. So, affection based on her results are a little skewed."

Mikhail walked into the room, catching only the tail end of the conversation. "What's this about skewed affectionate?"

Phenex rolled her eyes. "Oh, just planning on making out if you didn't come back. Looks like we'll have to save our passion for later, Sprocket."

"First off, gross. Sprocket, you can do better," she replied, her tone a mix of disgust and playful teasing aimed at her younger sister. "Second, Colette understood. I mentioned your head injury to her, and she said she'd check it out after her shower. Speaking of which, does it hurt?"

Phenex touched the back of her head, "No, actually, it's weird; it is just a small knot."

"How did you hit your head again?" Casey asked, moving into a sitting position.

"I fell into the creek by the falls; the current caught me and slammed me into the embankment." Phenex responded, "Trying to find Boomer Cave."

"Sooner Cave, Phe." Mikhail corrected, "Named for those who cheated and murdered to obtain land illegally, but we don't talk about that."

"It's only illegal if you're caught." Casey said pointedly, "So why were you that far out?" he saw through the excuse.

Sooner Cave was more than just a myth; it was an urban legend born from the imaginations of children, embellished with each retelling over the years. Initially, it sprang from stories of a smuggler's hideout during the Prohibition era, but as time passed, the narrative grew richer, weaving in tales from the Oklahoma land run. The legend held that Sooner Cave had served as a refuge for those trying to stake a claim to land before the official race began. It was said that a bloody conflict ensued as multiple claimants vied for the same plot, leaving only the children of the Sooners alive, hidden deep within the cave.

When the Land Run commenced, the cries of those children echoed from the cave, leading locals to believe the area was haunted. Fear of the supernatural powers kept people at a distance, allowing nature to reclaim the land. Over time, trees began to flourish, transforming the landscape into a small oasis amidst a fire-scarred region. The woodland expanded to nearly 800 acres, featuring hiking trails and campsites, though the nearby falls remained off-limits due to the risk of falling rocks. As the years went on, Sooner Cave's story faded into obscurity, whispered only as a cautionary tale to deter children from wandering too close to the falls.

In the back of Phenex's mind, however, Sooner Cave held a sense of significance that eluded her, especially in relation to her own and Mikhail's disappearances. Though uncertain of its exact meaning, she felt an instinctive urgency about it. With a resigned sigh, she declared, "Fine, the truth is I'm actually a time traveler who has come back to my fifteen-year-old body to tell you that the future is insane, and that the world ends during the millennium. So, be prepared." She locked eyes with Casey, delivering the line with a flat, calm inflection.

Casey raised an eyebrow, "Wha-what?" he stared back, looking into Phenex's eyes for any shift or clue that she was pulling his leg. "I… That's…"

"Not possible?" Phenex smiled, her expression mischievous and cunning like a fox. "Have you ever known me to lie, Sprocket?" A long, deafening pause followed before Phenex's smile erupted into laughter. "I wish I had my Polaroid! Your face," she said, chef-kissing the air, "is priceless."

Mikhail joined in the laughter with a relieved exhale while Casey rolled his eyes. "When did you learn to spin a tale like that?" he asked, laughing and impressed that he had nearly fallen for Phenex's joke, "You could never lie like that."

"She's always had it in her," Mikhail said, looking thoughtfully at her sister. "She's just too quiet for anyone to notice. Even when she tries to play it cool, it's clear she isn't as clever as she thinks. You can see the spark in her eyes when she's excited—she just needs to let it shine a little more." Mikhail smiled, a warm expression that conveyed both affection and gentle encouragement.

Phenex hugged Mikhail back, "Yeah, yeah, te amo."

Chapter 7
Waking Reality

Colette materialized in the doorway, her towel turbaned around her head and a lime-green and orange pajama set highlighting her vibrant energy. "Dinner's ready, girls!" she announced, her voice echoing through the house. "The kids have already scrubbed up and are waiting at the table."

"Guess you're a girl, Case," Mikhail said playfully with a lighthearted laugh.

"If that means Mama Cole's cooking and Mr. Nemain's grilling, call me anything you want, just not late for dinner," Casey responded joyfully jumping to his feet following Mikhail out of the room; his voice trailed off, "That's the saying, isn't it?"

"Don't leave yet, nenita," Colette said, entering the room. "¿Estás bien?"

Phenex nodded, her voice steady, though her heart quivered. "I'm okay, Mami." She bit her lower lip, fighting against the tide of tears that threatened to overflow. Just two days had slipped by since she last saw her mother, but with the weight of her future knowledge, it had been nearly five years.

Her gaze lingered on her mother's face, and a rush of nostalgia flooded her. She noted with a pang of surprise that she had almost forgotten how her mother's dark hazel eyes sparkled with unexpected delight. Mikhail shared that same gleam, the flecks of gold within changing flashing shades with every subtle mood: warmth, joy, worry.

Colette's eyes reflected a tenderness, a soft golden brown that seemed to wrap around Phenex like the warmest fluffiest blanket. They glowed with maternal softness, radiating both care and concern. It was a gaze that spoke of unspoken love, a soothing presence that reminded her of home.

"Actually, I know Misha mentioned that I slammed my head the other day. It's just a little goose egg now—maybe a duck or large chicken," Phenex said with a playful smile, trying to lighten the mood. She studied her mother's face, absorbing every detail: the gentle laugh lines that framed her mouth, the small wrinkles that danced at the corners of her eyes, each a testament to shared laughter and years lived. Colette's deep chestnut hair was laced with shimmering strands of grey and blonde, delicate threads showing that she was aging.

Her mother's pale skin seemed to glow under the soft light, an ethereal vision that mingled admiration with a deep longing. Taking a small step forward, Phenex hesitated, her heart heavy with the weight of what was lost or would be. She yearned for the easy bond they once shared, those moments of laughter and intimacy before the arrival of Enoch and Thana. As she watched her mother, she understood the younger siblings needed Colette's attention, yet Rhett's growing distance stung more sharply. He carved a wedge between them, labeling Enoch and Thana "his kids" while pushing Phenex and Mikhail away, making them feel like ghosts in the space they used to fill together.

Rhett had locked his and Colette's bedroom door at night when they were younger, keeping Mikhail and Phenex out. But for Enoch and Thana, he would carry them in, letting them snuggle in bed while he shooed Phenex and Mikhail back to their rooms if they dared to knock after a nightmare. Most days, Mikhail was expected to pick up the younger kids from school while Rhett lounged at home, engrossed in Mario Bros on Nintendo.

Though Rhett had always been kinder to Phenex, she now recognized the complacency in her demeanor compared to Mikhail's combative nature. After Mikhail vanished, that complacency shifted, making her the target of Rhett's rising frustration. Anger bubbled within her as she thought of the questions she wanted to ask Colette: *Why didn't you leave him Mother?! How can you be so blind to my fear, the pain? Why did you defend him, simply because he never hit us?* Phenex clenched her fist, feeling her anger rise like a cork, threatening to explode if left unchecked.

As these thoughts churned, Colette touched the cut lightly, inspecting the injury on her daughter's head. The bump had a long cut, it was already scarring over. "Well good news I don't think we need to chop it off. Though it looks like you're going to have a scar there." Colette murmured, her touch gentle as she brushed against the bump. "From what I heard, it sounds like quite an adventure."

"If that's what she said," Phenex replied with a shrug, "it's all kind of a blur. I've had a headache all day… Probably tension from Phys-ed," She stepped forward slowly, pulling away. "Lo siento, Mami. It's been a long day."

"¿Estás seguro que estas bien?"

"Yeah, Mami, I'm good. Promesita." She paused at the door to her room, hesitating. "Hey, Mami… just know…" She unclenched her fist as a sigh escaped her lips. "Never mind, I'm sorry." With a quick turn on her heels, she hurried away to join everyone else for dinner.

The conversation during dinner was mostly random, polite inquiries about each person's day. Phenex listened to everyone around her, moving her food around the plate. Her mind was preoccupied with the thoughts of her present and the future that seemed predestined.

Sooner Cave... the falls... Mikhail's disappearance... Rhett and Colette's deaths... Taking care of my younger siblings. Were all these events connected? Could I actually prevent any of this? Why am I even here if change feels so impossible?

Her breath caught in her throat, tightness gripping her chest as if she had just sprinted a marathon. She stared blankly at her plate, panic swirling in her mind, clouding her vision.

"Looks like you've finally shut up," Rhett said, glancing her way. "You're usually a non-stop chatterbox at dinner." The laughter in his voice was sharp, barely masking the malice that lingered beneath. It felt like a twisted form of revenge for her earlier remarks about telling time.

"Sorry," Phenex murmured, forcing the words past the knot of anxiety in her throat. "I have a headache."

"A headache? That's what you said the other night. Your excuse is starting to sound like just an excuse." Rhett's eyes narrowed, his tone dripping with skepticism.

"How articulate," Phenex muttered under her breath. "Excuse me, I don't feel well. I'm going to bed." She placed her left hand on the table to push herself up, preparing to stand.

From across the table, Casey observed with concern. He was familiar with the turbulent dynamics of the Nemain household. As she began to rise, he reached out and gently grasped her hand. "¿Estás bien, Phenex?" His eyes radiated genuine worry.

Phenex stood, shaking off Casey's gentle, concerned touch, and headed to her room, her shoulders squared as anger simmered within her.

"Headache is code for your presence, Rhett," Mikhail said with a mocking sweet smile, "Though personally, your presence tends to cause a pain in my—"

"Claudia Mikhail! Basta! That's enough." Colette snapped, "Rhett, you should apologize."

"Sorry, Mother," Mikhail said almost too sweetly, though it seemed Colette allowed it to slide. "Sorry, Rhett, what was said was unnecessary," she spoke flatly, making complete eye contact ensuring that he understood her contempt.

"It's not my fault she's so sensitive, Cole. Shit happens." Rhett rolled his eyes, irritation etched across his face. "She needs to grow up, get over it. No one is going to coddle her in the real world." With a final exasperated huff, he pushed back from the table and stamped out of the house, the door slamming behind him, punctuating his exit.

At the table, Colette turned to Casey, her voice a soft murmur of apologies, while Mikhail muttered curses under her breath, irritation simmering just beneath the surface. Thana and Enoch, however, seemed oblivious to the tension in the air. They devoured their food, their attention already drawn to the flickering promise of

"The Care Bears" movie on VHS. Beneath Enoch's stoic exterior, enthusiasm bubbled; though he would never admit it, he was just as excited as Thana. He would insist his eagerness was only due to the promise of playing soldiers in the park over the weekend if she got to choose the movie tonight.

As the children became engrossed in the flickering colors of the television, Mikhail busied herself with the leftovers, methodically packing them away. Casey, meanwhile, rolled up his sleeves and approached the sink, ready to tackle the dishes.

After returning with a cola from the gas station he had stormed off to, Rhett leaned against the doorframe, a hint of annoyance in his voice. "Oh, don't worry about that, Casey," he called out, having arrived only half an hour earlier. He had grumbled under his breath, brushing aside Colette's attempts to engage him in conversation. "The girls can take care of it."

Casey paused, glancing over his shoulder, determination still set in his features. "Now, Mr. Neiman, you know my 'rents would kill me if I didn't repay you for feeding me," he replied, his tone light but earnest. The splashing of soap and water filled the kitchen, becoming a soothing backdrop against the tension that lingered in the household.

After the dinner dishes had been cleared and the kitchen tidied up, Casey stretched as he reached for his jacket by the side door. "Nixx feeling okay?" he asked Mikhail, pulling the fabric over his shoulders.

"I think so; she's just been having some, let's say, growing pains." Mikhail smiled, though her eyes were more sad than happy. "You have a good night. See you in school tomorrow."

She embraced him tightly, their foreheads touching in that familiar gesture that dated back to their first days in daycare. "Te quiero," she whispered softly. As he turned to leave, she watched him wave at the end of the sidewalk, a ritual that had become a comforting symbol of their close bond. Casey had been there for her through the toughest moments—when their father, Alejandro, passed away and when Rhett moved in. His older sister had even babysat during the nights the little ones were born. Although Casey wasn't biologically related to Mikhail and Phenex, he felt like family, woven into the fabric of their lives. He spoke Spanish, learned from his own father, Carlos, as well as from the girls' father, Alejandro, and Alejandro's parents. At home, he also picked up Korean, influenced by his grandparents' heritage.

When she walked into her shared bedroom, the lights were off, and Phenex was lying in bed. "Hola," she murmured, her voice barely above a whisper, as if she were fighting back tears or had already been crying. "¿Podemos hablar?" She sat up slowly, the moon casting a pale light around her, leaving her eyes shrouded in shadow.

"Yeah, of course, Phe-Phe." Mikhail sat crisscross at the foot of the bed facing Phenex mirroring her composure feeling the weight of unspoken words hanging in the air. "I'm always here if you want to talk. What's on your mind?"

Phenex shook her head, her features twisting into a mask of uncertainty. "I'm not okay," she admitted, her voice trembling as the truth bubbled to the surface. "I feel so lost. It's like I know what's about to happen, the reality looming over me, but it's also like I've never experienced it before. It's all so surreal." She reached out, her fingers brushing against Mikhail's hand, seeking connection but not making eye contact. As she spoke, her voice wavered, and when she pulled her hand back, a flicker of guilt crossed her face. "Sorry," she added, letting out a shaky sigh as she fought back the tears that threatened to spill over. "But today... something changed.

"I chose to go home for the first time I went through this instead of going to Bryce's. Rhett yelled at me, screamed, and hit me because I stood up for myself. I don't want to say I blame him for what he did; looking back, I realize it was more reactionary than deliberate, but that doesn't lessen the impact of his actions." As she spoke, it was clear she was reflecting on herself from the perspective of her twenty-six-year-old self. "But still, he never apologized. It's like his pride was too big to let him admit he was wrong.

Her voice grew softer as she continued, the painful memories spilling out. "When Mami came home, I had a busted lip, and she just..." Her brows knitted together in concentration, a flash of hurt crossing her face. "...brushed it aside. As if I somehow deserved it. She made it seem like I was in the wrong for speaking up when he belittled me. But this time... I chose to break free. I chose to pick up the littles with you and Sprocket."

She paused, a distant look clouding her eyes as the weight of her words sank in. "But after I made that choice today, to go with you, my head has been hurting. I can feel the old memories fading, like they're slipping through my fingers, like sand. The worst part is, I don't know if the memories have changed completely for the future; it feels like the memories of the older me are fading too. They're dissolving as I speak." A bittersweet laugh escaped her lips, an odd blend of relief and despair. "It's like I'm losing pieces of myself in my present, and now, this entire displacement in time just makes everything so much worse." She wiped away a stray tear, her resolve warring with the vulnerability bubbling beneath the surface.

Mikhail listened, her heart aching for her sister. She nodded slowly, feeling her chest tighten. Words eluded her; it was as if she couldn't even take a breath amidst the unsettling realization spreading between them. When Phenex fell silent, they shared a moment of quiet understanding, staring at each other as though they were trying to bridge the vast chasm of experiences that lay between them.

"Okay…" Mikhail finally said, breaking the silence. "So how long do we have to stop my disappearance?"

"Sunday, May tenth," Phenex replied, her voice steadier now, though the dread lingered in her eyes. "That's about ten weeks—seventy days. After that…"

Mikhail leaned forward quickly covering Phenex's mouth with her hand, her eyes wide with determination. "No, don't even finish that thought. It is not going to happen. We'll figure it out, manita," she said firmly, her voice steady despite the urgency of their situation.

Phenex blinked at her, a mix of gratitude and fear reflected in her eyes. Mikhail's confidence was like a warm blanket amid a chilling storm of uncertainty. "For now, just go to sleep," she urged gently. "You've had a long day."

With a reluctant nod, Phenex let out a deep breath, each exhale carrying away a fragment of her worry. Mikhail, sensing the weight on her sister's heart, leaned back slightly, releasing her grip but still close enough to provide comfort.

As the room fell into a soft silence, Mikhail watched Phenex's eyelids flutter and drift closed. The long day, filled with heavy revelations and buried emotions, began to take its toll. Mikhail remained by her side, positioned protectively at the edge of the bunk.

⏳ ⏳ ⏳

Sometime after Mikhail had climbed into the top bunk, Phenex found herself unable to sleep. She lay wide awake, her gaze fixed on the underside of the upper bunk, tracing the shadowy shapes that danced there in the dim light. The room felt stifling, the air thick with unspoken thoughts and the weight of confinement pressing against her chest.

"Misha!" she whispered urgently, her voice barely a breath, but the quiet stillness of the room felt heavy. "Misha, are you awake?"

Silence enveloped her, punctuated only by the distant howl of the wind outside, rustling through the trees like ghostly whispers. Frustration simmered within her. Sighing, she turned onto her stomach, trying to find a comfortable position, but the restless energy inside her refused to settle.

Then, with a sudden spark of rebellion, she slinked off the edge of the bed and onto the floor. The thrill of sneaking out gripped her, leaving her heart racing. The thought of escaping the confines of the house, just for a moment, felt intoxicating. She glanced back at the sleeping forms around her, and the pull of adventure tugged at her.

Fresh air, freedom—she could almost taste it. Gathering her courage, she tiptoed toward the door, excitement coursing through her veins as she prepared to step into the night, far away from the worries that had kept her awake for too long.

As she considered a solitary morning stroll, her thoughts drifted to Casey and the possibility of sharing breakfast with him though she doubted he would be awake at such an early hour. Instead, the image of Bryce's friendly smile filled her mind, and she imagined herself tapping on her bedroom window, the way they often joked about waking each other up. Shaking her head, caught in a swirl of confusion and curiosity, she silently crept toward the door.

The possibility of spending a quiet morning with Bryce made Phenex's stomach flutter. After all, Bryce always seemed to light up her day, her laughter lifting Phenex's spirits like a ray of sunshine breaking through the clouds. Still, the thought of waking her felt like a breach of some unwritten rule in their friendship—an intrusion on the tranquility of early morning moments they both seemed to cherish.

Phenex hesitated by the door, weighing her options. Would she risk wandering into the familiar warmth of Bryce's company, or should she embrace solitude for a little while longer? The allure of quiet conversation, shared smiles, and the comforting hum of their routine tugged at her, and she found herself caught in a delightful dilemma.

Casey's friendly smile floated back into her mind, again. His easygoing nature had always been a source of comfort, but the prospect of adventure felt more tangible with Bryce. *Would it be fair to disrupt Bryce, Saria or Casey's sleep just to satisfy my own want for company?* With a deep breath, Phenex decided to take a step into the unknown. She would forge her own path this morning

When she crept into the living room, she froze at the sight of her mother sprawled on the couch, her face buried in a book that had slipped and fallen over her eyes. Colette snored slightly, oblivious to the world around her. The old wooden floorboard at the end of the hall creaked underfoot, as if a banshee were trapped beneath it, howling in protest at any weight. Colette flinched, roused briefly before settling back into a deep sleep within seconds.

With a sigh of relief, Phenex continued toward the front door, carefully opening it as quietly as she could. Once outside, she dashed down the street, glancing back periodically to ensure no lights flickered on behind her. The fresh, dewy morning air filled her lungs, invigorating her spirit. It wasn't until she was nearly a mile away that she realized she had forgotten her shoes. Nixx laughed softly, rolling her eyes at the memory of summers spent barefoot, wandering wherever her feet took her.

As she strolled, her memories began to shift. Thoughts of a walk intertwined with the decision that had presented itself to her before in this reality. She recalled lying on her floor, gazing at the waxing crescent moon through her bedroom window.

She happened upon Casey's house and noticed Mr. Hahm outside. He waved enthusiastically, shouting a cheerful hello as she passed by. Mr. and Mrs. Hahm were Casey's grandparents, and she remembered how, five years prior, Mr. Hahm suffered a stroke that prompted Mr. Cabrera to insist his in-laws move in with them. "No one is more qualified to help Sung-ki than I am," his father had told the family.

Her thoughts roamed freely as she walked, memories shifting like clouds in the sky. Pondering her interactions with Bryce the day prior filled her with uncertainty about what might have caused her return to this moment in time. Calculating the days in her mind, she counted them down again—just under seventy days remained. What had she been doing in 1998? The further she wandered, the more she felt like she was operating on autopilot, moving through the motions of a life that once felt familiar but now felt almost foreign.

She began to contrast her current thoughts of Hunter and Ryder with Thana and Enoch. In this moment, Thana and Enoch felt like bothersome younger siblings she would rather ignore. Yet, she knew that in just a few weeks, everything would change—she would be fiercely protective of them after Mikhail's disappearance. Her twenty-six-year-old self, wrestled with the urge to keep them safe from their mother and Rhett, to spare them the pain that loomed on the horizon, even if just a little.

"If today is... that means Easter is forty days later... April nineteenth. I'll have to double-check during class," she mused. Her thoughts drifted into a fog of uncertainty. Here she was, in nineteen eighty-seven, a fifteen-year-old girl navigating the complexities of adolescence yet burdened by the memories and experiences of a twenty-six-year-old woman. *How strange it felt to be so young, yet so old inside...*

As the early morning light began to break over the horizon, she found herself walking toward the school. She paused to admire the dew sparkling on the grass of the baseball field just north of Wakford Public. Mrs. Schon's pea green 1959 Volkswagen Beetle was already parked in the teachers' lot, easily recognizable by the vanity plate that read "SOUP."

For a fleeting moment, the reckless thought of stealing the car crossed her mind, a desperate escape from the cruel reality of her life that seeped into her consciousness. The weight of her relationship with Mrs. Schon loomed over her like a storm, tumultuous and unrelenting. Memories surged back, reminding her how her classmates had cruelly dubbed her "Link" after Mrs. Schon referred to her as "the weakest link" one too many times. They mocked her after Mikhail's disappearance, spreading vicious rumors of a pregnancy, and with her friends away at college, she felt more isolated and ostracized than ever.

She quickly dismissed the notion, feeling the burden of potential consequences settle heavily on her shoulders. If she wanted to make significant changes in her life, she'd have to bide her time. Right now, ensuring her sister's safety and, by extension, her own, was all that mattered.

With a resigned sigh, she trekked toward the secondary gymnasium. She slipped in through the back entrance, making her way to the weight room and then to the boys' locker room, where she borrowed Casey's old basketball shoes; they were of no use to him anymore. Making a mental note to thank him twice before leaving the locker room, she glanced at the clock in the lobby. The analog readout displayed at 07:15.

As she began to make her way toward her first class of the day, she found herself fingering the small, polished moss agate that hung from her necklace. It felt cool and smooth against her fingertips, the surface gleaming softly in the light. The white stone, streaked with delicate shades of green and gray, felt reassuringly weighty in her hand, grounding her amidst the chaos of the day ahead and the swirling thoughts of her displacement in time. Its contours were gently rounded, silky to the touch, offering an unexpected sense of calm. Wrapped around it was a rusting paperclip, once shiny but now dull and roughly textured, the iron oxidizing into a mottled brown. And in that moment, as she hesitated at the threshold, she drew in a deep breath, bracing herself for whatever lay ahead.

CHAPTER 8
DIVERGENT PATHS

Phenex sat at her desk, writing out her plan of action to ensure that Mikhail would be safe. The notes appeared chaotic, with scribbles and doodles in the margins; Rhett's name had been crossed out under 'reasons/suspects', a look of frustration on her face as she did. She sighed, twirling her pencil like a baton between her fingers. She kept lifting her feet out of the back of the shoes she was wearing. The Adidas were too large for her feet; having borrowed them from Casey's locker in the weight room, she had also grabbed his Wakford Red Warriors hooded jacket before slipping over to the girl's locker room and stealing Bryce's letterman jacket and a pair of her jeans she had left last week.

"Phenex, what were the primary goals of the Civil Rights Movement, and what strategies did leaders like Martin Luther King Jr. and Malcolm X use to achieve these goals?" Bernard Dickerson was easily the best but also the most boring teacher in Wakford High. He was passionate about history and taught it well. Nearly every student passed. The only way anyone could fail his class is if they didn't try at all. Unfortunately, he had a voice that could put even Randy Gardner to sleep before the eleventh day; his voice was more soothing and relaxing than boring.

"What?" Phenex snapped out of her daze, "Sorry, Civil Rights Movement. The Civil Rights Movement aimed to end racial segregation, secure equal rights, and achieve social and economic justice for Black Americans. Martin Luther King Jr. promoted nonviolent protests, marches, sit-ins, and speeches. Malcolm X, conversely, advocated for Black empowerment, self-defense, and racial pride, often emphasizing separation from oppressive structures."

"And where would you say we are at with those today?"

She swallowed, feeling entrapped by the question, "I feel that my opinion on the matter would be more suited for a debate discussion rather than a flat answer as my perception may not match those who are among my peers."

"That's a thoughtful response, Phenex," he said, leaning back in his chair with a hint of admiration. "I appreciate your acknowledgment that perspectives on such complex issues can vary widely. These topics are often shaped by personal experiences and context.

"Since you mentioned your perception, I'd love for you to share it, even just a piece. How do you see the progress since the Civil Rights Movement? Do you think we still face significant barriers? Remember, this isn't a debate; it's a conversation. Your insights could spark meaningful discussion."

Phenex raised an eyebrow, scanning the room and catching hostile glares directed at her. Kiera Hurst sneered, mouthing, "Shut up, wetback," while Nolan Ravel clenched his fist in a mimicked violent gesture that sent a shiver down her spine. She exhaled slowly, feeling the weight of their hostility. Years of similar experiences had deepened her understanding—an insight she hoped Mr. Dickerson would appreciate.

"I don't think we have enough time to discuss this thoroughly," she said, her voice steady but low. "Could we delve into it next class?" She held her breath, glancing at the clock as the second hand ticked agonizingly past twelve. Just as her words lingered in the tense silence, the sharp ring of the bell sliced through the air, marking the end of class. A wave of motion surged toward the door, the chatter a chaotic backdrop to the unresolved tension hanging in the room.

The familiar chatter and energy of students filled the corridor as Phenex hung back, allowing her classmates to bustle past. As Nolan walked by, he took the opportunity to shoulder-check her, his smirk all too evident. Kiera followed, stamping her foot dramatically, and whispered with venom, "Beaners have no place in civilized society," as she nudged her with just enough force to seem accidental. "Learn your place," she added, striding away with an air of superiority.

Phenex slung her bag over her shoulder, the weight of it feeling oddly reassuring as she navigated the crowded hallway. She'd just run into Mikhail between classes to reclaim her backpack after first period, a small but meaningful connection in a whirlwind of busy schedules. With Mikhail in grade twelve and her still in grade ten, their paths rarely crossed during the first half of the day.

Though relief washed over Phenex at the sight of Mikhail, a knot tightened in her stomach as she processed her sister's expression. Mikhail's amber-orange eyes shimmered with an unsettling blend of anger and confusion. Their warmth dulled by an invisible veil of sadness. Her jaw was set tight, an unspoken battle unfolding behind her composed exterior—as if she were biting her tongue to keep words dangerously close to spilling out. The intensity of her grip was evident; her knuckles gleamed white, straining against the tension, a sure sign of frustration barely held in check.

"I'm not dismissing you, Nixx," Mikhail forced out, a smile attempting to break through, though it fell short of reaching her eyes. Yet there was a flicker of reassurance there, a quiet promise as if she were silently vowing to be okay. "But I'll have to fill you in later. Your absence this morning put me on edge, and I might have… gone full Chernobyl."

Even amidst her turmoil, Mikhail took a deep breath, easing her grip just enough to meet Phenex's gaze with a flicker of determination. The warmth in her eyes suggested that, despite the chaos swirling around them, she still held a thread of control. But before Phenex could press for more, Sibyl Corwynn swept past, urgency radiating from her as she grabbed Mikhail's arm, shouting about needing to grab the good camera for yearbook photos.

Phenex couldn't help but smile at the familiar sight, rolling her eyes at Sibyl's frantic energy. "Catch ya later!" she called out, feeling a lightness settle in her chest from their brief interaction, even as unease about Mikhail's situation lurked in the background.

But the moment Mikhail's smile slipped away, the weight around Phenex's heart grew heavier. What had happened before she arrived? Waves of worry crept in, overshadowing the bright moment they had shared. Thoughts of Rhett tugged insistently at her—his intimidating presence a constant source of dread. Had he confronted Mikhail again? Memories of their last heated argument surged back—Mikhail standing her ground, fists clenched, defiance burning in her eyes; she had fought with every ounce of desperation. That day had changed something within her; Mikhail had transformed her frustration into a shield.

And then there were their parents. Phenex recalled the rising tension in their household, how it often left Mikhail feeling boxed in. She could imagine her sister maneuvering through the minefield of conflicting emotions, where small disagreements could erupt into chaos. The image of Mikhail's jaw set in concentration replayed in her mind a silent plea for calmness, for a return to equilibrium amidst the surrounding turbulence.

What if the argument had spiraled out of control? The thought twisted in Phenex's stomach. She wished she could shield her sister from the burdens of their home life, from the suffocating expectations and fears that shadowed Mikhail like a specter.

Focusing on the memory of Mikhail's slight smile, even if it was forced, sparked a flicker of hope in Phenex, though the worry lingered. There was an undeniable strength in Mikhail that Phenex admired, but at times, it felt fragile, a mask that could crack under pressure.

As Sibyl tugged Mikhail away, laughter and urgency echoing in the air, Phenex remained still, a soft frown creasing her features. Beneath the vibrant chaos of youth, she couldn't shake the feeling that her sister might need her more than she let on. Balancing the lightness of the moment with the weight of her concerns, Phenex resolved to keep a watchful eye on Mikhail, ready to step in when the burden of it all became too heavy to bear alone.

Lunch, science, and English—those were the pockets of time she eagerly anticipated. At lunch, laughter bubbled around the table, her friends filling the air with stories and jokes, even as a shadow loomed over the knowledge that they'd be parting ways at the end of the year. She cherished those moments, the shared warmth and camaraderie that made it feel as if they could stretch time, if only a little.

In science, she found joy in playfully distracting the teacher with offbeat questions about hunting, her curiosity igniting friendly debates amongst her classmates. English was the least enjoyable of the three; Mrs. Schon's droning lectures could drain the life from even the most exciting topics. Yet, even in that drudgery, Phenex found solace in the small sparks of joy—sitting next to Bryce, her friends gathered around, and her sister not far away. Those moments, fleeting but bright, filled her with a sense of belonging, a bittersweet reminder of what was to come.

"Is that my varsity jacket?" Bryce asked, her eyes brightening as Phenex slid into their usual seats in the bustling cafeteria. The familiar buzz of chatter and clattering trays enveloped them, but Bryce's gaze lingered on the jacket, a smile tugging at her lips as a rush of warmth crept into her cheeks. "Did I leave it at your place last time I visited?"

Phenex shook her head, a sheepish smile creeping onto her face. "No, I borrowed it from your locker," she admitted, the warmth of the fabric enveloping her as she adjusted it around her shoulders. "I went for a stroll around town this morning and... well, I ended up not being able to make it home to change into real clothes."

As she spoke, a weary laugh escaped her lips, tinged with a hint of embarrassment. "Sorry. I also borrowed your jeans, Casey's basketball jersey, and some socks and shoes." She threw in a halfhearted sign, attempting to mask her fatigue with her usual playful posture.

Bryce's eyebrows shot up in mock outrage, though her smile betrayed her delight. "That explains why it looks like you fell into a hamper." she exclaimed, laughter ringing out, infectious enough to draw the attention of their friends at the table.

"Sporty grunge is a thing?" Phenex quipped, though uncertainty laced her voice as she feigned a pout. She tugged at the jacket's sleeves, pulling them back over her wrists and hiding her hands in the fabric of the letterman. A familiar yet faded scent of sandalwood and lemon enveloped her, playfully teasing her senses. She pulled her hands out of the jacket's cuffs again, signing a greeting to Saria.

For their tight-knit group of friends, communicating through sign language had become second nature. Most students in eighth grade and above could sign at least conversationally, thanks to Saria's arrival in Wakford, which prompted the school to introduce sign language classes, an unusual positive in an institution that often seemed trapped in a cycle of resistance to change, much like the town itself.

While many students stopped using sign language after Saria received her first set of hearing aids, the five of them continued to practice and learn, enhancing communication eliminating the need for passing notes. Though they still resorted to that from time to time, they found signing much more convenient for quick exchanges.

"Jesting and teasing aside," Bryce smiled, "I think my jacket looks good on you."

Phenex felt her cheeks flush, "Thanks. Ripley." She returned the smile, "Hey, you guys want to go camping this weekend? The five of us?"

"After this morning—after yelling at Colette—I think I'd like to start that camping trip today," Mikhail said, her voice barely above a whisper.

"Wait, you yelled at your mom?" Saria's eyes widened in disbelief, and for a moment, she seemed to forget her usual graceful signing, caught off guard by the unexpected revelation.

The cafeteria buzzed loudly around them, but their friend group leaned in, eager for the details about Mikhail's confrontation with Colette and Rhett's role in the drama. Mikhail sighed, feeling the weight of their expectations as she gathered her thoughts.

"It all started with the alarm going off," she began, recalling the tension of the morning. "I kept calling for Nixx to wake up, but when I checked the bottom bunk—she was gone. Panic set in, and I rushed to the window, half-expecting to see her sneaking out. Thankfully, it was locked." The memory came rushing back, the pressure in her chest easing only slightly. "But with Rhett around, it's like we've all trained ourselves to tiptoe around everything, trying to keep the peace."

She continued, her frustration bubbling to the surface, "When I finally made it to the kitchen, Mother was all smiles, covering for Nixx. She insisted she left for a study session. Then, when I said 'yeah' instead of 'yes, ma'am' while I was scrambling to remember to grab Nixx's backpack, Rhett jumped in with a lecture about manners. I snapped back without thinking. Can you believe that?"

Bryce nodded, her expression turning sympathetic. Mikhail pressed on, her voice rising with anger despite her earlier hesitation. "Mother half-heartedly tried to calm Rhett down, but she just doesn't see how wrong he is! It's infuriating!"

Mikhail paused, recalling the car ride to Sova's Diner. "She finally asked if I was okay, and I lost it, pointing out Nixx's weird behavior since she hit her head. I told Mother she couldn't ignore Rhett anymore, but all she did was apologize. I was so frustrated that I just walked out." She shook her head, frustration evident in her voice. "Every step toward school felt like a fight. I'm tired of pretending everything's fine. Nixx deserves better, and so do I."

"All the more reason to escape this weekend via a camping trip." Casey agreed, "Where do we want to go? I'm sure Dad will let me borrow his truck."

As though reading her sister's mind, Mikhail answered, "Actually, we just need our bikes."

CHAPTER 9
SHIFTING FRAGMENTS

The rest of the week seemed to fly by. Like most Fridays, the moment the final bell rang, the hallways erupted into a stampede of adolescents racing to exit the building, like the Road Runner escaping Wile E. Coyote.

"Oye, Bryce," Phenex called, jogging lightly to catch up. The late afternoon breeze a welcome refreshment compared to the stale air of the classroom, a picturesque clear day over Wakford, Oklahoma, "Sorry I kept your jacket," she laughed, "kept forgetting it in my locker." She held the red and black varsity jacket out on her arm like a towel; she shivered slightly as the cool breeze traveled up her spine.

Bryce turned to her, a beaming smile lighting up her face. "Honestly, I thought it looked great on you." Her smile faded when she noticed Phenex shiver, "Well, if you're not going to wear my letterman," she pulled her black, hand-embroidered Muttering Gibberish Medusa jacket over her head, the pink and green polo clung to the hoodie with static, momentarily revealing her toned abs. "do me a favor. It's cold; I'll wear my letterman, but please, wear my jacket."

Phenex's eyes widened in surprise just before she caught the hoodie Bryce playfully tossed her, its fabric landing squarely on her face. The familiar yet elusive scent of lemon, jasmine, and sandalwood wafted into her nostrils, wrapping around her like a warm embrace. "Damn! You don't let anyone touch this one." she blurted out.

Muttering Gibberish was Bryce's favorite band and made groups like *Cheap Trick, Vixen, and Van Halen* seem like amateurs, at least in Bryce's likely biased opinion. They were an all-girl rock group, with their drummer, Theodesa Lancaster, as the lead singer. Though they mostly played small clubs and bars across the USA, it seemed unlikely they would meet the right people to truly "hit the big time," much to Bryce's dismay.

"Misha said she'd meet us at our house; she wanted to grab something from Sinclair's room," Phenex said before Bryce could ask.

"Hella cool, that gives us time to hang out." With a playful wink and her signature crooked smirk, Bryce started walking backward before spinning around and half skipping away.

As they walked side by side, their movements began to mirror one another's subtle rhythm in their pace. Occasionally, their arms brushed, a fleeting contact that sent an unexpected thrill skittering through Phenex. A spark of impulse nudged at her to reach out and take Bryce's hand, a protective gesture to keep their swinging arms from colliding. At that moment, her heart fluttered, warmth blooming from her core as she caught herself staring at Bryce, her thoughts drifting into the past.

They had become friends just before starting first grade. Bryce lived in the rundown apartments across town, where hope flickered like a dying candle. One rare moment of solitude drew Phenex outside, and as she wandered into her backyard, she caught sight of a figure bent over, plucking berries from a vine. Intrigued, she crept closer, half-expecting to find a raccoon or some other wild creature.

Instead, her heart stirred at the sight before her: the disheveled girl she'd initially mistaken for a boy, who would soon be known as Bryce. Barefoot and untamed, Bryce's hair was unevenly shaved, a clear sign of hurried grooming. She looked as if she hadn't known the comforts of a warm meal or a calming shower in days. Yet, what struck Phenex most were the bruises across Bryce's arms and legs; some faded, others fresh, blooming in shades of purple and yellow against her skin. Each mark spoke of unspoken struggles, a rawness that both intrigued and concerned Phenex, awakening something deep within her as she remembered that first moment. An undeniable urge to bridge the gap between them, to offer warmth and safety Bryce so desperately needed, rose within her. Looking back, she now understood the gravity of Bryce's situation.

"Don't say anything, please," Bryce murmured, her voice low and urgent. Her large crystal blue eyes shimmered with a mixture of pleading desperation and fear, darting around as if the very air might betray her.

Even before their friendship truly blossomed, Phenex sensed Bryce's silent fears and led her into the sanctuary of her yard a sanctuary that stood in sharp relief against the chaos that clung to her friend like a second skin. Sunlight filtered through the leaves, casting dappled shadows on the grass and creating a cocoon of warmth and safety. Phenex's heart raced as she dashed inside, not to alert her mother or Rhett, but on a mission to provide sustenance. Moments later, she returned clutching a lopsided peanut butter sandwich, a bag of chips, and a bright red cup of overly sugary Fruit

Punch. This small act not only ignited a spark of hope for Bryce but also solidified their friendship.

In the following weeks, their bond deepened, and their roles began to evolve. Gone was the vulnerable girl nervously plucking berries. In her place stood Bryce, fierce and unwavering, radiating strength as she confronted school bullies who loomed like dark clouds. With each showdown, her squared shoulders and lifted chin transformed her into a shield for those who needed protection. Phenex often found herself captivated by Bryce's laughter—rich and unrestrained—it broke the heavy silence like music, chasing shadows into the corners and filling even the darkest days with a light that felt almost magical. In those moments, as Phenex gazed at Bryce, she saw beyond the surface. Her eyes flashed like lightning, her jaw set in a fierce line, and she held her shoulders squared against the world. The air around her vibrated with unyielding energy, as if the very foundations of the earth had been stirred.

Years later, they moved through life like intertwined shadows, their friendship as effortless as breathing. There was the summer when they were eight that Bryce launched her dog waste removal service to earn money to escape her parents' abuse. Phenex worked alongside her, accepting only a quarter of the profits—a decision beyond her years of understanding. During Phenex's hospital stay at nine, Bryce never missed a day to visit, often arranging rides with the Shelley cousins and even paying them to stick around Caldwell, Kansas. Years later, they discovered that the cousins had put the money into a savings account for Bryce, a silent testament to their bond.

Between them, the air hummed with an unspoken understanding, a closeness that felt palpable, almost electric. Phenex often found herself stealing glances at Bryce, her heart fluttering with a mix of excitement and apprehension. Moments stretched longer than they should, their laughter echoing with an undercurrent of tension. In the quiet spaces, when their hands brushed or their gazes lingered a moment too long, Phenex sensed a shift beneath the surface, an electric current of emotions that quickened her pulse. As she navigated this new terrain, she felt both exhilarated and uncertain, caught in the delicate dance of what they had always shared and what they might become.

"Alejandra!" Bryce exclaimed, breaking Phenex's reverie, her voice playfully joking. Only she called her by her middle name, and only in moments of absolute privacy. Twirling around with hands on her hips, standing like Lynda Carter's Wonder Woman, she grinned. "C'mon, spill the weekend plans! Hiking, camping, are you planning on killing us?" she sang in a playful tone, laughter bubbling up as her smile beamed.

"It's not a surprise if I tell you how I plan to kill you." Phenex offered a playful smile, her eyes glinting with mischief. "Do you need to grab anything from your place?"

As they strolled past the narrow alley that led to the back door of her home, the familiar sights of their small town surrounded them. Most folks here walked everywhere—the sidewalks and streets worn by countless footsteps. Just a few buildings away, the silhouette of Bryce's garage loomed, sheltering her car that rarely saw the light of day. It was a relic reserved for journeys beyond the hour-long bike rides they often took.

Bryce slowed down, reaching for Phenex's hand and tugging her playfully through the narrow alley between Oak and Poplar. "If we're going camping, I want to grab a few things first. I definitely need my sleeping bag, and anything else we should bring. Snacks? Drinks?"

"Got whiskey?" Phenex asked, her voice light and teasing as they approached the back door, still hand in hand as she was pulled along by Bryce. The instant the words escaped her lips; she felt a rush of heat flood her cheeks. Swallowing hard, she quickly pulled her hand away, embarrassment washing over her like a cold wave. "I-I didn't mean that," she stammered, her heart racing as she fumbled for a change of subject. "Do I need to grab anything while you look for your sleeping bag?"

She glanced away, her eyes darting around for anything to distract from her slip. At the parties they attended, neither she nor Mikhail ever drank; they typically nursed a single drink all night—apple juice, water, or the occasional 7-UP, just a hint of orange food coloring to mimic the look of beer. The thought of whiskey felt so out of character, and she wished she could take back the joke that had spilled out unguarded.

"Hey, if you're going through something, you can always talk to me. I care deeply about you, Alejandra. You're my constant." Bryce's voice was sincere, and she offered a solemn smile as she placed her hand under Phenex's chin, lifting her gaze to meet her own. A spark ignited between them, and time seemed to stand still, the only sound the gentle rustling of leaves around them.

Phenex's heart raced as Bryce moved closer, her palms growing hot and clammy while her mouth felt dry. She could feel the warmth of Bryce's breath and the subtle hint of mint from the gum she had been chewing. In an attempt to steady herself, Phenex held her breath and began counting by threes. "Claro, pro -promesa. I promise." Slowly, she used her left thumb to rub the back of Bryce's hand while her right rested lightly over Bryce's heart.

When Bryce's forehead touched hers, Phenex felt her breath catch in her throat. "Good," Bryce said with a soft smile before pulling away. "You are my closest friend, Alejandra, and I love you with my whole heart." As their faces drew closer, warmth surged through Phenex; a sensation she had never experienced before. But suddenly, she felt the urge to retreat, her heart pounding fiercely in her chest. A line had been crossed, a line that left her feeling unsteady and unsure.

What was that? A tempest of confusion and denial whirled within her mind. *Pull yourself together. She's always been like this, affectionate with everyone in our friend group. You're confusing yourself.* But as the warmth lingered where they had touched, and emotions danced like dandelions in spring, it became harder to silence the flicker of something deeper.

Phenex stepped through the back patio doors, her gaze wandering as she entered Bryce's home. This spacious two-story house was owned by the Shelley cousins, who had graciously allowed Bryce to live there. The open layout welcomed her, with the living room flowing seamlessly into the kitchen and dining area, where the enticing scent of something delicious lingered in the air. A wall discreetly divided the living space from the more private areas, hinting at the quiet retreat that lay beyond.

Upstairs the three bedrooms awaiting their occupants, complemented by two practical three-quarter baths. At just two hundred fifty dollars a month, the rent felt almost too good to be true—another perk of living in a small town.

In contrast, the Shelley cousins thrived at their bustling Pages and Pastries bookstore downtown. The rich aroma of fresh coffee mingled with the excitement of discovering new stories. Above this lively hub, they lived together in a loft that radiated warmth and camaraderie. Their bond transformed the space into a welcoming home that felt familial.

Bryce often spoke of how much she owed to Lucille (Lucy) and Renee. They had given her a job at their store when she was just twelve, nurturing her ambitions and guiding her path to independence. Their relationship went beyond mere familial ties; it was built on mutual support rather than competition. This partnership was evident in the way they navigated life together, often including Bryce in their adventures—taking her on vacations and making sure she was part of their holiday photos. In many ways, she resembled a middle-American version of Anne of Green Gables, embraced by a duo of strong, caring women who treated her as if she were their own.

"Oh, speaking of things to bring," Bryce said, straightening up a bit, "that book I mentioned on Wednesday, *The Price of Salt*? I enjoyed it. I thought you might like to read it too." She rummaged through a bag near the couch and pulled out a gently worn but well-loved copy, its cover showing the effects of time and frequent reading. Faded notes in the margins and the warm patina of age give it character, revealing the thoughts and insights of previous readers. The pages are softened at the edges, and the spine bears the creases of countless openings, making it a cherished companion that has held many stories within. "Here, take this." A sly, sheepish smile spread across her face. "Let me know what you think."

"Thanks, Bryce," Nixx said, tucking the book into the hood of her borrowed jacket. The fabric crinkled slightly as she closed it, a casual gesture that belied the excitement bubbling beneath her calm exterior. "So, I'll snag the food; you grab your sleeping bag, but don't worry about pillows. The campsite's decent—maybe just poles? It's near the Triplet Ponds, about three miles by way of the bird."

Bryce laughed, her eyes sparkling as she took a step back, cheeks tinged with a light blush. "As the crow flies!"

"Yeah, that's the idiom!" Phenex chimed in, a grin stretching across her face, her cheeks warming as she rolled her eyes playfully. She hoped her flush would be mistaken for embarrassment over her own slip.

"True! Try signing 'you want coffee' and accidentally asking Saria's mom if she wants to make out." Bryce's laughter bounced off the walls as she dashed upstairs, her voice trailing down the stairs like a mischievous breeze. "That was mortifying!"

Phenex made her way to the kitchen, signing the two signs to herself and laughing. "I can see how that one was not only confused, but that mistake is hilarious. What did her mom say?" she shouted back as she looked in the cabinets for s'mores-making material ingredients.

"She laughed, saying she appreciated my boldness, but the age gap was too great, and she had a husband." Her voice was much closer as she set a military-style bag with a sleeping blanket already secured to the top on the large center island. She smiled. "S'mores, juice, honey sticks, and toilet paper?"

"Yeah... You're probably right. We usually keep our camp supplies stocked; however, paper is always a necessity, and leaves are the worst."

They finished gathering supplies and left through the garage. Bryce grabbed her bicycle, and Phenex borrowed Saria's as they rode to her and Mikhail's house. The streets were nearly empty as they navigated the sidewalks, cut through alleyways, and ignored stop signs. The trip wasn't far, a little over two miles. Even at their leisurely pace, they arrived quickly, but there was no sign of Mikhail or the others.

For a heartbeat, the house seemed to shimmer, the familiar white facade with its expansive wraparound porch blurring like a mirage in Phenex's vision. She stood rooted to the spot, the weight of her fifteen-year-old body brushing against the tumult of a twenty-six-year-old mind. The porch swing morphed before her eyes, transforming from its weathered, sun-bleached wood into a sleek, modern design. Gone was the rusty old lamppost; in its place stood two shiny motion sensor lights, blinking curiously in the sunlight.

A low hum pulsed in the back of her head as she sensed a new presence—a home security system she had engineered now nestled within the familiar walls. It felt like grappling with fog, her mind reaching back through the layers of memory to the warm, sun-soaked days of 1998, even while she wore the untested skin of her past.

She had started calling these episodes "phasing" or "shifts." They lasted mere seconds yet left traces of urgency and intensity, her headaches morphing into vivid flashbacks that pierced through the haze of youth. As reality sank back into focus, Phenex blinked, and Mikhail, Saria, and Casey emerged on the porch, as if stepping through an unseen doorway, their camp bags slung over shoulders, oblivious to the surreal transformation that had just unfolded.

In no time, they were off, a joyful blur of laughter and pedals spinning in unison, their giddy voices rising like balloons against the clear canvas of the sky. The wind whipped through Phenex's hair, sending a rush of exhilaration through her as the familiar path stretched out before them, beckoning them toward their hidden sanctuary.

"Come on, Casey! You're just looking for an excuse to inhale half a pound of pot!" Saria shouted, her laughter ringing out with a bright clarity, each word carefully shaped like a note in a familiar tune. As they wheeled down the street, the sunlight danced on the pavement, but the rhythm of the conversation sometimes slipped in the chaotic rush of cycling. "He may have the right idea." she added, a playful tease in her tone, emphasizing the joy of the moment even amidst the hustle.

Saria rode at the helm, her figure lean and steady, while someone stood the pegs behind her one hand gripping Saria's shoulder, the other hand flying in precise gestures that sliced through the air. With a tilt of her head, Saria caught every sign and syllable, understanding dawning in her keen expression. It wasn't flawless—words sometimes flitted away—but the essentials flowed seamlessly, laughter weaving through the air like a shared secret.

This time, it was Mikhail perched on the pegs behind Saria, her hands dancing in the air to capture the essence of their banter while Saria pedaled, laughter spilling from her lips and mingling with the rush of the wind. The connection felt as natural as the rhythm of the wheels beneath them, each inside joke and playful jab exchanging like fireflies caught in twilight as they glided down their familiar path.

Pulling into Ray's Good Day, the bell above the door jingled cheerfully. They grabbed a few sodas, the crisp cans cold against their palms, and shared a few quick laughs with Jay. After securing permission to stash their bikes in his shop for the weekend, they set off again, the excitement palpable in the air.

Casey took the lead, his confidence guiding them toward the favorite camping spot. "Oye! This way!" Phenex called out, darting toward a fallen tree just off the V. Richard Hiking Trail. She climbed onto the trunk, its bark rough beneath her palms, her heart racing. She balanced herself, glancing back to Casey with a grin. "It arches down, so jump onto the giant rock at the end." At her invitation, her outstretched hand promised support, a bridge between the earth and the next adventure waiting just beyond.

Casey scrambled up behind Mikhail, who was already down on the ground ahead. "Serio? Phenex, ¿estás intentando matarnos?" Casey's voice carried a playful edge, but there was an undercurrent of genuine apprehension.

"You know I joked about them trying to murder us," Bryce chuckled as she helped Saria onto the tree, staying close behind her, her hand at her back for balance.

As Casey's foot slipped, his body teetered precariously, but he reached out just in time, fingers brushing against Phenex's steady grip. Caught in the moment, he let out a breath, laughter bubbling up as he regained his balance. "Aww, you're my hero too," he teased, a mischievous sparkle lighting up his eyes. The memory of Phenex snatching Bryce from a tumble days earlier flashed through his mind, and he smirked. "So, I guess you don't actually want us dead," he quipped, shaking his head lightly as the last remnants of fright slipped away, replaced by the warmth of camaraderie. "Bodies need to be in perfect condition—no broken bones," Mikhail shouted from the large rock below, laughter following her words. "We're finally taking you to our secret campsite!"

Just over an hour later, they emerged into a serene clearing, the man-made cave tree house rising like a secret from the ground. The air hung still, each of their breaths a gentle puncture of the quiet. A distant chorus of birds filled the space, mingling with the soft trickle of a nearby stream—a soothing melody in the hush of nature.

The grass towered nearly a meter tall, swaying gently as they ventured deeper, creating a lush, untamed carpet beneath their feet. A small path wound its way beside a colossal fallen tree, where the closeness of the surrounding trees knitted a leafy canopy overhead, leaving the ground below bathed in dappled light. Rays burst forth through the leaves, spilling like liquid gold, casting playful shadows that danced around them in the evening dusk.

As they approached, a red fox froze, its bright eyes wide with surprise. An instant later, it was gone, slipping gracefully into the dense underbrush. "Wow... this place is amazing," Saria breathed, her voice barely a whisper, savoring the stillness that enveloped them. "No lie, it's gorgeous this little hideaway," she added, a hint of awe in her tone, fully taking in the beauty around them.

"You said it, Sari," Bryce murmured, her fingertips trailing over the tips of the grass, feeling the coolness beneath her touch. "I smell roses?"

"It's possible," Mikhail replied, her gaze sweeping across the landscape. "Some of the wild strawberries and other bush and vine fruits are starting to flower; they smell a bit like roses in their early stages." she paused, a playful glint in her eyes. "But don't be too impressed just yet. This place is gorgeous, but this is just the preview."

With a wink, she beckoned the others to follow as she knelt and gripped a sod-covered plywood circle, about two meters in diameter. With a swift motion, she peeled it back, revealing a shadowy entrance nestled beneath the ancient tree, inviting them into the hidden depths of adventure.

"Preview?" Saria raised an eyebrow, her hands moving slowly in sign language as she took in the quiet beauty around them. "Elaboration, please." She let her words hang in the air, the soft rhythm of her speech blending with the peaceful atmosphere.

Mikhail pulled a flashlight from her bag, its click echoing in the stillness as a bright beam spilled into the underbrush—but no light shimmered back. "Come on, let's be troglodytes," she grinned, leading the way into the depths below.

The underground house came to life as the solar-powered lights flickered on, illuminating a space just under four-hundred square feet. Gasps of astonishment filled the air, their friends' expressions shifting from disbelief to sheer wonder as they explored. Phenex and her sister felt a small swell of pride, delighted in sharing their creation, a feat made possible, in part, by the uprooted and half-rotted tree that served as their foundation.

Inside, cozy living quarters revealed divided sleeping areas, while a small kitchen radiated the heart of the home. The bathroom, surprisingly well-constructed, rounded out the essentials. Surrounding the outside, a small garden flourished with wild fruits, nurtured and expanded over time by the sisters.

An inviting couch, crafted from pallets, sod, and the fabric of old t-shirts, beckoned them to sit, while two chairs—similar but enhanced with egg crates and four soft bean bags—offered additional comfort. The beds, made from pallets and straw mattresses, boasted a unique treasure: a futon they had meticulously disassembled and salvaged from the side of the road.

Mikhail gestured toward the kitchen, where mud bricks formed a sturdy wall, with a small chimney extending through a dead branch. A hidden metal pipe snaked its way through, adding a rustic charm. The stove functioned as an oven, thanks to the lid of a small camp grill purchased with their saved allowance.

In one corner, herbs and flowers hung on a makeshift string, filling the air with their fragrant promise, while shelves lined with jars added a homey touch. Each detail told a story, wrapping them in the warmth of their shared adventure.

"I don't know to be mad or impressed." Bryce started.

Casey shouted from the back of the bedroom. "How could you not tell us about this?!"

"Seriously, how you two manage to create all of this?" Saria's words flowed from her hands with speed and precision, "This is truly impressive," she added, her excitement shining through in both her voice and gestures.

The voices of their friends overlapped with questions and comments, mostly repeating the same question, just in a different way each time: How? And why keep it a secret?

Chapter 10
Fate's Divergence

"I'm sorry," Phenex and Mikhail said in unison. Though it might have seemed rehearsed, in high-stress situations, their minds truly functioned as one, a shared intuition honed by their bonds as sisters "We thought about telling you but ultimately decided against it."

"We wanted to give you plausible deniability in case we ever ran away," Mikhail added, her voice shaking. "We've kept this place for a few years. It's where we escape on some weekends, especially in the summer."

"Please, you all know how Rhett can be," Phenex continued, her voice trembling. "We wanted to protect you and ourselves. Being… family." Her gaze locked with Casey's before drifting to Saria, lingering just a moment longer on Bryce.

The room hung heavy with unspoken thoughts, each person grappling with the revelation that lingered in the air. Shadows danced across their faces, and the silence seemed almost tangible. Finally, a sliver of laughter escaped Bryce, breaking the heaviness that filled the room. She shook her head, disbelief etched on her features. "Of all people, I think I'm the most offended," she said, a spark lighting her eyes. "But I get it. You remember how my so-called *parents* were."

Her voice softened, and a hint of pride crept into her tone. "I emancipated myself at fourteen just to escape them." A small smile tugged at her lips, as though relishing her own defiance. "So, if you two decide to run away, it looks like you'll be bringing all of us with you now." The words hung in the air during a brief moment of silence, "Though, with half us going to university soon, we can just kidnap you Nixx."

Laughter erupted among the group. "Is it really running away when I'm the only one who won't be eighteen?" Phenex asked playfully. "Kidnapping?"

"Hey, I'm only six months older than you, Nixx," Bryce shot back, grinning. "Though I'm not sure if emancipation would qualify me for adulthood if kidnapping is claimed... semantics, I guess."

They nestled into the warm glow of their gathering, the air thick with laughter and excited chatter. As they shared tales of clandestine adventures in the hidden treehouse, their voices danced around the flickering lantern light, each detail igniting anticipation for the summer plans that lay ahead.

As the night drew on and the time on their watches crept closer to midnight, a hush settled over them, the easy camaraderie giving way to palpable apprehension. Eyes darted toward one another, and the question that had hung just beyond reach finally broke the surface, the weight of it palpable in the cool night air. "Why show us now?" Casey's voice cut through the stillness, the uncertainty hanging heavily between them.

Mikhail's chest rose as she drew in a deep breath, her eyes fixed on their friends in the dim light. She held that breath for a moment, her voice and tone steady as she exhaled slowly. "About my dreams," she said, her voice low and measured. The others nodded, their expressions a mix of curiosity and apprehension. The night grew quiet around them, the only sound the distant hum of a cricket.

Mikhail paused, collecting her thoughts before continuing. "You know about the one where I met Phenex?" The others nodded again; their eyes locked on hers. Mikhail took another deep breath. "Well, I think that dream... was real. I know it sounds crazy, but what if I was actually there?"

Phenex rolled her eyes, a sharp sigh escaping her lips, the sarcasm barely masking the gravity of the situation. "We're going to sound crazy no matter how we tell this." She began tapping her fingers against her thumb, the rhythmic ticking of her anxiety echoing in the silence. "So here's the short version." The tremor in her fingers betrayed her calm façade. "I'm mentally in my mid-twenties; it's been just over eleven years. I have two more siblings, and I'm raising them because Rhett and Colette died. Mish has been missing since May tenth. Our goal is to prevent that."

She paused, scanning their faces, gauging their reactions.

"You need to explain better," Casey said, leaning in and clasping Phenex's hands. His gaze was steady, a quiet insistence in the way he searched her eyes. "That was direct, but I need details. Start from the beginning, Nixx."

⧗ ⧗ ⧗

"That's hella weird," Casey said after over an hour of explanation, scratching his head, confusion drifting over his expression though understanding the urgency. "So, if we don't figure this out, Mikhail goes missing?"

"That's just the cliff notes," Phenex replied, her voice faltering slightly. A flicker of doubt crossed her eyes, and she bit her lower lip, a telltale sign of her rising anxiety. "I think there's a way to communicate with my older self." She glanced away, brow furrowing as the weight of time pressed down on her. "We have about sixty-three days until... well, we run out of time." The words hung heavily in the air, and she exhaled slowly, glancing back at them. "That doesn't feel like much, especially with school and the three of you juggling work."

"Hey, no, ¡no hables así!" Bryce exclaimed, the sudden burst of Spanish catching everyone off guard. "I know you, Nixx." She slid off the pallet couch and sank to the floor, wrapping her arms tightly around Phenex.

Phenex stiffened for a moment, the unexpected embrace surprising her. Time seemed to slow as warmth enveloped her. She breathed in deeply, the cool leather of Bryce's letterman jacket soothing against her skin, mingling with the comforting scent of sandalwood. Gradually, she melted into the hug.

"I believe in you." Bryce pulled back slightly, her hand resting on Phenex's shoulder, while her other arm leaned against the ground for support. She leaned closer, her right hand gently gliding along the scar that traced Phenex's cheek up to her temple. Though she hadn't been there during the attack, she had witnessed the aftermath— the nightmares, the tears, the slow journey of healing. "You and Misha can accomplish anything you set your minds to. Plus, you have us, Nixx."

"Thanks for the vote of confidence, but I'm more impressed by your Spanish," Mikhail laughed easing the tension. "So, we need to figure out if this follows more H. G. Wells or *Back to the Future* rules."

The atmosphere grew heavy for a few moments until Casey finally broke the silence. "What's our next step?" He stood, stretching and rubbing the back of his neck, feeling the weight of their predicament settle deeper, mingling with a glimmer of hope.

"I've been thinking about that," Phenex replied. "Mikhail's dreams are helpful. It's strange to explain, but I've retained memories from both this experience and the first time I went through it. So far, I have two distinct memories for the day I went to Bryce's and the day I took that morning walk." She hesitated, searching for a way to articulate the shifting realities. "It feels like I'm living in two places at once. It's hard to put into words, but I have memories of my past and present… and what's happening right now. That probably sounds confusing."

"Is that why you seem suddenly more confident?" Casey asked gently.

"Because I have a twenty-six-year-old mind with two young kids at home?" Phenex paused, contemplating. "Not mine—Rhett and Mami had twins."

"Aww, gross," Saria laughed, her fingers mimicking disgust with a lively flair.

The group laughed, momentarily setting aside the enigma of time travel as they chatted about school and upcoming admissions. For a brief instant, they were fully present, anchored in the now.

Phenex yawned and stretched. "I think it's time for me to sleep. Obviously, we have the room. Pick a spot and crash. Night, everyone. Te quiero, Mikhail." She stretched again and added, "We can come up with a real game plan tomorrow… or later today, I guess."

As Phenex disappeared into the other room, Casey looked at Bryce and Saria, who were still processing everything they had just heard. "So… what do you think?" he asked, running a hand through his tousled hair, trying to shake off the unease that had settled in his stomach.

"Honestly, if it wasn't for my dreams, I don't know how I would feel about it." Mikhail spoke first, "It's hard to believe, but her shift in personality since she cracked her head open…"

"You think it's a TBI? You mentioned she cracked her head open." Saria interjected, her hands signing faster than her spoken words, "Did she lose consciousness?"

"Traumatic brain injury? No." Mikhail shook her head firmly. "She did have an outburst of anger, but that was the day it happened. Other than typical frustrations of teen-hood and a bit of surprising wisdom occasionally, she's normal. But… not normal in the way she was before. There's an intensity to her now, an understanding of things."

Bryce remained silent; her gaze fixed on the doorway Phenex had exited through. She listened to Mikhail and Saria, the logic of their doubt clear. A traumatic brain injury could explain a personality shift. But it couldn't explain the feeling. The absolute, unshakeable certainty that hummed within her whenever Phenex spoke about the future, about the missing sister, about the urgency. It wasn't just a story; it felt like a fundamental truth, woven into the fabric of reality. She didn't need proof. She just knew.

"It's..." Casey started, searching for the right words, his skepticism warring with the conviction he saw in both Mikhail and, surprisingly, the usually pragmatic Bryce. "It's a lot to take in. Time travel? Or... time displacement? Whatever it is." He rubbed the back of his neck, the weight of the revelation settling in his bones. "I mean, I trust you guys. But this is... wild."

Saria nodded slowly, her initial skepticism giving way to a more thoughtful consideration. "The dreams... and the change in her. It's hard to dismiss completely. But it's also... terrifying. If this is real, what does it mean for everything else?"

Mikhail met their gazes, her expression serious, "It means we have a chance. A chance to change things."

Bryce finally spoke, her voice low and steady, cutting through the uncertainty. "It's real. I don't know how. I don't know why. But it's real." Her eyes, usually full of playful defiance, held a quiet intensity that silenced the lingering doubts in the air. "And we have to help them."

Casey hesitated, not wanting to pull away from the seriousness of the moment. "Yeah, thinking about it. I've had some scholarship offers, but I don't know. Nixx being here alone doesn't really seem fair, you know?"

"I understand that sentiment," Bryce said, her tone firm. "But—Nixx would be upset if we prioritized her over ourselves, though admittedly, I am considering Baylor. You guys know I got early acceptance to them in December."

Mikhail motioned for Saria to follow her outside while Casey and Bryce continued their discussion. She held the makeshift door open for Saria to follow.

As they settled outside, Saria and Mikhail found a quiet spot beneath the tree's canopy, bathed in the remaining moonlight just as dawn was beginning to show itself. The cool night air wrapped around them, but Saria felt a mix of anxious anticipation and determination. She turned to Mikhail, hands poised in front of her, beginning to sign with fluid confidence.

"*Are you okay?*" she asked, her eyes searching Mikhail's.

Mikhail took a deep breath, leaning against the rough bark of the tree. "*Honestly? I've felt better,*" she signed back, her brows furrowing slightly. "*How do we even prepare for something we barely understand? I keep thinking… Is it fate that I abandon… that I leave her?*"

Saria nodded, her expression softening as she considered Mikhail's words. "*You're not alone in this. We'll figure it out together.*" She could sense Mikhail's unease and wanted to anchor her friend's spiraling thoughts.

"*I know, but I feel like everything falling apart is my fault,*" Mikhail signed, her emotions stacking up within her, clenching her fists momentarily before relaxing. "*Especially for Phenex. She deserves a normal life, free from this burden. If I am destined to go missing… I don't know what it will do to her, Sar.*" Her hands began to shake as her voice caught in her throat. "At least she was unaware the first time she was in ninety-eight, but now… she'll grow up aware and blaming herself if this fails, and we don't even know what the THIS is yet!"

Saria reached out, placing a hand over Mikhail's clenched fists and squeezing gently. "Stop! Stop, Misha." She shifted her weight to better face Mikhail. "Listen to me. You and Phenex are a wonder team—there isn't anything you two cannot do. Just look at this place." She gestured toward the treehouse and their small garden, their personal sanctuary hidden from most of the world. "*Now you have us too. We are aware, and not only can we help, but we will. You've always had our backs; we'll always have yours.*"

Mikhail met Saria's gaze. "You're right." She paused, closing her eyes for a moment and inhaling deeply, feeling the crisp, cool air filled her lungs. "*Thank you for listening.*"

Saria could see Mikhail's face soften as her jaw unclenched, and she began to relax. "We got you."

Mikhail's lips curled into a small smile as she leaned onto her friend's shoulder. "Yeah, yeah," she laughed, shaking her head. "You always have the wisest words, Saria," she spoke aloud as she signed. She jumped to her feet and yawned. "*Come on,*" she said, extending a hand to Saria.

⏳ ⏳ ⏳

Phenex glanced up as Bryce stepped into the room, her silhouette framed by the dim light spilling through the doorway. She lay on a small pallet, the makeshift mattress rustled slightly beneath her. Straw poked out from the edges, evidence of its rough construction. "Ugh, I can't sleep," Phenex said softly, propping herself against the gently curved mud brick wall. Small fingerprints dotted the walls, a random pattern left by both her and Mikhail.

Bryce approached with a warm smile. "Mind if I lie down with you?"

"Psh, there will always be room for you in my bed," Phenex teased, her cheeks turning pink the instant the words left her lips. "Um… that didn't come right out… out right." She laughed, the sound blending with the cozy atmosphere as Bryce settled beside her, laughter sparkling in her eyes. "What I really meant was, you and I can always… you know, hang out, do an activity. Ugh, it's going to sound wrong no matter how I phrase it."

"Just tell me how you feel, Alejandra," Bryce encouraged, her grin wide and inviting. The playful wink she shot Phenex coaxed another laugh from her.

"No, shush," Phenex giggled, her laughter spilling out as she playfully covered Bryce's mouth, burying her face into her shoulder in a flurry of warmth. "I haven't slept yet—my wires got crossed in word talking."

Bryce replied with a snort, a teasing glimmer in her eyes that eased some of Phenex's embarrassment. "You really need some sleep, kid."

Tilting her head slightly, Phenex rested it against Bryce's shoulder, savoring the comforting presence she felt. The steady rhythm of Bryce's heartbeat beneath her ear calmed her racing thoughts, making it hard to resist nuzzling deeper against her. "You're not wrong," she admitted, stifling a yawn and feeling a warm blush creep to her cheeks. "I'm really glad you're here, Ripley. Thank you for listening and believing us. I know it sounds ridiculous." Her voice softened, revealing the depths of her gratitude—and perhaps a flicker of something more that she dared not voice just yet.

Bryce shook her head, leaning in closer. "You've always had my back. I will always have yours. Tell me you're gonna walk on the moon; también Nosotros estamos llegando la luna para que puedas comida."

Suppressing a giggle, Phenex replied, playfulness in her voice just barely evident as she gave in to the heaviness of her eyelids. "The good news, your Spanish is improving—secretly practicing, huh? But the bad news? You just promised we'd eat on the moon. I'm pretty sure the restaurant up there wouldn't have much to offer, especially with the whole lack of atmosphere situation."

Unfazed by her words, Bryce laughed, the determination in her eyes sparkling. "You know what? If you want to walk on the moon, then we'll figure out how to eat it too. Always aim higher." She draped her arm over Phenex, pulling her closer. The gentle warmth of their closeness enveloped them, creating a space where worries fell away, if only for that moment.

As Phenex felt her eyes grow heavier, she felt her jaw relaxing, letting the rhythm of Bryce's breath lull her toward sleep. Relaxation enveloped her as she nestled closer, resting her hand gently on Bryce's chest, just beneath where her head rested. It was a moment filled with warmth and the promise of solidarity, a perfect escape from the chaos of everything else.

CHAPTER 11
BUTTERFLY KISS; PARADOX

Mikhail stretched and suppressed another yawn, fighting to keep her eyes open as she stepped into the bedroom of the tree house. The sight that greeted her made her smile: Bryce and her sister were leaning against each other on the same bed, fast asleep in what had to be the most uncomfortable position imaginable. Phenex was curled up in the fetal position, her knees hanging over the edge, while Bryce's head tilted back at such an angle that it almost looked like it was going to roll off entirely.

Suppressing a chuckle, Mikhail tossed a blanket over them, tucking it in around them before making her way to the futon that served as her bed during their stays in the treehouse. It wasn't long before she succumbed to sleep herself. When she finally stirred, the sun was high in the sky, and it was noon by the time she joined the others by the creek's embankment.

Saria and Casey were sitting nearby, fishing poles in hand, casting their lines into the water. Phenex was at the back of the tree house, absorbed in a book, while Bryce was nowhere to be seen. "Buenos días, Mana," Phenex said, not looking up from her reading. "I was just about to come in and wake you."

"Yeah... We all stayed up way too late."

"What's funny is that in ten years, I'm going to wish I could bounce back like this after an all-nighter." She chuckled, folding the corner of the page she was on before closing the book. "How did you sleep?"

"Como les muertos, como dice, ¿un zombie?" Mikhail said, shaking her head as she sat on the ground across from Phenex. "I dreamt I woke up covered in dew with a bird trying to eat my tongue like it was a worm." Her tone was playfully sarcastic. "What are you reading? Where's Bryce?"

"Oh, yeah, Ripley let me borrow it." She held the book up so Mikhail could see the front cover, "It's called *The Price of Salt*," Phenex said, her tone light yet tinged with curiosity. "At the beginning, it explores a young woman's internal struggle as she grapples with feelings that don't align with society's expectations." She stifled a laugh, the thought *feels a bit like an attack...* flitting through her mind. "Bryce went to Ray's to grab some candy and soda, but I think she'll be back soon; I gave her clearer directions to find this place."

Mikhail nodded, her gaze fixed on her sister as she committed every detail of Phenex's features to memory. In their conversations, an undercurrent of danger lingered in the air, making both of them uneasy about how events might unfold. Mikhail noticed the jagged scar on Phenex's right cheekbone—a stark line that extended nearly five inches toward her temple, fading into her hairline.

She sighed, biting her lower lip, an instinctive urge to protect her sister washing over her. It mirrored Phenex's own fierce desire to keep her safe. Yet, Mikhail couldn't ignore the weight of her past failures, each one a painful reminder of her limitations, none more so than the scar that marred Phenex's skin.

"So, do you have any theories?" Mikhail asked.

Phenex sat in silence for a moment, her gaze drifting as her thoughts wandered. "I have an idea—it's not fully formed, but it came to me last night," she said slowly. "What if saving you changes more than just the future timeline? Think about the Time Traveler; he can only return to the moment the Time Machine was invented. In this scenario, I'd assume I am the machine, so I can only travel back to the moment of my own existence. But the real question is how? Maybe I'm meant to help you or save you in some way. That could explain your dreams and my presence, even if it doesn't fully add up."

She giggled, the effects of the magic brownie bubbling to the surface, a hint of mischief in her eyes. "For now, it's the best line of thinking I have."

She began tapping her fingers against her thumb, a rhythmic distraction, before reaching for her necklace. As her fingers brushed her chest, a wave of confusion washed over her—*where is it?* She shook her head, reminding herself where she was, or rather, *when* she was. In that fleeting moment, her twenty-six-year-old self seemed to fade, leaving behind only a fragment of consciousness. She had momentarily forgotten that her necklace was no longer the class rings she'd worn for a decade, each one a reassuring charm.

When she returned to the present, she felt the clash of two minds within her: Her elder self and her teenage self seemingly at odds, each vying for control. The world around her threatened to dissolve, as if the water that once carried her back in time was trying to pull her under once more. As swiftly as the sensation began, it vanished. Her hand instinctively closed around the four stones that her closest friends had gifted her, grounding her in the reality of her teenage self yet again. Relief flooded over her as she sighed deeply, grateful to find the stones still dangling from their cord around her neck, tucked into her shirt—something she had almost lost in that moment of stress.

"¿Está bien?" Mikhail said, noticing Phenex's tapping fingers. "You only do that when you're worried about something."

"The term 'anxiety' comes to mind," Phenex replied almost instinctively. "It's only really talked about—never mind, future worries." She muttered a number under her breath as she slowed her tapping before stopping completely. "You haven't tried Sprocket's brownies yet; you need to."

Mikhail laughed. "That explains the Krispy Kreme-eyed look you have. Are you feeling okay?"

The corners of Phenex's lips lifted with an effervescent energy, but beneath that delightful exterior, a tremor rippled through her legs. It was as if her muscles had been replaced with a gelatinous substance, wobbling and quivering with every shift of her weight as if balancing on the edge of a cloud where gravity and buoyancy tangled in a mischievous embrace.

The world around her sparkled with an electric vibrancy; colors bled into one another, vivid and surreal. She could feel the thrum of music vibrating in her chest, resonating through her limbs like the gentle pulse of a heartbeat, each note coaxing her to let go of her inhibitions. In that moment, every sound felt amplified, the laughter of her friends in the distance floated around on the gentle breeze.

"Other than my legs feeling like green Jello and Pluto being within my sight and the theory I just dumped on you, I'm chill, Mana." The words flowed from her lips, buoyant and carefree, much like her current state. In the back of her mind, she thought of how absurd it was to feel so light-hearted yet grounded in that blissful wobble. The horizon stretched toward a kaleidoscope of stars, each twinkling light whispering promises of adventure, drawing her in with a gravity utterly different from the one that weighed on her limbs. "Didn't take much, same as last time, promesa."

Leaves and twigs crunched under Casey and Saria's feet as they returned, each holding a rope with several fish. "Check it out; we got a small haul, primas," Casey exclaimed, excitement clear in his voice. "We caught twelve—three catfish and nine bass!" He beamed with pride. Mikhail and Phenex exchanged amused glances, picturing a five-year-old Casey at the lake with them, their mother, and their father—back when making friends was easy, a simple "Hello, you like my fish?" could forge a lifelong bond between them.

"We also caught two crappies… carp, but they were small," Saira added as she held the largest bass, almost two feet in length, its scales glistening in the sunlight, "That's how we caught this guy!"

Bryce returned about fifteen minutes later, her arms loaded with snacks and a bottle of Pibb. "Oh, sweet! Wakford Foodlandia stopped selling Pibb in 1995; I haven't had one of these in—" Phenex paused mid-sentence, considering for a moment before a dry laugh escaped her throat, "I guess I technically have had one recently."

As they enjoyed their snacks, a few moments of comfortable silence unfolded between them, accompanied by the soothing sounds of nature – the gentle trinkling of the creek, the spring breeze playfully whistling through the trees. Saria's voice then floated through the air; a melodic lilt carried within her words. "I was thinking," she said, the subtle nuances of her speech emerging like a distinct fingerprint – a hallmark of her unique "deaf accent." Each syllable tumbled forth, slightly more pronounced and rhythmic, colored by the cadence of her thoughts.

The way she formed her sounds was immersive; she emphasized certain vowel sounds more fully, each vowel stretching slightly as if reaching for understanding. There was a slight tendency for her consonants to coalesce, creating a gentle fluidity that eased into the conversations around her. A casual smile lingered on her lips, the kind of confidence that was embodied best when she was sharing space with friends.

"What events do you change?" she continued, her hand slicing through the air to emphasize her curiosity. As she spoke, her eyebrows arched, drawing her friends in as if waiting for their reactions not just to her words but to the expressions that flared to life on her face.

Her friends noticed that her speech would occasionally slow down, a reminder that she sometimes forgot they were safe here together. Yet, her hands moved quickly in ASL, forming the signs with a fluidity that expressed her thoughts clearly. "I just... it makes me wonder; you know? What we could do differently."

"Going to your place," Phenex gestured in the direction of both Bryce and Saria, "the early morning walk, this." Gesturing to the campsite around them, "I didn't tell you all last time; after all, last time, I was fifteen, not rapidly approaching thirty in my fifteen-year-old body."

"So, you're old?" Bryce teased.

"Still six months younger than you, so I am still younger." She smiled. "Everything else has been the same or nearly the same. My vocabulary and cadence have changed a little, but the 'I'm a teenager' excuse seems to work out." She shook her hands as though doing jazz fingers as she said 'teenager'.

Casey threw the fish he had been cleaning aside and started to work on a second one. "So, what day does Mikhail… disappear? Or are we using that as a euphemism for…?"

"Disappear. It's Sunday, May tenth this year," Phenex replied quietly, her gaze dropping to the ground. "We don't know for sure if she's… dead. She just… was gone." The weight of her words hung in the air, heavy with unspoken fears and memories.

She sighed, her breath catching as a tidal wave of thoughts surged within her. *Should I reveal my truth? Should I finally share what I've kept locked away? Not yet; it isn't the right time.* Memories swirled in her mind, heavy and persistent. A faded news article flickered to life, its yellowing edges curling like old secrets. The stark headline "Missing" echoed in her ears, accompanied by the jarring sight of her name— "Phenex Alejandra López"—beneath her own photograph, a ghost from another time.

The article was unsettlingly detailed, recounting events and figures from her past that felt like shards of her own story. This clandestine knowledge pressed down on her like a stone, suffocating in its weight. Was she misinterpreting it all? Had her mind conjured her name from a haze of disbelief? The photograph of her sister Mikhail from 1987 haunted her; frozen at seventeen, Mikhail had been missing since. Yet when she had appeared before Phenex in

1998, she wore the same youthful glow, as if time had abandoned its march.

She wished the article she had found were true, that she could escape the pain of missing her sister—the only one who understood her when their parents fought. Without her best friend, there was no one to vent to about teachers and bullies, no one to share dreams and hopes with, or to whisper secrets in the dark. The absence of Mikhail left an ache that echoed through her days, a reminder of all the moments they could have shared.

Phenex stared at her hands for a moment, smaller and more youthful. She flexed her fingers, stretching them out and spreading them apart as far as they would go. A faint tremor coursed through her metacarpals—so subtle that she might have missed it herself had she not been hyperaware—like tiny electric jolts. In the stillness of the night, when vulnerability seeped through her defenses, she confronted her deepest fear: that it should have been her who vanished, not Mikhail. Living in the shadows of loss, she questioned her own existence, wondering if the world would be better off without her, just as she often wished it could be without the lingering pain of her sister's absence.

Phenex's voice, usually filled with playful banter, now carried the weight of a thousand unspoken words. 'I wish it had been me,' she confessed, her voice barely a whisper. "I probably shouldn't start with that..." Her laughter, once infectious, now sounded hollow, a stark contrast to her usual cheerful demeanor. "For nearly eleven years, I've wished it was me who disappeared. I... I was... am..." She trailed off, her words caught in her throat. The weight of her secret, a heavy burden she had carried for years, threatened to crush her.

Mikhail and Saria shared a concerned glance, struck by the sight of Phenex's uncharacteristic vulnerability. Her typically bright eyes were dimmed by a sadness that seemed to penetrate their very souls.

"I'm angry," Phenex continued, her voice rising with emotion. "Angry that I became Rhett's target. Angry that I'm trapped here, that I had to come back." Her words lingered in the air, heavy with unspoken pain and resentment. "I'm furious that we have no way of knowing if anything is actually changing because we can't see into the future. If I return… Dios mío… when I return, everything will be exactly the same."

A silence fell over the group, broken only by the distant rustle of leaves and the soft murmur of the creek. Mikhail reached out, her hand hovering over Phenex's, hesitant to touch. The weight of the unspoken words between them was almost tangible.

Phenex flinched, pulling her hand away. "Don't," she whispered, her voice barely audible. "Don't touch me." Her eyes, filled with a mix of fear and defiance, darted around the group. "I'm not the same person I used to be. I'm broken, and I'm afraid."

The revelation hung in the air, a heavy cloud that threatened to consume them all. As the sun began to set, casting long shadows across the forest, the group sat in silence, each lost in their own thoughts.

Chapter 12
Ebb of Time

Mikhail placed the slimy fish guts collected by Saria and Casey's earlier fishing expedition into a glass jar brimming with coarse salt, the briny odor wafting up and mingling with the earthy scent of aged wood that permeated the tree house. Nearby, the fish simmered slowly in a makeshift oven, its surface sputtering softly, sending up wisps of steam that curled into the warm, dim air.

Inside the tree house, shadows danced along the walls, alive with the flickering light from the lanterns perched atop the coffee table and suspended from the kitchen ceiling. The soft glow cast an amber hue over everything, creating an intimate cocoon that contrasted sharply with the weight of the unspoken words in the air.

Meanwhile, outside, Phenex stood alone beneath the sprawling branches of an ancient oak. The cool night air brushed against her skin, a stark contrast to the warmth of the fire that had recently flickered out. She gripped the rough bark, the splinters biting into her palm as she sought solace in the familiar texture. Her mind raced, replaying the words she had just spoken, each syllable echoing in her ears. The weight of her confession hung heavy in the air, a silent accusation that left her feeling exposed and vulnerable. The silence that followed was deafening, a stark reminder of the chasm that had opened between her and her friends. A wave of loneliness washed over her, a cold and isolating feeling that mirrored the chill of the night.

Inside, Bryce scribbled furiously in a battered notebook, the scratch of her pencil punctuating the quiet, occasionally accompanied by a soft sigh or a frustrated groan before she either erased her thoughts or resumed writing with renewed urgency. She was the only one who had not spoken since Phenex's confession, her eyes darting as if searching for answers hidden in the lines of her notebook.

Back outside, Phenex felt a shiver race down her spine, as if the very darkness around her conspired to draw her deeper into despair. She crawled deeper inside herself, retreating into the labyrinth of her mind, desperately trying to hold on to the split realities swirling around her like autumn leaves caught in a gust of wind.

Inside, Mikhail and Saria spoke quietly, their words barely above a whisper, the weight of the night's events painted across their faces. The conversation they'd shared during the twilight hours before felt fragile and insufficient now, incapable of preparing them for the depth of emotions Phenex had laid bare.

"She has never shoved me back that hard before," Mikhail said, her voice hollow, pained. "I knew that she was upset, that there was something she wasn't saying, but… I don't know if I could have imagined the pain she has been harboring."

Casey plopped down onto a faded bean bag, its fabric soft and worn beneath him, bringing with him the distracting scent of fresh air mixed with the lingering aroma of the compost barrel he had just tended to outside. He tossed some scraps from their earlier snacks into the thick burlap sack that lingered at the edge of the room, the crinkling sound of the material echoing softly as it settled.

Back in the shadows of the fallen oak, Phenex wrapped her arms around herself, trying to ward off both the chill in the air and the chill of her own thoughts. The night felt endless, each moment stretching into infinity. She tilted her head back, gazing up at the sky, where the stars twinkled like scattered diamonds against a deep, velvety purple blanket. The Milky Way arched overhead, a luminous river of light winding through the cosmos, and for a moment, she lost herself in its beauty.

She searched the night sky for any sign of the Crab Nebula, her favorite celestial formation. It fascinated her, a remnant of a once mighty star that could once be seen even during daylight hours. How had something so magnificent changed over time, fading from view yet becoming a beacon in her dreams? She felt an ache in her heart as she scanned the heavens; Phenex's thoughts drifted away from her worries, if only for a moment. The expansive beauty above her reminded her that there was more to life than the darkness she carried inside. Yet, as the realization came, so did the weight of her truth, pulling her back to the ground. She sighed, allowing the cool air to fill her lungs, but the ache remained.

Inside the tree house, Saria gestured lazily, her hands moving in a fluid motion that complemented her words, both a blend of thought and movement. Her fingers danced in the soft glow of the lantern light, creating soft shapes that seemed almost alive. "If Rhett starts taking it out on her, has he ever…" She paused, her brow furrowing slightly as the concern weighed heavily on her.

With a sudden intensity, she sucked her teeth, "Has he ever hit any of you?" she signed, her hands slicing through the air. The question spilled forth with urgency.

"No," Mikhail shook her head firmly. "No, he has never hit us. Grabbed me a few times, maybe shoved us in a direction, but has never fully swung at us." She paused, the weight of her words hanging in the air. "I think she just means the responsibilities that used to be mine have fallen on her along with the expectations."

Saria nodded, feeling the ripples of silence that followed Mikhail's words. The atmosphere in the tree house shifted as the reality of their lives settled heavily around them, the warmth of the lantern light only barely pushing back the shadows of uncertainty that loomed large in their hearts. Phenex's distant thoughts intermingled with their present, as they all grappled with what it truly meant to bear the burdens of the past and navigate the fragility of their present.

Casey and Saria nodded, the tension slowly dispersing as they tried to wrap their heads around the emotional currents swirling within the tree house. "That makes sense," Casey muttered, frustration creeping into his voice before he groaned. "How do we… No, that's not it. The issue isn't not knowing what we don't know; it's not knowing what we do."

"Say again, Sprocket?" Mikhail raised an eyebrow, a hint of laughter breaking through the somber atmosphere. "Maybe lay off the brownies."

"That's actually genius, Sprocket," Bryce chimed in from her corner, where she huddled over her writing, fingers moving quickly over the page. "You're saying it isn't that we don't know what we're missing; it's that we don't even understand what we already know, right?"

The soothing flicker of the lanterns persisted, casting a warm glow that wrapped around them like a comforting blanket amidst uncertainty. Yet, a heavy silence loomed in the air, thick and palpable.

Then, as if a light bulb had illuminated each of their minds, they all began to speak at once, voices overlapping in a rush of thoughts and emotions that filled the space, breaking the stillness with vibrant energy.

Bryce was the first to dart back outside. She found Phenex leaning against the back of the earth home near the embankment, "Alejandra! We figured something out. Casey did actually, inspiring, sparking the thoughts, believe it or not." Her words ran together excited as if trying to start multiple sentences at once.

Phenex jumped, startled by Bryce's sudden appearance and voice cutting through the air, shaking her from her innermost thoughts. She stared at Bryce, blinking, trying to ground herself and bring herself back to her reality that was. "Sorry about my depressive comments earlier. It wasn't at or meant for any of you; it's just difficult being here, knowing…"

"You can apologize for that later, Alejandra; I think we figured out what we can do to save Mikhail." She smiled, stepping close to Phenex, "Casey said something that inspired me. His words: we don't know what we're missing; we don't understand what we already know." She laughed, "And that made me realize something; you said you're twenty-six, correct?"

Phenex nodded yes slowly as Bryce continued, "Well, what if that is part of the key." She held up the notebook she had been writing in; there were numbers and calendars scribbled all around.

"I couldn't figure it out at first. I was asking Mikhail a few questions, and she said that she had dreams of an older you for a couple of years; if that's the case, why haven't you fallen backward in time before? And you said that you only saw her physically just the other day, but eleven years from now."

Phenex nodded, cradling the composition book in her hands as she absorbed Bryce's words. Slowly, the numbers began to click into place, the dates aligning in her mind with a clarity she had not felt before.

Bryce had meticulously crafted a calendar spanning March to June for both 1987 and 1998. In the margins, she noticed rough calculations for '53, '81, and 2015, and 2025 with a hastily scratched '6' written above. The notes sprawled across the pages like an intricate web, figures jumbled and overwhelming when viewed individually. But as Phenex scanned the entire spread, connections emerged, weaving a coherent narrative from what once seemed chaotic.

Excitement spread across her face with a brilliant smile, "Bryce... this... this makes so much sense. Thank you." She brought her hand to her mouth, processing the revelation. "So, if the key is oddly tied to the calendar, it means we might not only move forward but could even return. Or go backward... Uggh! I feel like we're just completing a circumference back to square one." She paused confusion washed over her, "Circle... I meant circle."

"Po-tay-to, po-ta-toh," Bryce said with a grin. "I'm glad I could bring a smile back to your face. I have to admit, the brooding goth look is great for Patricia Morrison, but you're more..." She waved her hand through the air, as if painting a picture, "Elvira."

Phenex teased, "Is that supposed to be a compliment, Ripley? Really?" As she looked down, she realized she was still holding Bryce's hand, the notebook nestled in her other palm. A warm flush spread across her cheeks as her heart pulsed rapidly in her chest, the sound echoing inside her head. Bryce's vibrant blue eyes sparkled, her cheeks taking on a soft, rosy hue as she gazed at Phenex. "Um… Heh." Bryce began, her voice nearly silent, more of an exhale than a response. Their faces were just inches apart, and in that charged moment, the world around them faded away. Neither had noticed how close they had moved while discussing the notebook and theory, captivated by each other's presence. As the gentle breeze wafted the faint scent of eucalyptus and sandalwood between them, Bryce hesitated, uncertainty flickering in her eyes as she leaned a fraction closer, caught in the magnetic pull of the excitement.

Their hearts seemed to beat in unison as around them silence seemed to fall, only their breathing cut through the electrified air.

"I ho…" Phenex felt as though her heart may explode, a mix of anticipation and anxiety swirling within her. Her hands were clammy, feeling heavy with the weight of her own awareness as Bryce's hand brushed against hers their fingers resting against one another, begging to intertwine.

She could feel the warmth radiating from Bryce, the softness in her gaze drawing her in. Just as their lips seemed destined to meet, Bryce paused, her breath hitching the scent of Big Red Gum wafted in the air between them.

The sharp crack of a nearby branch snapping broke the spell, jolting them both back to reality. Instinctively, they each took a step back, putting space between them.

CHAPTER 13
FRACTURED DREAMS

Mikhail approached silently, the soft loam muffling her footsteps. Rounding the corner, she caught sight of Bryce and Phenex, suspended in a moment. A gentle breeze rustled the leaves above, blending the delicate scents of faint rose and crisp cool air. They hadn't noticed her as she froze in surprise, sensing a silent conversation flowing through the space that separated their bodies.

Her gaze lingered on Bryce, noting the flicker of uncertainty in her eyes as Phenex leaned in ever so slightly closer. As their lips drew near, hesitation washed over Phenex. Mikhail observed the mix of anticipation and trepidation flashing across her sister's face, almost feeling the hitch in Phenex's breath—like the reluctant pause before a secret was revealed.

Mikhail narrowed her eyes at their almost-linked hands. Just as she stepped closer, preparing to say something to draw their attention away, a branch broke under her weight, disrupting the tranquility with a sudden snap. The brittle sound reverberated through the silence, snapping Mikhail back to reality as a sharp jolt coursed through her foot. Bryce and Phenex's heads turned nearly in unison, retreating to increase the distance between them, their moment extinguished in an instant. Mikhail released the breath she had drawn, confusion swirling in her mind. *What was that?* She wondered, the thought made her stomach clench slightly, a feeling she couldn't quite decipher. She glanced between Bryce and Phenex, searching their faces for answers, but found only a mixture of surprise and confusion. The tension in the air dissipated quickly, leaving Mikhail bewildered by what she had just witnessed. Shoving the thought aside, she instinctively raised her hands to sign, hoping to redirect their attention. "Hey, what's happening?" she signed, a habit they all fell into, even when Saria wasn't directly with them; her movements were fluid.

Bryce turned her gaze to Mikhail, surprise widening her eyes, while Phenex struggled to mask her flustered reaction. "Ripley was just telling me about the *vision* you all had, and I was sharing some more details about what I'm experiencing," she explained, excitement bubbling to the surface as her notebook slipped from her fingers and fell to the ground. "I really think it relates to the Falls and Sooner Cave."

Her words flowed with enthusiasm, accompanied by animated signs, and the tension slowly dissipated. Bryce nodded, seemingly relieved to shift the focus back to the intriguing discussion, allowing the air to clear without addressing the moment that had just passed.

Back in the treehouse, the atmosphere buzzed with chaotic creativity as they scrawled theories and ideas across the mudbrick walls with vibrant chalk stone. "So, we figured out the calendar. Dates lining up perfectly—eighty-seven started on a Thursday, and it wasn't a leap year, just like ninety-eight. Eighty-one and seventy did, too, and twenty-zero-nine will as well. All the dates are exactly the same. The real question is: why are you being pulled back?" Casey wrote in his trademark beautiful manuscript despite the awkwardness holding the large soft rock in his hand.

"We were around the Falls, near where the alleged Sooner Cave is," Mikhail chimed in, her enthusiasm spilling over like. "That means—" she paused, her brow furrowing in deep concentration,

"I don't know what it means." She flopped onto the floor in a mock tantrum, "You think the valedictorian, co-salutatorians, honors and AP could figure out advance time theory."

A chorus of laughter erupted, "You had us in the beginning, and then—" Casey chortled as the group chimed in, whistling to mimic the sound of an atom bomb dropping before erupting into exaggerated, playful explosions.

Mikhail rolled her eyes, the playful smile teasing the corners of her lips as she settled onto her back, staring up at the ceiling. "Café, dude! What do you expect me to do with only a few blank hours of sleep? I need the hot bean juice fix to function!" She stretched her arms above her head, relishing the slight creak of her joints, the promise of energy and a fresh start hovering just out of reach.

"Dead brain buttons, obviously," Phenex teased, leaning over to grab the notebook Bryce had initially presented. "Cells, I meant brain cells," she said with a smirk. "I think you're part of the key, too." Gesturing to Mikhail, "Just think about it," she urged, her voice growing serious with purpose. "The years are seventy, eightyone, seven, and ninety-eight. Misha, born in seventy; I was born in seventy-two. If we're considering my years or my lifetime, that leaves two years unaccounted for, making Claudia the key."

She paused, looking up from the notebook to meet her sister's gaze. "Tus sueños, la clarividente, o como dicen... I don't know how to explain it. The dreams about the older me—when did they start?" Her expression was intense, searching for answers in the depths of her sister's understanding.

A brief silence fell over the room as everyone exchanged confused glances, taken aback by Phenex's slip of calling Mikhail by her first name. Nobody used that name but medical professionals. "A few years ago, I guess, but they seem to happen more frequently between April and May," Mikhail shrugged, a flicker of uncertainty passing across her brow. "This year felt different. I had a dream around the end of February when I missed school because I had a horrible reaction to whatever was used to clean our bathroom. Broke out in horrible hives."

"Yeah, I had to pick up your homework, but cara de perra wouldn't let me get it for you." Phenex rolled her eyes, laughter bubbling at the effortless memory that had surfaced, a snapshot caught in the frame of nostalgia. One of the things they hadn't tested yet was her ability to recall more recent memories before her twentysix-year-old consciousness emerged: "Not about her, sorry."

Saria leaned against the back of the pallet-constructed couch, its rough edges digging into her back. "How was the dream different?" she asked, her voice filling the space between them, prompting a return to the more pressing conversation.

Mikhail closed her eyes for a moment, lost in thought as she waded through the murky waters of her memory, trying to grasp the details of the dream that felt increasingly elusive. "I had two that day. The first one was standard. I entered the treehouse, made Nixx some tea, and then this loud alarm went off—just a piercing, awful sound…" She paused briefly, her brow crinkling. "You really need a new alarm clock; it's the most irritating redundant noise I've ever heard… I'll skip that joke for now, focusing on the issue at hand: I woke up just as Nixx was being ripped away. They aren't always calm dreams…" Her words picked up pace as she realized she had forgotten to draw a breath before speaking.

Mikhail sat upright and slid across the floor onto the pallet couch, her thoughts racing. "The second dream," she began, taking a deep breath to gather her swirling thoughts. "I was working on the time capsule for graduation and fell asleep with it beside me. When I woke up, I saw Phenex, but I didn't fully recognize her at first. Even in my dreams of an older version of her, I would watch her transform right before my eyes, taking on that familiar shape I know so well."

She paused, a playful grin breaking through her serious demeanor. "And yes, I see you as a five-year-old Nixx before you even ask. However, this dream was different. This time, I saw an adult version of you, kneeling and crying." The gravity of her words hung in the space between them, the dream's vivid imagery lingering in her mind.

Mikhail's voice dropped to a whisper as she recalled the vivid image, her brow furrowing slightly. "She was wearing an outfit that really caught my eye—the same shirt and jacket you have on now." Directing the last half of her sentence directly at her younger sister, a chill ran down her spine as the details flooded back to her, the resonance of the dream mingling with the weight of reality. "It felt… it felt so real, like a warning or a message I can't quite understand." Her gaze flicked to her sister again, searching for understanding, for confirmation that she wasn't alone in this strange experience.

Mikhail walked over to Phenex, lifting her arm to show the sleeve of her jacket. The stitching on Bryce's jacket was distinctive; thick red thread formed an X pattern around the wrist. "Mine is thinner, just the standard merch from their stand. I remember noting the details; it struck me as odd because it was Bryce's jacket.

But seeing her wear it now makes me wonder—maybe you two are still friends…" She paused, an almost knowing tone, "…Or maybe Nixx just decided to keep it forever."

Phenex laughed, placing her hands behind her head, "Let's not get into the nine-tenths of law rule."

"Stealing my jacket for eleven years? How rude." Bryce chimed playfully.

"Not the time to sort this out," Casey rolled his eyes, "Nixx, what other details are there that you can recall."

Phenex crossed an arm over her chest and held her chin with the other, careful not to cover her lips, "I know it is important that we protect Mikhail, but also," she sighed, "I only vaguely mentioned it, but Mami and Rhett die in ninety-three. I remember they died. I was still angry with Rhett, but I'm not the only one affecting our past… future… this timey-wimey stuff is confusing." She gave an exasperated sigh, "I am not the only one who has done things differently. Mikhail yelled at our Mami. Bryce allowing me to borrow this book," she pulled The Price of Salt out of the front pocket, "You gave it to me when you moved to Waco."

"I don't remember much," she continued, a sense of loss creeping into her tone. "It's getting harder to recall the future. I feel like I'm slowly fading back to myself here in eighty-seven. I did manage to write a few things down in the case that I…" she hesitated, remembering that she was the only one who knew about the news clipping. For an instant she considered confessing that it wasn't just Mikhail's life at stake, but her own. "Er… I… Sorry," she stammered, her frustration evident. "When the time comes to remember, it's as if everything slips away." Her brow furrowed deeper. "I've even started journaling each night to keep my thoughts anchored."

After a brief pause, she took a deep breath, gathering her thoughts. "All of that was a long way to say… I think we need to change Rhett and Mami, too. It's not just about us. Talking to them, yelling at them, threatening—none of those feel quite right. I don't know exactly how, but we have to find a better way to communicate with them." She bit her lip, glancing away as she pondered, "There has to be a more effective way to phrase that." Her eyes returned to Mikhail, searching for understanding, for support.

Chapter 14

Fractured Barriers; Converging Words

Sunday evening, Phenex stood in the kitchen checking the chicken in the oven, "About ten minutes and it will be finished." She informed Mikhail, who nodded, "You ready, *Carnala*?" she looked at her sister, who had finished setting the table.

"No," Mikhail's tone was flat, lacking all emotion, "But we might as well knock this one out and hope. Nothing is going to change if we don't try everything we can."

Phenex nodded, "*Claro*. Thana and Enoch are out with Casey and Saria. We have Bryce on call, and Daisy and Abuelos will be here to moderate. I think it will be safe to speak as candidly as we want. Maybe not swear as much as I usually do." She smiled teasing, "You have what you want to say written down, or are you winging it?"

"Winging it like the day I yelled at our mother," Mikhail said, "I think I do better when speaking from my heart or off the cuff."

"I brought notes to pretend to study." Phenex laughed, pulling a small stack of note cards from the front pouch of the Muttering Gibberish jacket, the jacket she had originally borrowed from Bryce; she hadn't removed the hooded pullover since Friday except to shower. Bryce had tried to take it from her, but Phenex held up the book she had also borrowed in front of her like the world's smallest shield and promised to return both when she finished.

Mikhail had noticed that Phenex and Bryce seemed to be trying to hang out as often as they could; she overheard them making plans to hang out the following weekend as though wanting to make the most of their time together before Bryce went off to university.

She smiled at Phenex's over-prepared notes to speak with Rhett and their mother, "Think we can refrain from sarcastic comments?"

Phenex raised an eyebrow but refrained from responding; the cat-like smile that crept across her was all too telling. "Look at that beautiful crispy skin!" her voice filled with excitement as she pulled the roasted chicken from the oven. She placed a tent of aluminum foil over the chicken, "Just needs to rest for a bit. The nice part about being trapped in my fifteen-year-old self is I can cook like my twenty-six-year-old self." She laughed as she started the gravy, "Dinner will be ready in half an hour, so in about twenty minutes, everyone should be sitting down."

"I thought about asking how you learned to cook like this," Mikhail said, a playful smile tugging at the corners of her lips, "but I assumed it had to do with your mind." With a spark of excitement in her eyes, she leaned closer to the small tin foil tent, its shiny surface glistening under the soft kitchen lights. Gently, she ripped off a piece of the perfectly cooked chicken, the tender meat practically calling her name. She couldn't help but sneak a quick bite, letting the burst of rich flavors dance on her tongue—savory spices mingling beautifully with the juiciness of the meat. In that moment, as she savored the small bite, "Hmm. Okay, that's amazing, and now I am mad I have to wait half an hour." She sighed, "I will go inform Mother and Rhett and the grandparents that dinner will be ready soon."

Phenex carefully set the platter of chicken at the center of the table, a masterpiece of golden-brown skin and fragrant herbs that filled the air with mouthwatering aromas. A sense of pride swelled within her as she admired her handiwork, the culmination of her efforts for this family-style dinner. With a gentle smile, she released the messy bun that had been hastily thrown together earlier, allowing her hair to cascade down her shoulders. As her fingers ran through the strands, her thoughts drifted to the future—an uncertain path that beckoned her forward.

What would it hold? She pondered if the choices she was making now would lead to a life different from the one she envisioned. Would the memories she forged tonight give her a glimpse of what was to come? She took a deliberate breath, momentarily closing her eyes to summon any fleeting insights or dreams, hoping they might offer a clue as to whether their collective efforts had truly meant something.

In the background, she could hear the bustling sounds of Mikhail and the adults gathering in the kitchen, chatter blending together. The urge to shout out to them flickered in her mind, but she chose instead to maintain her quiet anticipation. Peeking around the doorway, she called out, her voice bright and inviting, "I got everything moved already! Drinks and all are in the dining room. Come. Sit. Enjoy."

Mikhail and Phenex sat in silence, allowing the adults around them to share their thoughts. Most of the comments focused on the dinner. "Wow, Phenex, it smells amazing," Colette said, taking a deep inhale of the herbal aroma.

Alejandro's parents, Abuelo Serjio and Abuelita, sat across from each other at the table. Despite his limp, Serjio gently pulled out Abuelita's chair and kissed her cheek as she settled in. His struggle with tasks highlighted the tenderness of the moment. Once she was comfortable, he walked around the table and sat opposite her. Though others suggested sitting beside her, he preferred to look at her face; their love unmistakable, soothing the nerves bubbling in Phenex and Mikhail as they braced for the conversation ahead.

Phenex had insisted on inviting them. They were supportive and loved Colette as their own, often treating her with kindness, even if they favored the girls. When it came to discipline, they believed in a "*spare the rod*" approach. Still, Phenex trusted they could navigate this conversation diplomatically, as she and her sister were growing into young adults.

Daisy, Rhett's mother, eyed the food with suspicion. "Er you shurr this iz cooked all deh wayh through?" Her thick accent matched her stout frame, and the venomous smile revealing her half-missing teeth soured the atmosphere. Years of smoking had left her voice raspy, mirroring her harsh demeanor. Since Thana was born, she had openly detested Mikhail and Phenex, making her disdain clear with snide remarks.

Rhett often recounted the painful truth of their childhood comparing it to his own as though fond or even playful memories— how she'd lock them in a closet while babysitting. "At least she let you have a light and a couple of toys," he would mock, the memory sharp and bitter, "I didn't get that luxury when I was a child."

Fortunately, their mother, Colette, had put an end to Daisy babysitting them, ensuring they wouldn't have to endure her presence any longer. Instead, Casey's older siblings took turns looking after all of them. As they prepared for dinner, however, they realized Daisy could be a key player in the discussion. While she might side with her son, she could also provide a neutral perspective. If they could get her to act as a mediator, it might ease the tension in the room. Alternatively, if she couldn't be neutral, Daisy's presence might at least make Rhett feel less isolated in the situation. They hoped her presence would give weight to their arguments and lead to a more constructive conversation. Though she could be intimidating, they needed her to see the value of being diplomatic.

"Si estás tan ofendida, Daisy, entonces tal vez las chicas puedan ofrecerte un trozo de sándwich de mortadela o guisantes aplastados, si eso le complace a tu paladar," Serjio spoke in the direction of his wife but it was clear he meant as a taunt toward Daisy.

Daisy turned to face Serjio, "Sucuze me? Waht'd ewe says?" her face a slight tint of purple from near-instantaneous anger, "Diz iz Emrmuraka, we speak English."

"I speak English, as does my wife," Serjio started, his voice was soothing like that of Ricardo Montalban, "You speak, eh… how is the term—"

"Abuelo! ¡Basta!" Mikhail quickly interjected, "Esta noche no hablas español, habla inglés y se amable por favor." Her voice was firm as she spoke quickly, "Sorry, Daisy, Abuelo was just asking how we acquired such an expensive wine since it was Nixx who set it all up." She lied but it seemed to satisfy Daisy, "It's actually not real wine, just a really good grape juice, brought from Spain. The Shelley cousins and Bryce brought it back from their last vacation."

Phenex swallowed, trying to laugh at the blatant misdirection of what their grandfather had said, calling Daisy's taste in food childish and immature.

Rhett was the last to join, looking similarly at the food as his mother had but he did not say a word.

Colette smiled sweetly at her husband as he sat at the table, "Doesn't this look delicious, love?"

He grunted a snorting response, "Since when can you cook, Phenex?"

Phenex had prepared roasted chicken and root vegetables, mashed potatoes, gravy, roasted asparagus, and dinner rolls. It didn't include the finger food that was snacked on as dinner was being prepared, and the cheesecake she had made for dessert was in the fridge along with some fruits she had made into a compote.

After everyone had placed what they wanted on their plates from the spread, "Thank you for joining us for dinner everyone." Phenex started, "Obviously we value each of you in our lives."

"Before we go into all the details, we ask that English only. No leaving the table until everyone is finished with dinner and dessert. And please, be open-minded. We want to discuss our treatment." Mikhail said her voice straining to hide her nervousness.

Rhett slammed his hands on the table it rattled the dinnerware as he stood, "This is ridiculous already. You are children, yelling at your mother the other day; your utterly disrespectful and despicable attitudes need adjustment, and it's high time the belt was not only enforced but used copiously."

Phenex and Mikhail both flinched. Mikhail's voice, though steady, carried a hint of defiance despite her effort to hide it. "This isn't about disrespect, Rhett. It's about fairness and understanding. We're not children anymore. We deserve to be treated with respect."

A vein pulsed in Rhett's temple as he glared at his stepdaughters. "You two have overstepped. Your mother's patience has worn thin, and now you've pushed her to the brink."

Phenex, ever the mediator, interjected, "We're not asking for special treatment, just a fair chance to explain ourselves. We've made mistakes, but we've also grown. Can't we talk about this calmly?"

"I believe I can speak for myself, honey." Colette said, "My patience is wearing thin with you, Rhett. Please, sit and be civil. The girls worked hard. The least we can do is allow them to speak and eat, or I will get you a bologna sandwich."

Phenex bit her lower lip, stifling a laugh, "We asked Daisy and Abuelos to be here because we wanted someone who could be outside the scope of the house. Daisy has always treated us with," she paused, fighting her fingers from tapping together at risk of criticism from Rhett or Daisy, "differently" she changed her mind on the word she wanted to use attempting civility and diplomacy, "than her biological grandchildren. Typically, she sides with her son on everything. We thought it would be fair. Abuelos though they typically side with us on several things, they are fair when it comes to parenting and discipline."

Mikhail glanced between Colette and Rhett, her expression serious. "I realize now that I may have been unfair to Mother, especially on Wednesday or Tuesday—whenever it was we went to Sova's for breakfast," she began. "Nixx and I wanted to have an open and honest conversation, and I keep reminding myself that we're seventeen and fifteen. But as for you, Rhett…" She paused, choosing her words carefully. "I'm sorry; I promised I wouldn't be harsh, but you pointed out that I'll be turning eighteen soon. The truth is, my time to develop a relationship with either of you is limited. It's difficult to admit, but you're the only father figure I've really known."

She took a moment, gazing away as if weighing her next thoughts. "The kids have noticed how Nixx and I are treated, and they've started asking questions. How long before they decide they don't like how their big sister is treated? Time is running out for us to build a real relationship. I've expressed my desire for one for years, yet you keep pushing us away. You called me a problem, but the real issue is that in just a few months, when I turn eighteen, I might walk away completely."

Mikhail sighed, the weight of her words hanging in the air. "If I'm truly honest with myself—and with you—I don't know if that's what I really want or if I just feel forced into it." Her gaze finally settled back on Rhett, seeking both understanding and an opening for change.

"Thank you," Colette started, "I appreciate your apology but I will admit you were right in your anger. I should speak up more, and Rhett could be less... abrasive."

A tangible heaviness hung in the air as Mikhail and Phenex allowed the silence to intensify their words. Rhett's face softened slightly for a moment, in contrast to Daisy, who glared at the girls with disdain and anger. "Idn't idt juz like thez spoy'lt brats to try'n make demands, how sick'nin."

"Could you repeat that, please, Daisy? For someone who demands English be spoken, yours is horrible." Serjio said, his accent and smooth voice made the words sound almost less insulting than they were.

"Waht eaz det 'posed tuh mean?" Daisy's voice rose to a shrill shriek.

Mikhail and Phenex exchanged a glance, their expressions mirroring a shared uncertainty. They stared at one another, silently weighing the consequences of intervening in the escalating argument. Should they step in to diffuse the tension or let the situation unfold? The unspoken question suspended forcefully between them as they considered their options, the air heavy with unresolved emotions.

Phenex's brow furrowed as she glanced around at the chaotic scene unfolding before them. Daisy's voice grew progressively shriller, her words escalating into a full-blown tantrum reminiscent of a toddler throwing a fit. It was clear to both girls that the anger— or perhaps embarrassment? —in Daisy's voice was bubbling over, and the potential for catastrophe was rising by the second.

Mikhail shifted her weight in the chair as she felt a tight knot of unease growing in the pit of her stomach. Instinct told her that the interaction could lead to something worse if they did not intervene, but experience told her if there was intervention it would be worse.

"Mom, stop!" Rhett snapped, "That's enough, Serjio, please." His tone was firm but was not angry; rather, it conveyed a blend of surprise and concern, "Could you watch the insults, Mom? They are my in-laws… sort of. It's confusing." He waved his hand in 'it doesn't matter' type of way rather than dismissive.

Serjio and Claudia welcomed Rhett into their family with open arms when Colette married him, embracing him as if he were their own son. While it was clear he could never replace Alejandro, they were grateful that he made Colette happy and treated their grandchildren with care and warmth. There was a sense among them that Alejandro, rest his soul, had somehow orchestrated Colette and Rhett's union, watching over them from afar. Almost instantly, they included him in family gatherings and traditions, weaving him into the fabric of their lives and hearts.

Once again, Mikhail and Phenex exchanged puzzled glances. "Did I miss something?" Phenex mouthed, confusion etched on her face. Mikhail merely shrugged, equally startled by Rhett's shift from what seemed like kindness to an unexpected display of empathy or understanding.

"Let's please refocus on our conversation and the reason we're here," Phenex said, her tone edged with barely concealed sarcasm. "We can save any personal grievances for another dinner night."

Rhett's presence felt heavy, and Phenex pressed on. "I'm afraid of you. You loom over us like a dark shadow, imposing expectations on us to take care of your children. Mikhail is on her way out the door, and I'm not far behind. I know we keep recycling the same points, but this is what we need to concentrate on. I'm tired of you and Misha fighting; I'm exhausted by Mami working constantly and stepping back while you dismantle us, even when she's here. You treat us as if we're separate from Thana and Enoch, as if you haven't been in our lives since near infancy."

Her voice faded from a tone of confidence to one tinged with sadness, the weight of her words hanging heavily in the air.

Abuela had been silent since she arrived at the table, her presence both commanding and enigmatic. A strong, stoic figure, she rarely spoke, yet her expressive eyes conveyed unspoken words, brimming with wisdom and intensity. As the tension in the room heightened, her demeanor shifted subtly; she leaned back in her chair, arms crossed, observing everyone with a penetrating gaze.

They could feel the atmosphere change as she leaned forward on her elbows, resting her chin on her knuckles, an icy chill seeming to fill the air around her.

Suddenly, it felt as though the lights had dimmed in acknowledgment of her presence, casting shadows that danced across the table—a stark contrast to the chaos that unfolded before them. Abuela, a woman embodying the strength and resilience of her Aztec heritage, commanded the room like a conquistador, her legacy deeply rooted in a history of fortitude.

The others fell silent, drawn to her as if the strength of her spirit had tethered them to the moment. Abuela was poised to break her silence, her thoughts swirling beneath the surface. In this charged atmosphere, each word would be chosen with care; her insights were like ancient stones tossed into a still pond, their ripples destined to change everything.

"Look around you," she finally said, her voice low yet resonant, slicing through the lingering tension like a blade. "We are a family, bound by history and choice. Yet here we are…" Her sapphire eyes locked onto Rhett's. "You need to listen to these girls; they are your first children. They may share my son's blood—may he rest in peace—but he has blessed them to you. It pains me to hear that my granddaughters are suffering because of their father."

She punctuated her words by tapping her knuckles on the table, the sound echoing through the stillness like distant thunder. She took a long, deep breath, then exhaled slowly, exuding a terrifying calm. "Have you forgotten what truly matters? Have you forgotten your responsibility?" She turned to the girls with a gentle smile. "Mujeres fuertes. They are being raised right, though I know much of that is because they have raised one another. Even our Pájara Tímida seems more confident now. I hope that, in part, it is because of you, Rhett, and of course our Alejandro's prima vida, Colette."

Her gaze returned to Rhett, her expression shifting from warmth to a stern, motherly gaze. "So what is your choice, Rhett? Will you listen to the words of your eldest daughters, pleading for one last chance, or will you walk away and keep your distance from them until they are gone?"

The challenge hung in the air, a mixture of expectation and urgency. The entire room, even Daisy, seemed to be holding her breath, waiting for Rhett to respond. Serjio was the only one brave enough to breathe as he finished his mashed potatoes and used the dinner roll to wipe the rest of his plate clean. "I don't know who suddenly taught you to cook, Pájara Tímida, but that was excellent. If the dessert is half as good, I may need to move your abuela and me in."

"As I say, Rhett, this is up to you to bridge the gap now. These girls, these strong girls, have built the foundation." Abuela smiled, lifting her glass of sparkling juice as though she had finished a speech intended for a toast. "For the memory of my Alejandro, and for you, I hope you choose connection."

Rhett sat in silence, the weight of her words settling over him like a heavy blanket. The room was still, each person feeling the gravity of the moment. The path forward would not be simple, but something had shifted in the air—an unspoken understanding that open communication would be essential.

CHAPTER 15

TIME'S RIPPLE, WATER'S DROP

Phenex perched on the kitchen counter, a Wibbly Wobbly Wonder in hand, her mind drifting as she stared blankly at the wall before her. The popsicle, a vibrant mix of strawberry and banana, was melting into a sticky swirl of yellow and pink, tainted only by a single bite taken from the upper half—the part Phenex believed was the best, with its light lemon flavor encased in a delicate layer of chocolate.

In the two weeks since the dinner they would forever refer to as "Dinner Interrupted," things had gradually been improving. Rhett had made an effort to be kinder and more considerate in his words. Colette was spending more time at home, and Mikhail was striving to be less combative. Unbeknownst to them, Rhett had begun seeing a therapist, and though it had been just fourteen days since that fraught evening, the subtle changes were becoming evident. Phenex often reminded Mikhail that significant transformations take time and can't be rushed. One day, after Mrs. Schon's class, Mikhail joked in a huff that the wisdom of her twenty-six-year-old sister was the second most annoying thing about her.

Phenex understood Mikhail's teasing was just playful sibling banter, yet they both felt the weight of the uncertain days ahead. With less than fifty days until May tenth—marking either Mikhail's or her own disappearance—the pressure loomed large.

Lost in her thoughts, Phenex felt the world around her fade as she contemplated their next steps, particularly the electric moment she had shared with Bryce in the woods. They hadn't yet addressed that suspended moment, overshadowed by the nagging question of 'what if.' In the two weeks since, they had both avoided each other—not entirely on purpose, but it seemed they were unsure how to interact. Their usual banter had been replaced by awkward smiles and hesitant sidesteps.

In the back of her mind, Phenex felt a desperation to speak with Bryce and explore the lingering tension from that day. Yet, there was also a part of her that wanted to shrink away, especially in front of Mikhail, who had witnessed that charged moment that hovered in uncertainty, leaving them both questioning what it could have meant.

With a heavy sigh, she brought her hands to her face, momentarily losing track of the nearly melted popsicle until the stick nearly jabbed her eye. The sharp realization jolted her from her stupor, prompting her to slide off the counter and rush to the sink. The warm, soapy water washed away the stickiness from her fingers and face, shaking her from the haze of thoughts that engulfed her.

As she rinsed off the last remnants of the melted popsicle from her hands, the comforting stream of the water running over her hands slowly brought her back to reality. She dried her hands on her jeans and glanced at the clock in the kitchen. Late afternoon sunlight streamed through the bay window, the solar rays bouncing off the dust motes in a poetic, albeit gross, tango. She needed to snap out of the haze in her head. So much was changing that she felt her head may explode from the new memories as they erased the old. She was afraid to admit that she could feel her future mind slipping away, her fear of losing her future-self seemed to be becoming a certainty.

Phenex thumbed through the wall calendar, her eyes tracing the days to come as they had since her twenty-six-year-old consciousness began cohabiting her fifteen-year-old body. She found herself tapping her fingers absently against her thumb, fixated on May 10th. The sixteenth was circled in bold, harsh scrawling—"Muttering Gibberish!" written in Bryce's slant cursive. *How could I have forgotten?* The excitement surrounding the band was palpable, but that date meant more; it was also Prom night.

Memories rushed back to her: Bryce, Casey, and Saria had skipped Prom altogether because of Mikhail's disappearance. Mikhail had become an honorary Prom Queen, not attending but crowned in absentia when Helga Sinclair took the official title. It was no surprise that Casey had been awarded Prom King, but since he had dropped out of the nominations, the honor went to JJ Baker, whose father owned the largest farm supply store in the Tri-County area.

Bryce had been thrilled, despite the Camelot theme, they had managed to secure a live band. Years later, she'd sheepishly admit it was because she personally tracked down the group and convinced Theodesa Lancaster to play. Phenex had pushed them to go, not wanting her friends to miss out. In retrospect, she felt an overwhelming wave of gratitude toward them for refusing; the bittersweet feelings rushed back with an intensity that nearly brought tears to her eyes.

As her anxious tapping slowed, an image flickered in her mind—a vivid memory of Mikhail shoving her away, urgency evident in her voice. "GO! ¡Ir! ¡Correr! ¡Fuera de aquí! GET OUT!" The memory was punctuated by the thunderous roar of water crashing against them, then an engulfing darkness. Phenex gasped, jolting back to the present when her younger sister, Thana, tugged at the sleeve of her jacket.

"Hey!" Thana exclaimed, her excitement bubbling over. "I was asking if you would walk to the bookstore with me? Mom and Dad are having their date tonight. They said they could take me tomorrow, but I could ask you if you'd go today. If you say yes, they'll pay you extra, and you can get a book too!" She spoke quickly, her words tumbling out like a chipmunk's, adorned with the kind of infectious enthusiasm characteristic of Brittany or Alvin. "I was supposed to ask if you had plans first before offering the money… Whoops! Can I try that again?"

Phenex laughed, her earlier thoughts fading. "Um, sure! I don't have any plans. Most went to Friends University for a tour and Bryce is working. What books are you after?"

Thana beamed, her smile like a hundred-watt bulb. "No book for me. Bryce said she'd save me a Hitchcock Mystery Magazine! When I saw her in the school library, she told me it was in." She bounced with excitement. "She said the cover is 'Death of a Poet.'"

"Surprised she didn't mention it to me," Phenex said. "But I suppose if she saw you first, she figured you'd tell me."

"That's exactly what she said!" Thana laughed, playfully pulling at Phenex's arm, careful not to tug too hard at the sleeve of the jacket sensing the love and care she had for it, "Come on! If we go now, Ms. Lucy Shelley might have some fresh pastries!"

The scent of lemon bars, chocolate chip cookies, fresh baked croissants and other pastries felt like a warm embrace as Phenex and Thana entered the bookstore, Pages and Pastries.

"'Allo, Nixx an' Thana! You're right on time! I pulled some lemon bars an' just put some fresh ones in the case—they're yours if ya want one, Nixx," Lucy shouted, her warm Kiwi accent sweet music to Phenex's ears from behind the counter. "An' I've got two fresh cookies for ya, Thana, if ya brought a trade in!"

"Hey Luce," Phenex smiled and waved as she walked up to the counter, Thana close behind her. "Did you know I'd be in today?" She grabbed one of the lemon bars Lucy had set on a napkin for her. "How's Renee?"

"Ai, she's just up the road at the bank, showin' Bryce a few things before we head back to New Plymouth for a short holiday," Lucy replied, her voice lilting with that familiar accent. She picked up the copy of *Many Waters* by Madeleine L'Engle and carefully flipped through the pages, givin' the flaps on the inside cover a quick once-over. "Looks like you took my advice, addin' your own notes. On page… that tiny choices can lead us down completely different paths, and… that experiences shape us—and the same experience can affect each of us differently, right? Brill… sights! Here's a question to ponder: how does… challenge the characters' ideas about fate?"

As she finished, Lucy handed Thana two cookies of her choice. Phenex was only half-listening to what Lucy was saying to her younger sister; her gaze was caught up in some photos on the wall, the words drifting in and out of her focus.

"I reckon we've got a magazine for you too," Lucy continued with a bright smile. "An' don't forget to grab the next book in the series, *An Acceptable Time*. I'll sort you out a two-for-one deal, but you've gotta promise to take excellent notes, alright?"

"Yes ma'am," Thana beamed as she skipped off toward the children's section to find the final book in the *Wrinkle in Time* series.

Lucy Shelley has a striking appearance and a commanding presence that belies her age of around thirty. She was an amazon of a woman just under six foot tall, her a statuesque figure that exuded confidence and strength. She had a well-defined physique, athleticism and a healthy lifestyle. Her long, dark brown hair usually worn in loose waves or straight, gracefully framing her face with expressive green eyes that added a depth to her empathetic and caring nature making her captivating to those around her. Her facial features are strong and symmetrical, highlighted by high cheekbones and a warm smile that spread all the way to her eyes that could be both inviting and fierce.

"How's the family?" Lucy asked, brushing a few crumbs off the glass countertop into her hand and tossed them into the waste basket.

Phenex jumped onto one of the bar stools and swung "Alright, so it looks like Mikhail, Saria, and Casey went on a weekend trip to Friends University. Rhett and Mami have a date tonight, and Enoch is spending the night at a friend's house." she took a bite of the lemon bar, the tangy sweetness exploding in her mouth like a burst of happiness. She imagined it was what sunshine would taste like, with a subtle hint of earthy herbal mint adding the finishing touch.

She gave a half smile, "Dios mío, Luce, your lemon bars are heaven. If this was the last thing I ate, I would die happy."

Lucy laughed, "Try this one, it's something I am experimenting with." She placed a lemon bar on a plate in front of her. The lemon bar was its usual pale yellow green, but with tiny red flakes throughout and some sprinkled on the top, they appeared like large red salt flakes. Noticing the confusion on Phenex's face, "Try it, I promise it isn't a lethal dose of arsenic. No *Flowers in the Attic* reenactments here."

"Well, if it isn't a lethal dose, I have no interest," Phenex shrugged as she pinched the lemon bar between her fingers and took a bite. The flavor was familiar, but the addition of the strange red salt crystals brought an unexpected extra zing of lemon-lime and a satisfying crunch of chili, the spice perfectly complementing the tart sweetness of the lemon and the refreshing mint base of the bar, "Wow... Weird..." she mumbled taking a second bite, this time allowing the flavor to sit for a moment as though trying to dissect the flavors. She covered her mouth with her hand to speak, "What is it?"

"Luce, are you using Nixx as a Guinea pig?" Renee said coming out of the back room, "Good to see you sweetie, are you here for Bryce?" she put her arm around Lucy's waist for just a moment before registering that there were others in the store and pat Lucy on the arm near the shoulder.

"Lab rat actually," Lucy winked with a sly smile, "It's a spice from Mexico, Tajin. We picked it up when we were visiting family in Texas."

"It's strange but I like it. They're like those con chili candies you bring us." Phenex's voice was soft, noticing the connection between Renee and Lucy for what felt like the first time, "No, I'm here with Thana, but I do have the book Ripley let me borrow with me," she pulled the thin paperback copy from her back pocket and set it on the counter.

Renee took the book from the counter and looked at it, "Aw, 'The Price of Salt'. Patricia Highsmith under pseudonym Claire Morgan. What were your thoughts?"

Phenex looked over at Renee, a hint of shyness creeping into her expression, looking down at the counter trying to shrink herself. "I didn't know it was Patricia Highsmith's pen name. I didn't really think about the author when I was reading it. I just got lost in the story," she said, she started to tap her fingers to her thumb but caught herself and stopped. She sighed, before taking a deep breath "It… beautiful and heartbreaking. I mean, it makes you think about love in a way that feels really raw and real."

She hesitated for a moment, her thoughts swirling as she remembered how she felt while reading—the excitement, the longing, the confusion. Feelings that followed her into adulthood, feelings that still confused her at twenty-six. "At first, it seems familiar, but then there's this kick that surprises you. I guess I'm trying to figure out if that's how I feel…" she closed her eyes, allowing her mind to explore her present self at fifteen and explore more understanding she had at twenty-six.

The words escaped her, she knew how she felt. Bryce made her feel seen, but Casey, Saria, and her sister made her feel seen too. It wasn't the same. "I don't know the words. Therese, her emotions were palpable, the uncertainty. I feel I can relate." her hands shaking slightly.

Renee raised an eyebrow, intrigued. "Take your time, Phenex. We're here for you," she said gently, her sweet Texas accent imbued with a melodious Southern drawl. Her dark brown hair caught the light in soft waves, framing her face with an almost ethereal quality. In her soothing presence, Phenex found refuge, enveloped by warmth and encouragement that flowed effortlessly. Renee's hazel eyes sparkled with understanding, their sincerity making it easy for anyone to open up beneath her gaze.

"Yeah," Phenex replied softly, her voice almost a whisper. "It makes me wonder if I'm more than just confused. Like, what if I'm not just figuring things out? What if… I don't know, what if this is really me?" She glanced quickly at Lucy, feeling a spark of something she wasn't ready to name yet. "It's made me think about how I connect with people, especially my friends. My best friend gave it to me, and now I keep wondering, was that a hint? Or did she just love the book and want to share it? And that weekend camping… Am I reading too much into it?"

Her voice trailed off, and silence hung between them. Renee and Lucy exchanged glances, something unspoken passing between them—support, curiosity, or maybe both. Before anyone could respond—

"Nixx, what are you talking about?" Thana's high-pitched voice startled all three at the counter. "Ha-ha! I scared you!"

"Ay! Necesitas una campana," Phenex blurted. "You need a bell around your neck, Thana. Find your book?"

"I did, and Bryce went to the back to get my Hitchcock Mag," she said, grinning wide as she teased, "Don't think I didn't see you jump too!"

Chapter 16
The Price of Fragments

"Ya, ya, que trae suerte plantaina," Phenex teased, ruffling Thana's hair. A wave of relief washed over her as the interruption broke the spell of her thoughts.

"Did you just call me a lucky banana?" Thana rolled her eyes, a grin pulling at her lips.

Bryce returned, a knowing smile playing on her face as she handed Thana the magazine. "Here you go, Banana-butt. 'Death of a Poet.' Perfect for a rainy day."

The warmth in Bryce's gaze lingered on Phenex, making her heart flutter unexpectedly. She caught herself fidgeting with the jacket she was wearing, a silent plea for understanding, the fabric a makeshift shield against her vulnerability. "I didn't wear anything under it—just this jacket like a long-sleeved shirt. Unless you're willing to trade," she added with a hint of mischief.

Bryce chuckled, amusement lighting up her features. "Lucky you're my best friend, and it's getting harder to imagine you without it."

Renee stifled a laugh, her eyes shimmering with amusement. "Is it appropriate to make a 'that's what she said' joke in front of two teenagers?"

Bryce rolled her eyes playfully, feigning exasperation. "Aw, Ma, that's not funny. It wasn't funny on Saturday Night Live, and it's definitely not funny in person."

"You made a 'that's what she said' joke at lunch just last week," Phenex chimed in, a mischievous glint in her eye.

"Nooooo, don't call me out!" Bryce laughed, a light blush creeping up her cheeks. "It's only okay if someone our age makes the joke."

"Bit of a double standard, innit?" Lucy teased, a knowing smirk curving her lips.

"I'm sixteen, so it's fair. No other reason than I say it is," Bryce declared with mock seriousness.

"We can't ground her, can we?" Lucy asked Renee, her tone playful.

"Not without risking a riot," Renee replied, a bright grin on her face. "Besides, we need all the help we can get from our resident teenagers." She paused, her expression shifting as she turned her gaze to Phenex. "So, do you girls want a ride home?"

Phenex hesitated, feeling warmth creeping into her cheeks. "Mami and Rhett should be home by now. If you two don't mind, could I hang out here with you and Bryce? I kind of wanted to continue the conversation we were having, and I'm sleeping over at Bryce's tonight anyway." As she spoke, she sneaked another glance at Bryce. The way Bryce looked at her, with that soft smile, made her heart race. Would she read the unspoken longing in Phenex's eyes? She hoped Bryce couldn't see the blush flooding cheeks.

"Call 'em first," Lucy suggested, nodding towards the phone behind the counter. "Just make sure that plan's all good, eh?"

⧖ ⧖ ⧖

"What is the weirdest thing about the late nineties?" Bryce asked, leaning forward with curiosity.

Phenex settled into the recliner, her expression pensive, as if she were caught between two realities. She folded her hands thoughtfully and gazed into the distance. "People are terrified that the world will end in the year 2000—Y2K, as they call it. There's this pervasive fear that computers, which control so much of our lives, won't be able to handle the transition. Programmers are working tirelessly behind the scenes, debugging systems and reinforcing protocols, but you know how the masses can be," she reflected, shaking her head lightly.

"It's like shouting 'fire' in a crowded room and then asking everyone to trust you for an escape, all without presenting any real plan." Her expression shifted slightly, losing the warmth and animation it usually held, replaced by a seriousness that felt almost unsettling. "The problem is that when enough people buy into the hysteria, those who say things will be fine—those who offer concrete plans of action or backed-up evidence—are often ignored. Their voices get drowned out, suppressed under the weight of panic, and chaos ensues." She paused for a moment, glancing down at her hands as if contemplating the repercussions of such widespread fear. "It's a dangerous cycle, one where rationality is overshadowed by collective anxiety."

Bryce stared for a moment in awe but disturbed by Phenex's words, "I asked for weird... Not terrifying, so thanks for the Skynet related nightmares to come."

This seemed to snap Phenex out of the haze she was in, "Don't worry, I'll fight the terminators off with you." She smiled, "Disappointingly I have absolutely no combat or fighting skills, I'll be the brains to your brawn... though you have me beat in that too."

"Shut up Nixx," Bryce snapped, "You're talking caca about my best friend, I don't want to have to kick you in the shins."

"I—uh," Phenex laughed, momentarily at a loss for words. "Okay, okay, I get it. But you can't stop me all the time!" She blew a raspberry before standing up. "Pizza is done!" As she stretched, a delightful aroma wafted through the air, and her stretch transformed into a yawn.

"I haven't asked yet!" Bryce shouted from the kitchen, her voice muffled as she leaned in closer to the oven, reaching for a fragrant Hawaiian pizza topped with sweet pineapple, vibrant bell peppers, and a kick of jalapeños. Turning to place the hot pan on the counter, she exclaimed, "Ow, damn!" The pan clattered loudly against the stovetop.

"You okay?" Phenex asked, leaning over the breakfast nook with concern as she watched Bryce run her hand under cold water at the sink. "Did you burn yourself?"

Bryce growled softly, muttering under her breath, "Yeah, my hand slipped off the potholder." Although her voice carried a hint of pain, she managed to keep a calm demeanor. "Sorry about that." She spun on her toes, holding her right hand close to her chest as if to shield it from view. "Don't worry, it's just a little red." A small, reassuring smile crossed her lips as she assessed the situation.

"Anyway, back to what I was saying before this delightful injury so rudely interrupted me: what did you and Mrs. Shelley One and Two discuss?"

Phenex raised an eyebrow. She had heard Bryce when referencing the Shelley cousins as "Missus" before but had never given it much thought. She occasionally called them "Mom" and "Ma," as they had helped her gain her emancipation and treated her as if she were their daughter.

In their small town, most people referred to Lucy and Renee collectively as the Shelley cousins, but Bryce stood out as one of the few who addressed them as "Missus" when speaking of them together. It was a subtle distinction that hinted at Bryce's unique perspective on the two women, leaving Phenex curious about what lay behind it. She felt she might be starting to understand.

"Oh, it's just about the book. Thanks for letting me read it, by the way."

Bryce, with her typical nonchalance, took a slice of pizza, the gooey cheese stretching languidly until it finally surrendered between her fingers. "What were your thoughts?" she asked, biting into the slice with a contented grin. "Dissect it for me."

Phenex felt a thrill of nerves at the thought of sharing her reactions. She repeated most of what she had mentioned to Renee and Lucy, her throat tightening slightly as she carefully omitted the raw feelings of confusion that had settled within her. She focused instead on the beauty of Therese's character, the way the storyline evoked longing and uncertainty that resonated with her, albeit from a distance.

"It's heartbreaking," she said, her gaze momentarily drifting to the table as she contemplated the delicate unraveling of life and love that the story revealed. "It makes you think about love in a way that feels so raw and genuine…" Her voice faltered, caught between the desire to delve deeper into her feelings and the weight of vulnerability that restrained her.

Bryce nodded, her attention fully on Phenex as they continued the conversation after putting food away. They sat together on her bed at opposite ends, the two of them nestled in the sanctuary of her room. This was a space Bryce had truly made her own in the house she rented from the Shelley cousins. Their warmth and kindness had woven a tapestry of security around her, and she often expressed her gratitude for the love they shared. Though they weren't related by blood, it was clear their bond ran deep, a connection that Bryce admired. She caught herself smiling at their playful banter and tender glances, fully aware that their relationship but never speaking it out loud.

"You know, when it's just you and me, your accent comes out more," Bryce said, with a soft smile on her face. "It's subtle and cute. I like that you feel comfortable enough to relax around me. I've always appreciated that you drop your guard with me."

She was acutely aware of her accent, particularly with Spanish words, which usually remained hidden, tucked away unless she was speaking with her siblings. When she switched back to English, she made a conscious effort to shed the accent as quickly as it emerged. "I don't have an accent," she nearly whispered in quiet defense, her words barely audible.

As she caught herself reacting, Phenex felt a flush rise to her cheeks, and she hastily hid her reaction beneath the cozy confines of the Muttering Gibberish jacket she still wore. She had playfully refused to return it to Bryce since arriving at their place, claiming it was far too comfortable to part with. Every time Bryce suggested its return, her tone light and teasing, Phenex would merely shrug it off with a playful smirk, effectively silencing the request.

"Come on, you know you'll survive without it," Bryce would say, the corners of her mouth curling up in a teasing grin. But her insistence was gentle, never crossing into the territory of seriousness.

"Not a chance!" Phenex would reply, wrapping the jacket tighter around herself as if to shield her heart from the underlying emotions that simmered just below the surface. The hoodie had become a kind of armor, a way to navigate the warmth of their growing connection while keeping certain walls intact. In those moments, it felt like more than just an article of clothing; it was a piece of Bryce she wanted to hold onto, if only for a little while longer.

Her eyes sparkled with admiration as Phenex continued, "I really enjoyed it. I could relate to Therese's confusion at first—the way she grappled with her feelings as she grew closer to Carol and began to express that closeness. It felt so real to me, like a mirror reflecting my own struggles."

Her gaze drifting momentarily as she collected her thoughts. "It was powerful to see her ultimately choose to listen to her heart and reject the societal norms that sought to define her. It's such an empowering decision, but…"

She hesitated, biting her lip as uncertainty flickered in her eyes. "It's also terrifying, isn't it, Bryce? To truly embrace who you are?" Her cheeks warmed slightly as she returned her gaze to Bryce, revealing the depth of her feelings.

Bryce met Phenex's gaze with a blend of vulnerability as she spoke "I guess I see parts of myself in Therese. I want to be true to who I am, but sometimes I wonder if I have the courage to fully step into that." She admitted her voice trembling with hesitation, "There's something about you that encourages me to explore these feelings, though I'm not entirely sure what that means yet."

The words hung in the air, the tension palpable as Bryce's heart raced. "But the ambiguity of the ending..." she added, a hint of disappointment creeping into her tone, "it feels unresolved for me. Yet maybe that's what makes it hopeful too— encouraging readers to break free and find their own path."

Her voice softened, a smile slowly forming as she looked at Phenex. "Watching Lucy and Renee navigate their relationship has shown me that love doesn't always fit neatly into labels, you know? Their bond is a reminder that it's okay to embrace the uncertainty. I'm just trying to figure it out who I am and what I want, I hope to be like them someday."

"But the Shelleys are cousins, aren't they?" Phenex asked softly, her voice steady but laced with a hint of apprehension, as if she were trying to convince herself of a truth she suspected might not be entirely accurate.

Bryce shook her head no, "They are family, and that is what they call one another." Her words seemed to confirm some sort of relation, but the exact words nor confirmation was said, "Maybe it's not my place." She yawned, laying back on her bed patting the spot next to her.

Phenex lay next to Bryce, sharing the bed as they had done during sleepovers since they were six. Though the beds seemed larger back then, it felt easier to share than to make someone sleep on the floor, especially when they preferred to stay up talking all night.

"Hey Nixx," Bryce murmured, her voice groggy as drowsiness began to pull her under. "Do you think Mikhail will be safe this time?"

That thought weighed heavily on Phenex's mind, always lurking just beneath the surface. Her memories had become increasingly murky, making it difficult to distinguish the originals from her new reality. The original memories seemed to fade, gradually overridden by newer, although less frequent images of the future that were more vivid and detailed. Even the phases, those flashes of reality where she could glimpse the world of 1998, had become less common. They had once increased in intensity and duration, but that spike had subsided about a week ago. The warmth of the pallet couch, the quiet hum of the night – sleep was beginning to pull at her eyelids. Her thoughts began to blur, coalescing into fleeting images.

She saw, or felt, a scene from another time: Just the other day in class, she found herself sitting with a much older Mrs. Schon, who was still teaching high school English but had also taken on the role of librarian. A student had written in the margins of a book to correct a spelling error, but unlike the usual insightful annotations they had seen at home, this note only rectified the mistake left by the editor. Upon noticing three other names following on the checkout card, Mrs. Schon quickly jumped to conclusions, accusing Hunter of defacing the school's property. For just a few moments, Phenex found herself fiercely defending her baby sister before the image dissipated like smoke.

A disorienting sensation washed over her: It was always a bizarre feeling, straddling both the past and the future while anchored in her immediate present. It felt surreal, like an out-of-body experience, leaving her with an unsettling sense of disconnection.

Another scene shimmered into view as she sank deeper into sleep: As she walked to Sova's Diner after school the other day, the streets whispered memories, intertwining images from '87 and '98. One stood out starkly: the stoplight that had been proudly announced by the Wakford Tribute, renamed for Collete after her passing. Advertised as a sign of progress for the town's growing population, it had lasted less than four hours before the police officer inadvertently toppled it. A laugh escaped her, picturing the disbelief that must have rippled through the community. In a place where change came slowly, even that brief spectacle felt symbolic—an unmet expectation, or perhaps a misstep from the beginning.

The scene fractured, replaced by a jolt: Lost in thought, she suddenly found herself standing in the middle of the street, disoriented. A blaring car horn shattered the moment, pulling her back to the present. She blinked, startled, as the world around her rushed back into focus, her fifteen-year-old self.

The final image, dark and unsettling, appeared just before she succumbed to sleep: For just a moment, Phenex's mind wavered as she contemplated confessing her secret to Bryce. It was a news clipping that had shaken her to her core. The article was old, yellowed with age, but the words on the page were stark and clear: "Local Teenager Disappears." And beneath it, a name: "Phenex." Not Mikhail. Not her sister, the girl who had been her best friend and confidant for her entire life. But Phenex—her own name, which now felt as if it belonged to someone else, someone who had lived a life parallel to her own, yet entirely separate.

"I have hope. So much has already changed." Phenex's whisper was barely audible as she drifted off into a deep sleep.

CHAPTER 17
ORIGINS OF FRAGMENTS

Phenex awoke to the soft midmorning light streaming into Bryce's room. Bryce lay asleep behind her, her arm gently draped over Phenex's waist, holding her close. Normally, if they found themselves waking up like this, Phenex would have shifted Bryce's arm away, but this time the conversation from the night before lingered in her mind. The shared emotions they had confessed the night before swirled around them, laden with meaning yet untouched by words. With a quiet exhale, she moved slightly closer, sinking deeper into Bryce's warm embrace. She could feel the gentle rise and fall of Bryce's chest against her back with each breath.

Carefully, Phenex slid her hand over Bryce's, intertwining their fingers, her palm resting against the back of Bryce's hand. In that moment, she savored their connection, relishing the comfort and warmth that enveloped them both.

Phenex took a deep breath, but it emerged shaky and shallow. With each inhale, the air felt thinner, constricting around her lungs. She realized with a jolt that the tension was emanating from within her, a swirling tempest of emotions threatening to break free. Fear and anxiety coursed through her veins, heightening her senses until the reality of the bedroom began to warp.

The familiar surroundings blurred and twisted. Furniture faded into nothingness chaos enveloped her, spinning and twisting, and with it came a tidal wave of memories crashing against her consciousness, overwhelming her.

The sharp pain from that fateful fight with JJ Baker and Nolan Ravel surged from the depths of her memory, crashing into her like a rogue wave. She felt the gnawing agony of her broken arm, the white-hot shock that had rocked her eighteen-year-old self—a pain that reverberated in her mind until it threatened to fracture her thoughts. She clutched her head, fearing it might splinter apart chaotic, like a cubist painting by Picasso, disjointed and fragmented, impossible to decipher.

She pulled herself into the fetal position, locking herself in a small ball. As she was swept into a whirlpool of spinning colors—blues and greens coalescing into a tempest of emotion—What would have been Mikhail's twenty-first birthday flickered before her eyes like a cherished but haunting film reel. Joy and laughter as Phenex and the high school group of friends gathered, the clinking of glasses, the sight of her sister glowing with happiness, all beautiful moments that twisted sharply into a heart-wrenching void of those who should have been there.

The realization settled heavily in her chest, a profound ache rising like a tide. She could vividly recall the pain of her parents' fatal crash in 1993—the moment light and love were extinguished too soon, leaving an emptiness that gnawed at her insides. Yet, in this strange timeline, they were still alive—an unbearable contradiction that cleaved through her heart.

Colette had been a steady presence in Phenex's life, someone she had a complicated but nurturing relationship with. She mourned her mother's absence deeply. But Rhett—a once-wonderful father to her younger siblings—had been a storm of chaos and cruelty for Phenex and Mikhail, who had disappeared in 1987. Rhett's volatile temper and emotionally abusive nature cast long shadows over their childhoods, fracturing their bond in ways that had left scars deep enough to feel even now.

In this new reality where both parents were present, Phenex found herself grieving two sets of parents: the nurturing mother and beloved father who were no longer in her world, and the mother who still lived alongside the father whose presence was tainted with toxicity. Colette's warm embrace brought her comfort, while Rhett stirred a tumult of conflicting emotions. He was still the father who cared for his younger children with tenderness, yet for her and Mikhail, he had only ever brought pain and anguish.

This jarring duality twisted and tormented her heart, intertwining confusion and sorrow into a desperate knot that squeezed painfully within her. How could she find joy in this new reality, knowing the torment Rhett had inflicted? How could she reconcile the loving father her siblings adored with the man who had terrorized her childhood?

As the flood of emotions washed over her, Phenex struggled to catch her breath. Each pang felt like a cruel paradox, a reminder of what she once had and the complexities of what lay ahead. The pressure within her chest mounted, as if the weight of her thoughts might crush her. It was a tangled mess she had never fully understood, and now it felt all the more unbearable as she faced the haunting reality of having to coexist with the intertwined pain of her memories and the living specters of her family.

Phenex's breath quickened, each inhale coming faster as the familiar walls of the room seemed to close in and constrict. Her thoughts raced like a wild storm, threatening to engulf her entirely. Panic surged through her, a tidal wave of dread crashing over her senses. What's happening? The question echoed in her mind, an urgent plea as she felt the very foundation beneath her shift and tremble like the ground before an earthquake.

She fought the crushing weight pressing down on her, longing for escape. *I have to break free!* Desperation clawed at her throat, and suddenly she shouted, "Stop!" Her voice cut through the chaos, sharp and clear, slicing the frenetic energy like a knife through fog. In that moment, it felt almost magical—a desperate force that might rewind time itself, granting her just a moment to breathe, to regain control.

As silence followed her cry, she stood poised at the edge of a precipice, the chaos momentarily suspended, waiting to see if she could reshape the world around her.

To her astonishment, everything froze—time itself seemed to yield to her plea. She found herself suspended in an unfamiliar void, an eerie silence wrapping around her like a shroud. As the haze began to clear, she could see she was sitting at a table, Enoch or maybe it was Ryder, they looked so similar when they were little. She felt as though her consciousness was coming alive as if this were her destination.

"No, no! This can't be right!" Phenex cried out, her voice trembling as waves of fear rolled through her. Her heart raced, pulse pounding in her ears like a fragile drum. "I need to go back! How do I go back?" Desperation infused her every word as she screamed into the void, flailing against invisible boundaries that held her captive in this suspended reality. "Please, send me back!"

Suddenly, a jolt coursed through her, as though a rope tied around her waist yanked her backward, dragging her through a swirling haze of shifting sands—a surreal current of time eager to swallow her whole. The world shimmered and trembled in response, the air crackling with electric anticipation. Panic clawed at her throat like a wild beast, tightening its grip until she felt she might choke. What would it take to rewind time? The question spiraled in her mind, a desperate yearning to flee this ill-fated timeline that threatened to unravel completely.

The scene shifted, blurring the lines of time as a suppressed memory resurfaced, one that both she and Mikhail had long tried to forget. It was a warm, sunny day in the summer of 1981. Mikhail and Phenex pedaled eagerly through their small town, laughter echoing as they chased each other, pretending to be fearless explorers. Their mission: to reach Wakford Foodlandia for snacks and drinks to fuel their adventure to the secret treehouse hidden in the woods.

From her present self, she watched the memory unfold like a film, able to see through the eyes of her eight-year-old self, her fifteen-year-old self, and her adult self all at once—each older version powerless to intervene.

A pale blue '57 Chevy barreled down the street, screeching to a halt at the last moment, narrowly missing the girls. In a moment of fury, Mikhail kicked the truck's tire and shouted at the occupants—brothers Lukas and Markus Doogan, along with their friend Beau Baxter.

Mistake.

The boys in the truck retaliated, revving the engine as the girls attempted to ride away, momentarily detoured but unharmed. Mikhail had made her point; there was no damage done—neither to the girls nor to the truck. Yet as they began pedaling again, the Chevy roared back to life, its tires squealing in protest. The boys leaned out the windows, the threat palpable in the air.

"When we catch you, you dirty spics!" Beau's voice boomed; a sinister promise wrapped in rage. "You're dead!"

Panic surged through Phenex like a tidal wave as she pedaled furiously, her heart racing in tune with the looming threat. The truck roared behind them, a menacing growl that echoed in her ears. Mikhail shot ahead, leaving Phenex to grapple with her fear.

"MISHA!" she screamed, her voice fraying at the edges, swallowed by the adrenaline coursing through her veins. The world around her blurred as she lost control, veering sharply into a ditch and tumbling off her bike, the impact jarring her senses.

She felt as though she were standing on the sidelines, witnessing the chaos unfold from two perspectives at once. Desperation clawed at her throat as she caught sight of Mikhail, a blur of frantic motion dashing away from her bike and sprinting toward a nearby house. Her fists pounded against the door in a frantic rhythm, each thud resonating with the turmoil racing within her. Panic twisted Mikhail's features, mirroring the helplessness that enveloped Phenex like a shroud.

The truck's tires screamed as it screeched to a halt behind them, a banshee's wail slicing through the air. Luka and Beau exploded from the vehicle, their movements sharp and aggressive, while Marcus stayed behind the wheel, a cruel smile stretching across his face, sending chills racing down Phenex's spine.

Beau advanced on Phenex, his massive hands enclosing her arms with a grip that felt like iron. "Hold her still," he barked, yanking her forward and flinging her toward Luka as if she were a mere toy tossed aside.

Lukas obediently caught her, twisting her arms behind her back, rendering her powerless. Panic surged in her chest as she fought against him, her screams clawing their way into the open air.

"MIKHAIL!" she cried, desperation spilling from her lips, wishing for the rescue that felt so far away. The panicked shrill of her voice cutting through the air like a sonic boom.

"Leave my sister alone!" Mikhail's voice was barely able to penetrate through the chaos, fierce and unwavering, as she pounded on the door of the blue house. She glanced back, her heart collapsing at the sight of Phenex less than twenty feet away, trapped in the ditch, caught between the two men.

She pounded on the door harder, each desperate knock a flicker of hope against the suffocating darkness closing in around them. Yet, as the chaos intensified, dread tightened its grip like a vice, and the world spiraled out of control—the worst kind of nightmare; reality.

In a swift, calculated motion, Beau picked up a rock in his left hand and swung it hard toward Phenex's head. Time seemed to stretch, playing out in slow motion as she felt both the fifteen- and twenty-six-year-old versions of herself watching helplessly from the same moment, occupying the same space. She had been here before, haunted by the memory. Her hand instinctively flew to the scar on her cheek, a painful reminder of the past, blood pouring out like a grim echo of what was to come. She had to stop it; she couldn't allow this moment to unfold before her again.

"BASTA!" she shouted, her voice ringing with the fierce resolve of her eight-year-old self.

Beau froze, confusion flickering across his face. "What did you call me, you little beaner?"

"Vete a la mierda, ¡tu manzana!" Her voice surged with defiance, weaving together every version of her into a single moment of strength as she spat in Beau's face. The memories crashed through her: Beau Baxter had been eighteen when he attacked her as an eight-year-old, while Luka was sixteen, and Mark—the one who ignited the pursuit—had just turned twenty.

She felt as though she were simultaneously watching and experiencing the moment unfold. With a surge of adrenaline, she kicked both of her legs with full force into Beau's groin. He snorted, stumbling as the rock came tumbling from his hands.

A sharp laugh escaped her lips, a brief noise of triumph, but it quickly turned to pain as Beau's hand came full force connecting violently with the right side of her face. The force of the hit sent a shockwave through her entire being, disorienting her.

Just as she felt herself pulled from the icy river of the past, gasping for air, the warmth of the present enveloped her. She recognized Bryce's voice nearby, a lifeline amid the chaos. If she could just reach out... "Br-Bryce?" The word slipped from her lips, fragile and constrained.

Clenching her eyes shut, she instinctively reached for the necklace, her fingers sweeping across the empty space where the comforting weight of the stones usually rested. A cold wave of dread washed over her. It was gone. The necklace, a constant anchor, was missing. But then, a faint pressure registered, a feeling she almost dismissed – the delicate cord tight against her throat, and a dull ache at the base of her neck. She paused, a flicker of confusion turning into understanding. The stones weren't lost; they had twisted around, pressing against her back, a frustratingly inaccessible weight. Drawing her hand close to her chest, she clasped her fist, no longer searching for the absent stones, but feeling the persistent pressure of the cord, a tangible link to the comfort she couldn't access.

With her right hand, she started tapping her fingers against her thumb in counts of three, the steady rhythm grounding her amid the spiraling chaos. As she concentrated on slowing her breathing, a tingling sensation washed over her, a gentle pull towards something just out of reach. In that moment, she felt herself slipping back, the edges of her consciousness softening until the echoes of her adult self-seemed to blur, leaving behind a lingering sense of familiarity that was both disorienting and strangely reassuring.

Suddenly, the world sharpened around her. She felt a hand wrap around hers, warm and grounding.

"I got you, Nixx."

Bryce's voice sounded closer, comforting and steady. Phenex could hear her rhythmic breathing and felt the softness of her touch. Her heart fluttered, but she focused on the reality around her, anchoring herself in the warmth of Bryce's presence in nineteen eighty-seven.

As Phenex's eyelids fluttered open, her vision dissolved from vibrant colors to the soft hues of her bedroom. Bryce's concerned face floated above hers, their bodies entwined on the bed. Phenex's gaze drifted to Bryce's hand cradled beneath her head, the gentle pressure of her fingers a comforting sensation. The warm weight of Bryce's body pinned her down, holding her close.

Bryce's lips curved into a soft, silent phrase as she stroked Phenex's hair, the gentle touch sending a shiver through her. Bryce's fingers danced across her scalp, sweeping stray strands away from her face. The gentle rhythm lulled Phenex into a state of calm, but beneath the surface, a cold, hollow chill spread through her.

Her chest rose and fell with each slow breath, her lungs fighting to fill with air. Her mind struggled to grasp the fragments of her thoughts, but they slipped through her fingers like sand. Bryce's touch seemed to be the only thread holding her together, a gentle presence that allowed her to start to untangle the threads of her past.

As she breathed slowly, Phenex felt her memories shifting, like leaves on a gust of wind. She reached out for something to hold onto, a memory, a thought, anything to keep her grounded in reality. Her past seemed to be unraveling before her eyes, and she couldn't grasp it. Anger flared up within her, but the words eluded her. She tried to grasp something, anything, but her mind was a muddle of confusion.

Bryce's fingers continued to weave a soothing pattern through her hair, but Phenex felt herself slipping further into unconsciousness. Her memories faded, her twenty-six-year-old consciousness faded, and she was back in the darkness, trapped in a dream from which she couldn't awaken.

CHAPTER 18
TIME DIVERGING

Mikhail gasped, each breath a frantic struggle against the surging wave of nausea that threatened to consume her. "Estas bien, mija?" Carlos's worried voice cut through the fog from the driver's seat, his brows furrowed with concern as he used the rear-view mirror to look at her.

"Papa, pull over quick! I think she's gonna ralph!" Casey shouted, the urgency in his voice slicing through the tension. Without a second thought, Carlos rolled down his window, allowing a rush of cool air to counter the heat of panic, then veered off the highway onto a narrow dirt road that twisted away from the frenzied traffic.

Before the car even came to a full stop, Mikhail flung open the back door and tumbled out, landing hard on her knees in the ditch. Her stomach roiled as the world around her spun violently. With a painful heave, she bent over, retching like a cat battling a stubborn hairball, each convulsion shaking her entire body.

Saria was at her side in an instant, kneeling beside her and gently rubbing her back in soothing circles. Concern etched across her features, she kept her voice calm. "It's okay, just breathe, Mikhail. You're going to be alright."

In the trunk, Casey tossed aside a crumpled blanket and a couple of old backpacks, rummaging for something, anything, that might help. Heart racing, he spotted a half-empty bottle of water wedged among the forgotten items. "Found it." relief flooding his face as he sprinted back toward Mikhail, offering her the lifeline she desperately needed.

As Mikhail's heaving began to subside, the fresh air and Saria's steady presence anchored her back to reality. She looked up, her vision blurred but gratitude shining in her eyes. "Sorry," she gasped, wiping her mouth on the back of her hand. "I don't know what happened. I just suddenly felt horrible." Her fingers flew as she signed to Saria and Casey, *Nixx, something is wrong with Nixx.*

"You don't need to apologize," Carlos called out from the driver's seat, his worry deepening into a frown. "You scared us, that's all."

Kneeling beside her, Casey offered the water bottle. "Here," he said gently, unscrewing the cap. "Take small sips. It'll help settle your stomach." His expression was earnest, filled with empathy.

Mikhail eagerly accepted the bottle, tilting it to her lips as the cool water soothed her parched throat, offering a welcome relief. Just then, Rei-Lee stepped out of the car, her presence calm and authoritative.

"Slow down, sweetie, small sips," she advised, her voice a comforting blend of concern and warmth, a trace of her Korean accent weaving through her words. "Was it motion sickness?" She rested a hand on Mikhail's shoulder, grounding her in the moment.

Mikhail nodded, her thirst for a moment forgotten. "Yes, ma'am. I don't usually get this bad, but it hit harder today." With Saria and Casey's help, she pushed herself up, the world tilting for a moment before she steadied herself.

Rei-Lee's smile brightened her features, a warmth in her gaze as she gently patted Mikhail's cheek. "You can sit in the front for a bit. We're only half an hour from home. No arguments."

Mikhail hesitated, her eyes falling to the pavement as uncertainty flickered across her face. "Thanks, um, Rei-Lee, but I think I'm okay…" Her voice trailed off under the weight of Rei-Lee's steady stare. After a moment, she nodded, a hint of resignation seeping into her tone. "Yes, ma'am."

Sliding into the front passenger seat, she sank into the cool embrace of the leather. "Lo siento, Señor Cabrera," she murmured, the air around her thick with the scent of car freshener and the faint echo of voices.

Carlos gave a dismissive wave, his tone light. "No need to apologize, Misha, Mija. I saw you haven't eaten much this weekend. We're just outside of Anthony; we could grab some Pizza Hut."

"Gracias, pero no. I think I'll just close my eyes and enjoy the ride back to Wakford." A soft smile played on her lips, an unspoken assurance that she was alright. She turned her head toward the back seat. "And thank you too, Rei-Lee. I really appreciate it."

"You're sweet, Mish, but if you ralph again, please project it forward—not backward," Casey chimed in, his attempt at humor hanging in the air like soft laughter.

"Chakage gureo. (Behave)" Rei-Lee shot a look at her son, her tone playfully stern.

Casey met her gaze with a sheepish grin. "Mianhae, eomma, (Sorry, Mom)" he replied, chuckling. "I'll behave."

Mikhail leaned back, her eyelids fluttering shut as she tried to grasp the remnants of the dream that had slipped away just as nausea washed over her. She focused on her connection with Phenex, a bond akin to that of twins, though typically less intense. Yet this time, the familiar whisper in her mind erupted into an electric intensity, pulling her into a vivid whirlwind of emotions.

What had once been a sanctuary now felt like a lifeline, the current of their psychic link dragging her down with a force that left her breathless. Emotions crashed over her like relentless waves, tumbling her deeper into the depths of her own turmoil.

As she struggled to anchor herself, fragmented images burst into her mind's eye, a disjointed montage of sounds, scents, and sensations. The memories came in sudden, vivid flashes: the darkness of the dream, the Subaru's wheels screeching, the rush of adrenaline as she launched herself from the vehicle.

The scenes blurred and morphed, refusing to coalesce into a clear narrative, but the emotions lingering in their wake were unmistakable – fear, urgency, and a deep, abiding concern for Phenex. The bond between them pulsed with an otherworldly energy, as if trying to convey a message that Mikhail's conscious mind couldn't quite grasp.

Flash. Phenex's terrified scream pierced the air, her wide eyes locked in a desperate struggle against Lukas's grip.

The memory shifted focus. A blue truck idling nearby, the laughter of boys twisting into something dark and menacing. Mikhail's heart raced with each jolt of her sister's fear, a drumbeat of dread echoing in her chest.

"Leave my sister alone!" Mikhail shouted, fury igniting her dread as a protective instinct roared to life within her. With every ounce of strength, she pounded on the iron-plated door of the blue house, her knuckles bruising from the impact. She cried out for help, catching glimpses of fingers parting the blinds, eyes watching her desperate struggle from the shadows. But her cry was too late.

The focus of the memory blurred, then sharpened on a new horror. Flash. Beau lunging forward—no… Adrenaline surged through her veins as she reached for Phenex, acutely aware of the impossible distance between them, the gap feeling like an insurmountable chasm stretching twenty feet wide.

Each second felt like an eternity, an aching reminder of how far her sister was from safety.

Something shifted in the memory, an alteration in the fabric of the past.

A single word screamed out cutting through the air like a razor. "BASTA!" Phenex's powerful cry pierced the air, a wave of defiance radiating from her small body, igniting Mikhail's own resolve.

Flash. Beau hunched over, a rock slipping from his hand as he launched a brutal right hook, his hips twisting to deliver a devastating blow to the side of Phenex's face. Mikhail could have sworn she heard the sickening sound of bone fracturing as her sister's head snapped to the right, each vertebra in her neck popping like the crack of a firecracker.

As the adrenaline of the dream faded, unease began to rise within her, threatening to plunge her stomach back into turmoil. Mikhail opened her eyes, gulping from her water bottle to quell the churn inside her. She struggled to piece together the disjointed memories, each glimpse weaving a tighter web of anxiety that pressed against her chest. Taking another sip, she swallowed hard against the unsettling tide threatening to engulf her.

"You okay?" Carlos asked, his hand resting on her shoulder as he focused on the road ahead.

"Si." The word slipped easily from her lips as they turned onto a familiar street. Mikhail unbuckled her seatbelt, and the scent of warm asphalt filled the air as Mr. Cabrera eased into the driveway of Bryce's two-story home, a pale green structure with black shutters that had lost their luster over the years.

Even as late spring rolled in, Christmas lights dangled like cobwebs along the gutters and garage, remnants of a festive season left behind—not just from laziness but also practicality, a decision made easier by the adage: 'It's already done.' She glanced at Saria, "I think I'll stick around for a bit. Nixx was supposed to stay over this weekend anyway."

With a gentle push, she opened the door and hopped out, Saria falling in step beside her. Rei-Lee, lingering a moment longer, leaned in to wrap each girl in a warm embrace before sliding into the passenger seat. "Thanks for the ride to Friends University; I had a blast."

"Can I stay here too, Papa?" Casey asked, leaning back into the car, bags in hand.

"You girls aren't sick of him yet, are you?" Carlos joked. "If you are, I'll just drag him home."

Mikhail chuckled. "Nah, he's cool. With less than three months until graduation, we're just trying to make the most of our time together before college. Plus, he's a pro at carrying our bags." She winked and flashed a playful side smile.

Carlos and Rei-Lee waved goodbye as they pulled away from the curb. The moment they were out of sight, Mikhail dashed into the house. From the front room, she could see straight through to the back porch, where she spotted Bryce in her usual spot on the railing, leaning against one of the pillars with her legs crossed. Though Mikhail couldn't make out the details of what Bryce was holding, her posture conveyed unmistakable frustration.

"Hey, Claudia." Phenex poked her head around the kitchen wall into the foyer, the vibrant red pink can of Tab in her hand hissing as she popped it open. "How was the trip?"

Mikhail stared at her sister, confusion knitting her brow. No one called her by her first name, even the teachers at school and the bullies called her by her middle name or close variant. A strange chill ran down her spine, something was out of place, "It was informative, had some decent Mexican food at a restaurant I forgot the name of already." She laughed lightly trying to hide her hesitation. Unease creeped in as she stepped closer. Something was different about her sister; something had changed.

Phenex leaned against the wall as Mikhail and the others entered the kitchen. A bright smile lighting up her topaz eyes. "Well, hopefully you remember next time we go. My night was good, had a terrifying dream, Bryce helped pull me out of it though."

"Strange, I had a weird dream when I fell asleep in the car. Almost punched Sar in reaction." She leaned on the island in the middle of the kitchen facing her sister, a light laugh escaped as she stared at Phenex trying to judge her reactions. "What was your dream about?"

Phenex paused, her smile flickering away. A shadow crossed her features, as she clenched and unclenched her free fist three times, "It doesn't matter now," she said, her voice low, "Just drop it." Her tone was hostile. Harsh.

Casey signed rapidly to keep Saria updated on the conversation between the two sisters, although Saria brushed off any concerns about her hearing aids, indicating they were working just fine. Signing was the norm in their household; while Saria could hear with her aids, she still preferred sign as a means of communication most of the time. Nevertheless, she noticed a subtle shift in Phenex's demeanor; something that caught her attention, as she had learned to pick up details that others might overlook.

"You guys are being weird," Phenex remarked, raising an eyebrow as she noticed the concern etched on her sister's and friend's faces. "Whatever special brownies or cookies you've both had, lay off them." A dry chuckle escaped her lips as she walked toward the living room and out the patio doors to join Bryce.

"I can't be the only one thinking that's not my sister," Mikhail reiterated, turning to Casey and Saria. Casey was leaning against the fridge to her right, while Saria sat at the nook by the island.

The silence weighed heavily in the room, suffocating, as though they had all shared a bizarre hallucination. Phenex, usually sweet and a bit standoffish, now felt distant—an unexpected shadow lurking beneath her familiar surface. Anger and rage bubbled up from nowhere, creating the unsettling illusion of a pod person.

Saria slowly raised her hands, as if breaking free from a deep freeze. In silence, she signed, "No." Then, with a gentle gesture, she pointed to the right side of her face before voicing what they all realized simultaneously: "No scar."

Chapter 19
A Fracture in Time

Bryce tapped her notebook with her left hand, absentmindedly spinning a pencil around her fingers with her right while gazing up at the sky. The calm moment shattered as she heard Phenex step onto the porch and let out a sigh. "Everything okay?" Bryce asked cautiously. Since Phenex had woken up for a second time that morning, she had seemed on edge, her personality having pulled a one-eighty in less than twelve hours.

"Why does everyone keep asking that?" Phenex retorted, exasperation flaring as she threw her arms up. "I'm fine." She flung herself into a nearby patio chair, the sound of metal scraping against cement echoing through the air.

Bryce rolled her eyes and hopped down from the railing. "Sorry, Nixx, but ever since that nightmare you had last night, you've been hella tense, and you won't even talk to me. After everything, I thought maybe..." She paused, searching for the right words.

Phenex rotated her wrist and took a long sip from her Tab, a clear 'go on' gesture. "I've told you a zillion times today, how can you be so insistent on calling me by my first name? Is it, like, a dare or something? Alex, I've gone by Alex since I was nine."

"Right...Nothing, Alex." Bryce muttered, disappointment flickering in her chest, a mix of confusion and hurt settling over her. For a moment, when the others joined them on the back porch, she had hope but it was quickly squashed when she realized they each had the same look of concern and confusion on their faces, "Hey guys! How was Friends?"

"Not far enough away from Wakford." Casey laughed, "Though the campus was nice. Clean. Bit boring."

"Just glad we took the scenic route, as much scenery as Anthony, Harper and the back roads have anyway." Saria said, sitting on the ground, her back against the railing just under where Bryce had been sitting just moments before. She fiddled with her hearing aids for a moment before folding her hands neatly into her lap.

"How was your night, Ripley?" Mikhail asked taking her usual spot near Phenex.

Bryce raised an eyebrow, "Okay, I guess, closed up at PnP, Ma gave me a ride home because she didn't want Lucy to keep pestering Nixx... *Alex* and I with probing questions." She smiled, "Thana was excited for that Alfred Hitchcock Magazine, didn't you get her into those, *Mikey*?"

Mikhail shuddered at the tonal shift in Bryce's voice. Though she had braced herself for the casual use of "Mikey," it felt wrong coming from her. Fortunately, Bryce's confused expression mirrored her own discomfort as she uttered it. While the bonds of their friendship weren't as deep as those between Bryce and Phenex—or the sisterly bond Mikhail shared with Phenex—they had learned to read one another well. Phenex affectionately dubbed Bryce "Ripley", while Mikhail often faced the shorthand of "Mikey" from those who either struggled to pronounce her name or simply chose to bypass it. This moment felt significant; despite the turmoil of the previous timeline, Mikhail, Bryce, Casey, and Saria appeared untouched, yet something had undeniably shifted in Phenex's demeanor.

As the others engaged in conversation, Mikhail attempted to pull the fragments of a haunting dream back to the surface. Vivid images and raw emotions churned in her mind—an event they had all chosen to avoid discussing afterward. She recalled the day the Doogan Brothers and Beau Baxter had attacked Phenex, when her sister needed twelve stitches. Mikhail could still see the sharp, jagged line where Beau had smashed a rock against Phenex's face, tracing a path from her temple to her cheekbone, halting just shy of her upper lip.

The memory surged back painfully: Phenex lying limp on the ground, blood seeping from the devastating blow as the boys fled. Mikhail had rushed to her sister's side, pulling her close, tears streaming down her face. Thankfully, Phenex remained conscious… But then a piercing discomfort carved through Mikhail's thoughts. *No. That's not how it happened.* Panic fluttered in her chest as her eyes widened, yanking her back from the depths of chaos.

"Oya, ¿Cuál fue tu sueño sobre el nueve de julio?" Mikhail asked suddenly.

"You know I don't speak Spanish, Claudia." Phenex growled, "This is America, we speak English."

Casey put his hands up defensively, "We always speak Spanish, Nixx." He interjected.

"My god! It is Alex, are you all trying to piss me off?" she rolled her eyes her fist clenching and unclenching in anger, "Sure, you and my sister speak that *savage* language, but I don't."

"Whoa, what the hell, N-Alex." Bryce stepped towards her, "What is wrong with you?"

Phenex stood up abruptly, her topaz eyes blazing with hues of amber as she strode over to Bryce, squaring up as if ready to fight. "What's. Wrong. With. *You?*" Phenex retaliated, "*You* got me to read that ridiculous book, all while being creepy and 'calming down' from a nightmare," she said, waving her hands in front of her in a mocking imitation of soothing gestures. "And now *you're* offended by the way I'm talking? News flash, Bryce, nothing has changed. You all must have gotten a bad jazz cigarette or eaten a laced brownie.

Her irritation was palpable, she clenched and unclenched her fists, as if trying to keep her anger at bay, the muscles in her arms taut and trembling. "I'm going home. You all have annoyed me today." With that, she extended her middle finger in a sharp, defiant gesture, flashing it at them before she stormed off the porch and down the alleyway, each step echoing her fury as she disappeared from view.

The air hung with tension as her departure left a silence in its wake, the kind of silence that buzzed almost painfully. Mikhail exchanged glances with Bryce and Casey, the confusion in their expressions deepening. What was happening to them? Why was Phenex... Alex spiraling, and why did everything feel off-kilter? A sense of dread coiled tightly in Mikhail's stomach.

"Over reaction much." Casey said after a few moments while everyone processed what had happened before them. Phenex's nuclear explosion was unexpected, "What set her off like that?"

Saria was comforting Bryce who appeared to be fighting back tears, "That's not our Phenex." She muttered her voice barely audible, "That's not…" she whispered again, "Mikhail… What did you ask in Spanish?"

"I asked if the dream was about *that* day."

"The Doogan Brothers and Baxter?" Bryce's question was more for confirmation than an actual question.

Saria's gaze darted back and forth between Casey's brooding figure and Bryce's concerned face before locking onto Mikhail with an inquiring stare. Though she was unfamiliar with the specifics of the story that seemed to hover around its edges, she sensed the weight of its significance. A questioning furrow formed between her eyebrows as she glanced at Casey once more, noticing the intensity of his scowl. It was as if the very mention of those names had triggered something deep within him.

The air around Casey seemed to darken, like a storm cloud gathering on the horizon, and even Bryce, typically the picture of poise, appeared flustered by the undercurrents swirling beneath the surface. Yet, despite their close-knit relationships, a secret remained shrouded in mystery, one that had become an unspoken understanding, even among those who treated each other like family. It was this unspoken bond that had allowed for the ease of sharing cars and keys, a privilege reserved for those who trusted each other completely.

Mikhail's words lingered in the air like a challenge, her voice barely above a whisper. She drew a sharp breath and sank onto the coffee table with a quiet bump, her hands trembling like leaves in the wind. The others leaned in; eyes fixed on her as she spoke. Her confession was heavy, the weight of the pain almost tangible.

"We don't talk about it," she said, her voice cracking as she battled the anger and sadness. "It's hard to even think about... it feels like reliving that day all over again, and somehow, I have two memories of the same event."

She took a few moments to compose herself, her eyes drifting closed as she recounted the haunting dream, the image of Phenex's ghostly figure, older haunting her. As Mikhail spoke, the words lurched out of her, struggling to keep pace with the emotions flooding her. It was as if she was trying to grasp the slippery edge of a nightmare, one that refused to be caught. If her dream was any indication, then it seemed that the past was indeed malleable, susceptible to change. "If that's what happened," she said, her voice laced with desperation, "then we know that the past can be changed. We know that things can be altered... if the lack of scar isn't proof enough, then Phenex's sparkly new personality should be."

A heavy silence filled the air until Bryce finally spoke, drawing on Mikhail's earlier comments and pulling her gaze from her notebook. The only sound had been the soft scratching of her pencil as she wrote furiously, thoughts spilling out like an uncontained torrent.

"What if she couldn't pull her older self-back to our time? What if the events from age eight onward, those altered memories, are now her only reality? Nixx mentioned on that camping trip that she was afraid she'd wake up in her twenties and find nothing had changed. It is possible that's what happened, but instead of waking up in her twenties, she's trapped in a distorted version of her past."

"Along those lines, yeah," Mikhail muttered while everyone nodded in agreement.

"What if that's true? She wasn't able to pull her elder self-back, which could explain the sudden change. From age eight to now, those new events are what exist in her mind. Instead of just being hit by a rock and the cowards ran," Bryce swallowed hard, unwilling to repeat the twisted beating Phenex had endured as a child, "she was severely beaten. I can understand why she holds so much wrath."

The others nodded as Bryce continued "I have a theory." She paused for a long time, gathering her thoughts. "We don't know how you disappear, Mish. Though apparently the past can be altered, what if nothing changes going forward?"

Mikhail's tone was dry, but her friends picked up on a hint of excitement beneath the surface. "Well, at least we have that to look forward to!" she said with a wry smile, her friends confused for a moment unsure if she was being sarcastic, or was she genuinely excited about the prospect of facing their uncertain futures?

"Step one, we find her journal see if it has any clues that will help us. We have a lot to cover and with May tenth less than a month away, not much time." Casey said, at first his tone was confident but at the end he wasn't able to hide his worry.

"Step two, hope that we can prevent Mikhail's disappearance." Bryce laughed, nervously, but the longer she laughed the more real it became.

Saria started laughing, "So we have all lost it." She signed, "Step three, if that fails."

"I guess we will find out in the future, but we won't fail." Casey snorted as he and Mikhail joined in on the laughter, "Think about that camping trip. The five of us figured out the pattern. How the dates aligned. We know more than we think we do. We're unstoppable."

"And if we do fail we can wonder if there is a discount when it comes to group rate lobotomies," Mikhail said, her tone tinged with irony. "Well, you all can. Do lobotomies erase memories?" She put a hand behind her head.

After a fit of laughter that left their stomachs hurting, they agreed that if they couldn't save Mikhail, focusing on the future was the next best option.

"We will change the future, and I'll be a part of it," Mikhail declared, picking up the Tab that Phenex had left behind. She took a sip before handing it to Bryce. They each took a drink, passing the can around as if it were the pact that sealed the oath.

Chapter 20
Altered Future

The scent of stale coffee and the quiet hum of the engine filled the SUV as the beat of "Indigo" by *Muttering Gibberish* drummed on the steering wheel. Shades of grey and muted green blurred past, leached of color by the overcast sky. Each note resonated with unspoken thoughts—paths not taken and moments heavy on her heart. This song had a knack for pulling her into deeper reflection, stirring memories of the past and the anger that accompanied them. It was one of the band's slower songs, melancholic yet hopeful. Theodesa's low voice made the music feel rich and enveloping, and as the soft melodies flowed through the car's speakers, she felt a mix of nostalgia and yearning wash over her. Theodesa's vocal delivery was soothing yet burdened with the weight of shared complexities. A half-empty travel mug sat in the cup holder, its plastic worn smooth by countless trips.

Sighing as they shifted the car into park and turned off the ignition. "Ready for this?" she asked herself, stepping out of the Land Rover and pausing to gaze up at the majestic cathedral before her. Its grandeur was undeniable; she had always admired the artistry of the church's architecture. It had been years since she had visited Wakford, not since leaving for college.

She traced her cheekbone with her fingertips, a phantom yet familiar ache began to stir, creeping in whenever she pondered Wakford. It was always accompanied by a sinking feeling in her stomach. Now that she had returned, her mind was consumed with the reason for her visit, pushing aside the memories of the past. "It's not too late to turn back, is it?" she mused, as if seeking reassurance from the ghosts of the past that may still linger in the air.

With a deep breath, she gathered her courage and made her way toward the towering green doors of the church. The noon bell tolled, its ringing echoing through the chapel. Beau Baxter stood at the lectern, welcoming the mourners as they gradually settled into their pews. She slipped through a side door and made her way to the balcony. Over the past decade, the town has dwindled in size, resulting in the balcony being used less frequently; even during full service, it was rare to see it open. She knew this thanks to Casey, who still lived in Wakford. As children, they often found themselves up there together, reading the Bible and interpreting the scriptures in their own words. As they grew older, Casey continued to seek solace in the church, especially after May 10th of '87.

Beau Baxter launched into his sermon, quoting Ephesians. His voice boomed through the chapel, capturing the attention of mourners like a clap of thunder. "Let all bitterness and wrath and anger and clamor and slander be put away from you, along with all malice…" The words dripped with syrupy sentimentality, making her stomach churn.

"Dear friends and family," he continued, "As we gather here today to celebrate the life of our beloved Dr. Carlos Cabrera, who left us on April fifteenth, two-thousand and nine, we are reminded of the bittersweet nature of our time together. We come with heavy hearts, grappling with sorrow and loss…"

She felt trapped in a cruel joke. Clamping her lips shut, she stifled a scoff as she fought the urge to call out his hypocrisy. He and the Doogan Brothers remained pillars of the community despite their shared past of nearly murdering a child when they were teenagers. That was Wakford for you, a town shrouded in shadows and steeped in secrets; echoes of the past drowned out the whispers.

Dr. Cabrera's death struck a deeper chord within her—a jagged wound that demanded she return for this funeral, no matter the ghosts that followed her. The disappearance that affected her and friends. From her perch on the back balcony, she spotted Casey in the front most pew among his six siblings. Though she couldn't see his face twisted in grief, she could tell he was devastated. He sat next to his mother Rei-Lee and his grandparents, trembling as he subtly wiped tears with a handkerchief he kept in his pocket. A stab of guilt twisted in her chest, urging her to leap from the balcony and curl up next to him, offering solace.

Saria sat on the opposite side of Rei-Lee, her fingers gently entwined with Rei-Lee's in a comforting grip. Her magnificent black hair cascaded down her back like a waterfall. She had heard whispers of Casey and Saria's marriage, but the warmth and familiarity between them suggested that, at the very least, they had remained close friends.

"While it is natural to feel anger, anger at circumstances, at fate, or even at God—let us instead find strength in our faith. Jesus teaches us to surrender our burdens to Him. In moments of despair, we can turn our hearts toward Him in prayer…" Beau's voice droned on, fading into the background.

The door to the balcony creaking open suddenly behind her, snapping her back to reality. Panic rushed through her, instinct urging her to hide, but she took a steady breath. "So, you did make it," said a soft, familiar voice. "I thought if you had, you'd be up here."

She spun around to see a tall woman with sun-kissed skin and curly hair pulled back into a messy bun. Dressed in a black dress with a yellow belt—the very color Dr. Cabrera had adored—she mirrored the understated elegance of the moment. A shiny pin on the woman's collar caught her eye, emblazoned with the name "Nyx." The design was striking: a swirling, abstract pattern of lines and vibrant colors, embodying the chaotic yet beautiful nature of thoughts and ideas. It was an unmistakable symbol—the Muttering Gibberish pin—representing the energy and creativity that flowed through the mind like an endless dance.

She stared for a moment, her jaw set as she took in the woman's brilliant flashing eyes, which shifted from deep grey to a faded green as she smiled. The woman raised an eyebrow. "Well, you gonna stand there slack jawed, or are you going to say hello?"

"Mikhail." Bryce swallowed hard, fighting the flood of tears that threatened to spill over. An overwhelming urge surged within her to wrap her arms around the woman. "It's nice to see you." She smiled.

"Under different circumstances, it would be better," Mikhail agreed, her tone shifting slightly. "Can you believe that mouth breather actually went to seminary?" She scoffed and rolled her eyes.

"—journey of healing, reminding each other to find solace in community and in our faith," Beau's voice boomed as he wrapped up his final thoughts. "In closing, remember that while we mourn our loss, we do not mourn alone. God is with us today and always, guiding us to a place of peace. May our beloved Carlos Cabrera rest in eternal light and peace, and may we carry his love in our hearts forever.

In near-perfect unison, the congregation responded, "Amen."

"Thank you so much for making it, Mikhail. I know Carlos appreciates it," Rei-Lee said, wrapping her in a warm embrace. "How have you been? How are your siblings?"

"Thana is doing fantastic, the doctor esquire thing hasn't gone to her head yet." She laughed, "Enoch, I think he is competing for some MMA title? I'm not sure I just know when he tells me about it, he is extremely excited." she replied, "You know the twins graduate this year."

As they stood in the backyard of Rei-Lee's house, remnants of the past surrounded them. The patio, once a place filled with laughter and family gatherings, now felt steeped in silence under the overcast April sky. Nearby, mature trees swayed gently in the chilly breeze, their branches casting fleeting shadows on the ground. The cool air added to the heaviness.

Rei-Lee beamed with warmth as she wrapped a hand around Mikhail's shoulder. "That's wonderful. And, yes, the twins are no longer babies. You four are the last ones left in the neighborhood." Her gentle Korean accent filled the air as she smiled at Bryce, her eyes sparkling with genuine happiness. "You know, we really haven't been all together since oh… about ninety-eight, maybe two thousand was it not? Time truly flies."

Bryce's expression was tinged with a hint of nostalgia, but her voice revealed an underlying unease as she replied, "Yeah... I guess I forgot about that." The truth, however, weighed heavily in her mind. It had been over a decade since their last reunion—a reunion that had been doomed to fail. They had attempted to alter the past, but fate had other plans. As a result, Phenex was still missing. Unspoken words lingered, like an open wound.

The four engaged in lively conversation, reminiscing about shared memories while bringing each other up to speed on the moments they had missed. Saria and Casey had reignited the spark that once flickered between them in college, and now, with the ink barely dry on their marriage certificate, they felt firmly rooted in Wakford. Despite the familiarity of their hometown, their careers often took them on frequent travels, leading them on adventures that expanded their world far beyond the small town's borders.

Mikhail returned to Wakford just as Rhett fell ill about five years ago, a stark contrast to the man she once knew. With Phenex's disappearance casting a long shadow, something within him had shifted; kindness had replaced the coldness that had once defined him. Laughter and easy conversations began to fill the silence that had lingered for too long, gradually forging a tentative camaraderie between her and Rhett. As Mikhail settled back in to help her mother and support Rhett through his struggles, their connection deepened, each shared moment serving as a step toward healing.

Yet even as she witnessed this transformation, a painful knot of resentment tightened in her chest. She watched his gentle encouragement, the way he seemed to genuinely care, and it reawakened memories of her and her sister being pushed aside during darker times, Mikhail couldn't help but feel like a shadow.

"I cannot believe how much has changed," Bryce whispered, her voice barely rising above the rustling leaves of the nearby trees. The weight of her words hung in the air, thick with unspoken regrets and emotions that had long bubbled beneath the surface, "I'm sorry I missed so much. After Phenex disappearing and the failure to travel back in ninety-eight I just felt a little defeated. Not an excuse, just felt discouraged and I'm truly sorry."

Casey nodded, a hint of determination in his voice. "Well, there's a glimmer of hope, if we calculated correctly today is fortyfive days." He glanced at Bryce, his expression serious. "I think we can actually pull it off this time."

Saria smiled, holding out a worn composition notebook. "We've built on your initial theory, and we're factoring in Nixx's disappearance instead of Mikhail's. It's complex, but I think we've got a solid shot at making it work." She handed the notebook to Bryce, who took it with a skeptical look.

Mikhail raised an eyebrow as Casey nudged Saria's hand toward him. "Misha knows that book inside and out," he said with a hint of amusement. "Bryce's initial idea was a good foundation, and we just added some dimensional theory to the mix."

Bryce glanced at the figures and sighed. "Yeah… I'm not even going to pretend I understand any of that." She extended the notebook back to Saria. "I trust your math; these days, all I do is add and subtract." She let out a dry laugh.

"The essence of the theory," Saria began, her voice steady as she pulled a lap-top from her bag, "is that if one of us can tap into the minds of our younger selves—subconsciously." She paused as she opened a file on the computer turning the screen towards Bryce and

Mikhail, "Nixx's disappearance stirred the timelines, creating these ripples we never anticipated." She pointed at the spaces on screen that appeared to break, shooting into a separate directions like little exploding stars.

Misha leaned in closer, her gaze intense as her eyes flashed in the light of the porch. "Those ripples," she said, "they create resonance that could act as a dimensional anchor, in layman's; time where the mind is more susceptible to the entrance of the older consciousness. We're bridging our timeline and the one where we vanished. With your calculations, it's roughly a forty-percent chance of success."

Saria's fingers danced across the interface, the numbers shifting as she spoke. "We originally thought you," nodding her head toward Mikhail, "disappeared in nineteen eighty-seven, but it seems that our reality, Phenex disappeared. If we target the exact moment of that shift, we can rewrite it, ensuring neither you nor Phenex ever vanishes."

She paused, a spark of excitement igniting in her eyes as she calculated the variables. "The next ripple is in a few days. Before your original disappearance, Misha. It's risky, but the convergence might just work."

Bryce rubbed her temples before pinching the bridge of her nose trying to wrap her head around the theory. "And what exactly do you plan on doing once we're back in my younger self's mind?"

"Obviously prevent me or my sister from disappearing and thankfully we have all the clues, except for the answer of how, or was it why?" Mikhail responded with a shrug.

"Twenty-two years later, you really think this time it's possible? We don't even know how Nixx made it back the first time." Bryce's skepticism surfaced, her controlled voice tinged with the threat of rising emotion. "We're nearing our forties! Phenex is gone."

Casey nodded, listening intently. "Just hear us out. I believe Nixx only changed because she went back twice. We're only going to eighty-seven, and Nixx was there for almost three months. Four weeks should be nothing."

"Am I speaking French here?" Bryce crossed her arms, frustration edging her words. She shifted her weight, unable to hide her exasperation. "We tried this in ninety-eight and failed! Whatever happened in eighty-seven was a fluke—or just a shared delusion. Look at us," her voice softened as she glanced away. "We're in our late thirties now. This fantasy of saving Phenex? It's just that—a fantasy." Irritation mingled with pain in her tone.

Mikhail placed a hand on Bryce's shoulder. "You're right; we could fail again. But I believe my sister had it wrong. I'm not the key; we are." He gestured to the group. "Are you willing to try once more?"

"If we fail. Phenex sacrificed herself for this future, for our present," Casey said. "We owe it to her to try again. I think we figured it out. We haven't shown you our timelines yet." He entered a few numbers on the keyboard and hit return.

The screen burst to life, revealing four new lines, each marked with starbursts in different places. The top line was red, representing Casey; the second, highlighted in cyan, was Saria; Phenex's timeline was in orange, Mikhail's in purple, and Bryce's in goldenrod. Each ripple was unique, some larger than others.

"See? There's a single day where all five of us converge—the factor we didn't have before in ninety-eight," Casey explained. "Theoretically, we can go back to any date with a ripple. Look at March twenty-seventh; you, Mikhail, and Phenex all had ripples around the same time. We calculated it based on déjà vu moments."

"One last chance, Bryce?" Saria asked, sensing Bryce's resolve softening.

"Before you ask," Mikhail interjected, noting the question forming on Bryce's lips, "Return is simply aging. Remember Nixx's journal? She said she felt her elder self-fading, as if her fifteen-year-old self was taking over."

"That's right," Bryce murmured, memories surfacing. "It all comes together—the dates align: nineteen ninety-eight, nineteen eighty-seven, eighty-one, seventy, fifty-nine." Vividly, she recalled the camping trip, sitting in the dim light of the earth-house, sketching out the math in her notebook, eager to share her findings with her friends.

That memory, once shrouded in fog, now surged back into sharp focus: the moment in the woods with Phenex, electric and charged with uncertainty. It lingered in her thoughts, forever a haunting 'what if' that she revisited now and then. Her girlfriend, who hadn't joined her on this trip to Wakford and was back in their shared home in Massachusetts, knew the story but couldn't fully grasp the aching weight it held for Bryce.

In the stillness of that memory, Bryce felt the pull of the past intertwining with the present, a reminder of everything that had been left unsaid.

Casey made a finger gun gesture, clicked his tongue, and shot her a playful wink. "Bingo! Not to mention, my papa just *happens* to die, and suddenly we're all back together, ready to mess with time? Feels a bit dark to be convenient."

"Aw, yes, the ever popular we live in a simulation theory." Saria rolled her eyes at her husband, "Ever since the Matrix this one." She teased laughing.

"We're not getting younger. This is basically our last chance as next time we will be retirement age if the math is correct." Bryce said hesitantly, "Though it was my math originally, I assume it's correct."

Mikhail laughed, her boisterous laughter drawing everyone else in. "I thought you just added and subtracted these days?"

"It's true! That doesn't mean I'm overconfident in my mental abilities—at least not in my younger years." Bryce joined in the laughter.

After a few moments, the air around them buzzed with infectious laughter, their joy so intense that they all clutched their stomachs, the sound spilling out in bursts of delight that momentarily left them breathless. Even as the laughter brought with it a twinge of pain, it was a small price to pay for the happiness it conjured. Their smiles radiated warmth, a brilliant reminder of the bond they shared.

In that fleeting silence that followed, they collectively savored the moment—an unspoken understanding that resonated deeply among them. It was this laughter, this shared joy, that they had all missed the most during their time apart. Looking at one another, they recognized the truth: it wasn't Phenex that had kept them connected; life had gradually woven them into its own separate threads, pulling them away from each other until they felt their connections fray.

Yet, in that bubble of laughter and smiles, they found a renewed focus. Amid the warmth of camaraderie, they were acutely aware of the task that lay ahead. The urgency of their mission anchored their spirits, reminding them of the larger goal that awaited them. They had to return to 1987—not just for the sake of nostalgia but to secure their future with Phenex. As the laughter lingered in the air, they exchanged determined glances, ready to embark on the next chapter of their intertwined fates.

CHAPTER 21

CONVERGENCE

Bryce squeezed her eyes tight as her mind melded with the past, the scene unfolding before her like an old, grainy film. Hazy edges blurred, colors shimmering in shades of blue, green, and yellow that sparkled around her peripheral. At the center of the beautiful chaos stood Phenex, her presence commanding attention in an atmosphere thick with tension. The flicker of her topaz eyes ignited with fiery hues of amber, illuminating rage and a glimmer of fear as she faced Bryce mere inches from her face. It was as if a storm brewed between them, Phenex's body language radiating challenge, disdain, pain and confusion.

Bryce could see that Phenex's lips were moving, the tone of anger in her garbled voice as Bryce's mind settled in the vaguely familiar scene. Phenex's intensity electrified the surroundings, Bryce could feel her best friend's mounting frustration. There was a moment of confusion as she tried to gather herself. With a fierce declaration, Phenex stormed away, her middle finger raised in Bryce and the other's directions.

Before Bryce could fully process it, Phenex had vanished. She watched as Mikhail sprang away from the porch and sprinted after her sister; the surge of adrenaline palpable as she chased her. "PHENEX!!!!" Mikhail's voice echoed in the distance.

Bryce swallowed, her body shaking as she stumbled for a moment. Casey's voice came from behind her, "Well, I would say it worked then."

About The Author

Growing up in the small town of Wakita, Oklahoma, it is easy to understand why and how Jerrica K. Godwin (nee George) grew up to be resilient, strong, and passionate. But after careful discussion with her youngest sister, the decision to not use an obscene amount of sarcasm and self-deprecating humor in her about the author segment was officially determined. Unfortunately, the sarcasm could not be removed, but self-deprecation was omitted due to time, and readers likely prefer a more polished narrative.

A vivid imagination, Jerrica loved to tell her younger brother terrifying tales about monsters, werewolves, and a strange bloody monkey paw that mischievously stole underwear and tickled you till you looked like Batman's Joker. Video games, animated movies, and classic horror (Vincent Price forever! <3) became a lifelong passion. Passions she enjoys sharing with her elder godchildren.

When it comes to language, Jerrica has a complicated relationship. To quote, "Arithmetic is my first language; I am forced to speak English." As she has said to her parents and friends when she gets tongue-tied, "Numbers make more sense than the various ways people can mispronounce my name." It is clear that her journey into Computer Science was both inevitable and necessary!

Jerrica aims to merge her storytelling with her technological dreams. She lives happily with her wife, Cassandra, and their two cats, Kiki, the brooding teenager with a flair for the dramatic, and King "Moose," the ambitiously energetic younger brother who treats every surface like his personal playground.

Acknowledgments

Momma, your love of books was a gift I likely received even before I was born. I remember crawling into your lap, pleading with you to read whatever you had opened. You would read Robin Cook to me, and looking back, I realize there's no way you could have been following the words on the page. Yet, you captivated my three- or four-year-old mind as I declared, "I can't wait to read like you!"

Dad, your excitement for watching animated movies with me, especially those by Don Bluth or early Disney with the visible line art, was infectious. You taught me sleight-of-hand tricks and spent countless hours playing chess with me, hoping to impress my crush (It didn't work). When I felt the pain of a crush completely rejecting me, you were there with a five-gallon tub of ice cream, telling me about your first heartbreak.

Everett, my bubba and baby brother (though we are only fourteen months difference), you were the first to listen to my stories. Your encouragement fueled our imaginations, whether we were fleeing from the bruja del bosque (forest witch), traveling back in time to hunt dinosaurs for steak, or riding our mighty steeds (bicycles) to slay dragons. You'll always be the little dancing Superman.

Lexus, I don't think I can say it all here, you married my brother, as insane as that is I don't believe sisterhood was complete until you came along. The deep conversations we have shared, and the check-ins I hope they have meant as much to you as they have me.

To my bonus brothers and sisters: Billy, Rowdy, Dusti-Rae, and Emelia, "The Strays" as you called yourselves, our parents had more than enough love for all of us.

Dusti-Rae, I know we don't speak as often, but the memories, especially near Manchester Lake/Pond, will always be some of my favorite stories to tell "Do a sit-up, I dare you" (she can tell you haha). Or driving to Anthony just for french fries at McDonalds. Though our friendship approaches nearly three-decades (when did we get old??) we will always be those two tiny children sitting in the dug-out.

Rowdy and Billy, it's weird to think of one of you without the other, my brothers. We have lost contact over the years, but I love you both.

Rowdy all the time we would sit on the bedroom floor and talk, about life goals and our banter, have been stories I continue to share with my wife and present-day friends. Wild child but always willing to help.

Billy, you were always the first one to stand up for me and would seek my advice sometimes to my confusion. The calmer of my brothers. My gosh do I miss you.

Emelia, thank you for our conversations on the roof, late nights, sneaking in my bedroom window (short story), and all the escapes through the years. Macadamia to my Cocoa (long story). I am proud to call you my little sister. Te amo. Forever, and after that. Pop tarts and Dr. Pepper are our forever story and still my favorite breakfast especially before class.

Love you each with my entire heart.

Kinz-aroo, yeah, that name is going to live forever now. You'll likely read this first, second, and probably third. My favorite artist. Your love of books and art, along with your amazing skills and passion, are inspiring. You're so much more than you realize, and I hope to be there when you finally see that light within you. You're an amazing person and I love you.

Eli, *cough Elijah cough* my favorite little Bud—though you're nearly as tall as I am now (when I wrote this, you were just about my height, but now you've officially surpassed me!), your ramblings and insightful conversations while we played Minecraft have been a true delight. Watching you grow up, I see your intelligence, honesty, and humor shining through; you take after your Aunt Jerrica! XD (Your mom may have given birth to you, but I swear, you're my son at heart.) I am so proud of you. Remember to stop at the line, and to slow down BEFORE the turn.

Dani and Dax, I'm sorry I don't know you two as well, due to distance. I love seeing you both when your mom or older siblings and I video chat. Both of you are always excited to talk to me. I hope we can spend more time together. I promise I am trying… And depending on how popular this book is, I made this promise in front of hundreds, possibly more, so I best keep it, huh?

To everyone reading this as my test audience—friends and family alike—thank you so much. I truly appreciate your input more than words can express; I couldn't have improved without your help. To the team of editors, thank you as well. This experience has made me realize that I am better at spelling than I give myself credit for! It may still need work, but it's definitely an improvement.
Haha!

Jesse, my best man. I love you with my whole heart, and if you read this... The card is in the binding... Good luck. <3

Of course, my mother-in-law, Tracy who probably knew her daughter and I were dating before we even started dating. Treated me like family from the moment Cassie and I became friends. Thank you. Love you, Mom.

Max, my Canadian kiddo. Thank you for the cheers. I am so very proud of you. Congratulations on your recent marriage! I cannot wait to meet them in person, love you both.

I would like to express my heartfelt gratitude to my late high school English teacher in Wakita. I always promised you that I would thank you when I eventually wrote a book, and as a woman of my word, I say thank you now. While your treatment of my siblings— especially the blatant and subtle racism directed at Everett and me—was hurtful, it taught me valuable lessons about striving to be a better person than you ever were. I only wish I could share this moment with you as I celebrate my degree in computer science. It took time, but I have built myself up, and though your words sometimes linger in my mind, this achievement serves as proof of how far I have come. Ultimately, you were never as significant to my journey as you might have believed. Thank you, and I hope you have found the peace and warm embrace you sought.

To the many passer-byers and passengers in my life, some of whom may not have realized their influence on me: Some had a negative impact, like the woman who tore up my English paper in middle school or the kid who told me I could only be a maid while playing house because "that's what people like you do." Whatever that means... My OCD affects the number of things I have, not the dishes in the sink (to my wife's frustration... Lo siento, mi vida!). Some had positive impacts, like the little girl who kissed my arm because I had "ouch marks" and she found out my mom did not kiss them better. To be fair to my mom, I was seventeen at the time. So, to all those who passed through my life, thanks for the chaos and the kindness.

Speaking of my wonderful, amazing wife Cassie: to our future, whatever it may hold. Our adventures, pets, and children await. I look forward to growing old with you. Waking next to you, I get to wake up to that smile, I would not mind it at all.

www.ingramcontent.com/pod-product-compliance
Lightning Source LLC
LaVergne TN
LVHW061034070526
838201LV00073B/5034